ANCHOR OF SECRETS

SUPERNATURALS OF CASTLE ACADEMY

2

TESSA HALE

ANCHOR OF SECRETS

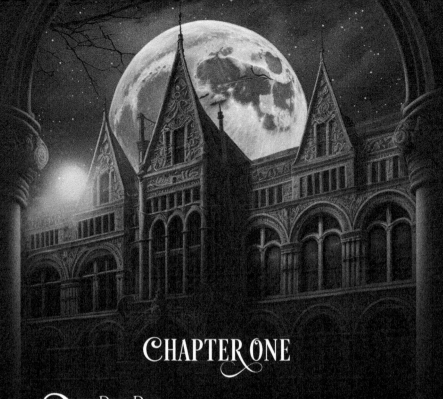

CHAPTER ONE

DRIP. DRIP. DRIP.

The sound pounded against my skull. Some part of me recognized that it wasn't actually that loud, but it felt like a marching band practicing on my head.

A soft groan escaped my lips, and I rolled to my back. A hard stone floor met my movement, and my eyelids fluttered at the assault.

The room appeared in flashes of vision. Snapshots. Each one more terrifying than the last.

Low light. Rock walls. Stone floor. No windows.

I forced my eyes completely open, fully taking in my surroundings. I was in some sort of basement with a crumbling staircase that led to a thick wooden door. I didn't want to think about what might be on the other side.

I struggled to push myself to sitting, my head swimming with the action. And that was when I saw it. Dread pooled in my belly as I took in the rusted chain from the wall to a shackle around my ankle.

It was almost as if my brain didn't want to fully compute the sight in front of me. As if there was some self-protection mechanism in place that didn't want me to come to terms with the truth. But it didn't change my reality.

My fingers trembled as I reached down to examine the cuff. It was held in place by a small padlock. I tugged on the metal, my mouth going dry. Though the chain and shackle were rusted, they held strong.

I was a prisoner.

Panic surged, but I shoved it down. I focused on my breathing, trying to keep it even as I searched my memory for the last thing I could remember.

Discovering the awful truth that the guys had known where I was my whole life. Confronting them. The fight. Running. Someone hitting me. That voice…

I tried to pinpoint the owner of the deep tone, but my mind wouldn't cooperate. The truth was, it didn't matter. The only thing that mattered was getting the hell out of here.

I pressed my hand against the wall for balance as I prepared to stand. The stone was damp, and the air smelled like mildew. I ignored it and shoved to my feet. My vision blurred, and a wave of nausea washed over me. The faint memory of someone striking me on the head and the raging pain there told me I likely had a concussion. I'd have to deal with that later.

The moment my vision righted itself, I followed the chain to the wall. If I couldn't get the cuff off my ankle, maybe I could remove the chain from the wall.

It took me far too long to cross the ten feet to where the metal was bolted into the rock. I studied it carefully. It looked like it had been there for decades, maybe longer. The chain was hooked into a metal plate that was fastened to the wall with thick bolts. Those, too, were rusted.

My fingers traced each one, testing its strength. Two of them were the slightest bit loose.

I quickly scanned the space again. In the far corner, in the shadows of the basement, I thought I could make out another door. It was likely some sort of closet or cellar, but a small part of me hoped it might be an escape.

Turning back to the bolts, my fingers worked the metal until they bled, but I didn't stop. I had to get out of here. To get free.

Images of the guys filled my mind. I knew those images were a lie, but my heart still longed for them. A time that didn't even truly exist.

A whirring sound had my head snapping up. That was when I saw it. The red blinking light.

My hand instantly dropped from the metal plate. I strained to identify the object in the low light of the basement. A camera. My stomach twisted.

Someone was watching.

I curled my arms around my middle, suddenly feeling as if I weren't wearing any clothes. Then I began searching the room again. This time not for an escape but for anything to use for protection. There wasn't a single item in the room other than cobwebs.

Footsteps sounded above, and my stomach cramped again. A key slid into the lock. Hinges creaked as the door to the basement opened. More footsteps on the stairs.

I made out boots first. Ones made of gleaming leather. Nice jeans over the tops of them.

Then a face appeared. One that had a chill skating over my skin. Damien stepped into the light. I couldn't help but take him in, as if somehow, I'd be able to spot a weakness that would save me. Dark hair, expertly cut. Pale but beautiful skin. And a deadness in his eyes that made me shiver.

He grinned at me. "Finally awake, Little Lamb?"

I swallowed, trying to clear the dryness in my mouth and throat.

His grin widened. "Nothing to say?"

My heart hammered in my chest. Could he hear that? The blood roaring in my ears? Suddenly, I wished I'd asked the guys a million more questions about the supernatural world. In movies, vampires always had a superior sense of hearing and smell.

Fear spiked somewhere deep. The memory of Damien's teeth plunging into my neck. The horrible pain. As if I were being burned from the inside out. Only now, I was totally and completely alone. No one to protect me.

My fingernails dug into my palms to keep me from screaming. "W-what do you want from me?"

I couldn't do a damn thing about the tremor in my voice, but it wasn't as if I could've hidden my fear from Damien anyway. Everything in his expression told me he'd already sensed it. And that he loved it.

Damien's eyes flashed, a quick burst of red in the deep brown. "What do *I* want?"

He prowled toward me. "I want what I've always wanted. I want my goddamned birthright. To be at the head of the Crescent bond and everything that comes with it…"

"W-what?" My mind whirled as an image of the guys' marks flashed in my mind. The crescent moon.

He bared his teeth. "They think they can steal everything from me, but now I've got what I need to get it back. I've got you."

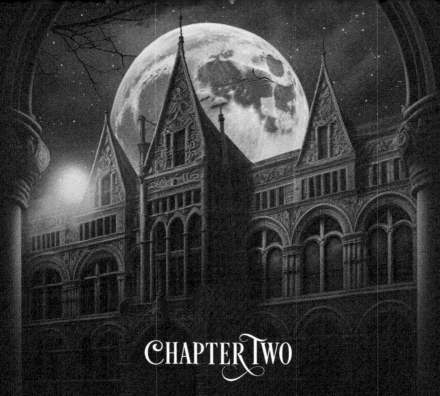

CHAPTER TWO

MY HEART HAMMERED SO HARD AGAINST MY RIBS IT WAS a wonder it didn't break free and fly right out of my chest. "What did they steal from you?"

My voice sounded remarkably calm. Almost too calm. As if I'd gone dead inside.

And maybe I had. Maybe that was what was necessary to make it through the nightmare. To keep my shit together and get *out*.

Damien's nostrils flared as he struggled to keep his composure. "They stole *everything* from me."

I didn't say a word in response. I simply waited. Because there was one thing I knew about guys like Damien. They loved to talk. To tell the whole world all the ways they had been wronged. I didn't have to wait long.

He began to pace back and forth along the stone floor. "The Laurents are one of the founding families. *I* am my father's heir.

Do you know how it looks when all their fucking marks appeared and mine didn't?"

I stayed quiet, my fingernails pressing deeper into my palms.

"It looks like I'm fucking weak." Damien's steps halted, and he whirled in my direction. "But I'm not weak. I know they did something. Something to cut me out of the bond. And I'm going to find out what."

My mouth felt like it was stuffed full of cotton. He was crazy. Full-on batshit crazy.

I didn't know a lot about bonds, but it seemed like they were destined by the Universe. The guys had been desperate to find a way to make me their anchor despite the fact that I hadn't manifested, but they hadn't found anything that would help.

Damien stalked toward me. "Tell me what they did to suppress my mark."

My eyes flared wide. "W-what?"

"Tell. Me. What. They. Did," he gritted out.

"They didn't do anything," I squeaked.

Damien's hand snaked out so fast I didn't have a prayer of blocking it. His fingers locked around my throat, squeezing hard. Panic surged as my air supply was cut off.

Damien let out a hiss and jerked his hand back.

I crumpled to the floor, coughing as air filled my lungs again.

"That goddamned caster," Damien cursed, examining his palm.

There, in the middle of his hand, was a burn in the same shape as my locket.

He glared at me as if I'd made the locket attack him. Then he tipped his head back and bellowed, "Lucien, Caspian, get the hell down here!"

My muscles locked, a new fear coursing through me. Being alone with Damien was bad enough, but three against one?

An image of Trace coming to my rescue flashed in my memory. Tears stung my eyes. Even if none of them had truly wanted me, not when it mattered most, at least they'd done what they could to keep me safe. I would've given anything for that protection right now.

Footsteps thundered above me and then down the stairs. Lucien and Caspian appeared. Lucien looked similar to Damien with dark hair and eyes, but Caspian was the light to their dark with blond hair and blue eyes. But no matter the color, all three sets of eyes held that same deadness that made unease wash over me.

They glanced at me on the floor and then at Damien.

"What do you need?" Lucien asked.

"Get me gloves and a set of bolt cutters," Damien growled.

Lucien immediately started back up the stairs, but Caspian glanced at him, a hint of wariness in his gaze. "What's your plan?"

He held up his palm. "I need to get that damned necklace off her if I'm going to question her properly."

My stomach pitched. I didn't have the answer to any of Damien's questions. The guys had left me completely in the dark.

Caspian looked in my direction. "Tell him what he wants to know."

Damien's eyes flashed red again. "This is the only chance you'll get. Tell me how they cut me out of the bond."

"They don't tell me anything. I was leaving because of all the secrets they kept. They didn't even want me. You think they would tell me their plans?"

A flicker of uncertainty flashed in Damien's expression, but then it was gone again. "You were living with them. You had to hear something."

I struggled to my feet, the shackle digging into my ankle. "I found out they were supernaturals. That I was an anchor who didn't manifest. That I'm their mate. That's all I know. I swear."

"She might be telling the truth," Caspian said in a low voice. "You know they keep things close to the vest."

Damien shook his head violently. "She knows more."

Footsteps sounded on the stairs again.

"Got it," Lucien called, handing Damien what looked like gloves for yardwork and some sort of intense clippers.

Damien yanked them from his grasp. "Hold her down. I'd hate to accidentally cut her carotid before she's useful."

"N-no. Stay away from me." I thrust my hands forward, but it didn't matter. They were on me in a flash.

I cried out as Lucien swept my legs out from under me in a single kick. I hit the stone floor with a force that knocked all the air from my lungs. But the moment the stun passed, I started kicking.

Lucien cursed, sitting on top of my legs. "Get that fucking necklace off. It's making me sick."

I remembered Dash's words about it protecting me from those who wished me harm. It hadn't protected me enough, though.

Caspian gripped my shoulders hard. "Stop fighting. Don't make us hurt you."

But I couldn't stop. Because if I did, they'd have free rein.

I twisted and bucked, trying to get free. But nothing worked. The two guys were unnaturally strong.

Damien bent down, his face twisting. "They can't save you. They never could."

His gloved hand reached out and tugged on the necklace. Then he slipped the clippers under the chain and pressed down.

I swore I felt it when the necklace broke, my last shred of hope along with it.

Damien sneered down at me, dropping the clippers and glove to the floor. He cracked his knuckles. "Now, you're going to tell me what the Crescent bond's plans are. If you don't, I'll just have to see what I can do to change your mind…"

CHAPTER THREE

FOOTSTEPS SOUNDED ON THE STAIRS. I JERKED UPRIGHT, OUT of my hazy half sleep, and scrambled back against the wall, as if that would somehow save me. It hadn't once so far. My muscles cried out at the sudden movement, pain still radiating through them at the faint memory of the burn.

Damien grinned as he took me in, dirty clothes and matted hair. But that was what seven days without a shower did to you. The only privacy I got was when I was allowed to go to the bathroom in a bucket.

"Ready to tell me?"

"I told you everything I know." My words were barely audible. A faint rasp from screaming so much.

His eyes flashed red, and a muscle jumped in his cheek. "Stop. Lying."

"I'm not lying. Don't you think I would've told you by now if I knew?" The truth was, I wouldn't have been able to hold back any information if I'd wanted to. The pain radiating through me was too great.

Damien cocked his head to one side, cracking his neck. He opened his mouth, teeth elongating into fangs.

I wanted to beg, to plead, but I knew it wouldn't do any good, and I refused to give him the satisfaction. But I couldn't hold back my shudder.

Damien surged forward, and his teeth sank into my shoulder. I was so covered in wounds, it was a miracle he'd found a new place to bite me.

I tried to brace, but it was never enough. The pain stole my breath. A blazing white-hot fire that surged through my veins, burning me alive from the inside out. Then the scream came. I didn't want to let it free, didn't want to give Damien that sense of power, but I couldn't stop it.

Damien jerked his teeth out of my flesh and straightened with a wince. "Damn, your voice is annoying."

The scream didn't stop, though. It kept going as pain ravaged my body over and over in waves of burning lava. It kept going until my voice gave out completely and even after that. It just turned to a silent scream then.

Damien let out a dramatic sigh. "Finally." He studied me. "I wonder if we're doing permanent damage to your vocal cords."

Probably. But I couldn't find it in me to care. All I could focus on was trying to breathe through the agony.

"Are you ready to talk yet?" he pressed.

There were no sounds that escaped my throat, and my only movements were those of writhing in pain.

Damien bent over me, tapping against my forehead. "Did I break you?"

A snort came from the bottom of the staircase. "Probably," Lucien muttered.

With my torture, I hadn't even noticed them coming into the basement.

Caspian's gaze locked with mine, and his jaw went hard. "This obviously isn't working, D. You need to try something else."

Damien whirled on his friend. "Are you questioning me?"

"N-no. Of course not," Caspian stammered.

Damien stalked toward him. "You don't think I know what I'm doing? You don't think I can lead our den?"

Caspian shook his head frantically. "You'll be an excellent leader."

But even through my pain, I could read the lie in his words. Caspian didn't think anything of the sort.

"I won't let that trash seize power. They'll sway The Assembly, turn our allies away from us. It's not going to happen," Damien growled.

"Damn straight," Lucien encouraged.

Damien jerked his chin at Lucien. "What do we know about the Crescents?"

Lucien straightened, but a smile played on his lips. "They're running around like chickens with their heads cut off. They have no idea where she is or who has her."

Tears leaked from my eyes. They were looking for me. Even if it was just because I was something destiny had ladened them with, they were still looking. I wanted to feel a flicker of hope that they just might find me. But I couldn't grab hold.

A beep sounded, and Damien pulled out his phone, scanning the screen. He cursed.

"What?" Lucien asked.

"The Assembly wants to ask me some questions about Leighton." His gaze jerked to me.

It was then I realized I was still writhing. My body still reacted to the pain, even though my brain had completely dissociated by this point.

Damien crouched in front of me. "If you get me into trouble, I will drain every drop of blood from your body, and I will do it slowly."

"Are you sure no one knows about this place, D?" Caspian asked.

"I'm fucking sure. It was abandoned almost a century ago. I found it by accident."

Caspian looked around as if he expected The Assembly to jump out at any moment.

"Grow some balls," Lucien snarled. "The Assembly can't rule us. The vamps should be leading the supernaturals anyway. Everyone knows we're the strongest."

Damien straightened from his crouch and grinned at his friend. "That's the fucking truth." He turned toward Caspian and glared. "Either you're with us or against us."

Caspian's already fair complexion paled even further. "I'm with you. You know I'm with you. I just think we need to be smart. Think outside the box so we make sure we get you to where you deserve to be."

Damien stilled at that. "Think outside the box, how?"

Caspian's mouth opened and closed as he searched for something, anything, to get Damien off his back. "We need to link you back to the bond so you can take over. Lead like you were always meant to."

Damien scowled at him. "Why do you think I'm questioning Leighton every damn day?"

"I know," Caspian hurried to say. "But there has to be a way to go around her. Someone else who can help. Maybe a caster who could work a spell?"

Damien stilled, his brain working over the problem. Then he smiled. It was an ugly, twisted curve of his lips. And it made me shudder, only intensifying the burning agony surging through me.

He turned slowly toward me. "If Leighton won't tell me what I need to know, then I'll bond to her. The Crescents will have no choice but to welcome me with open arms."

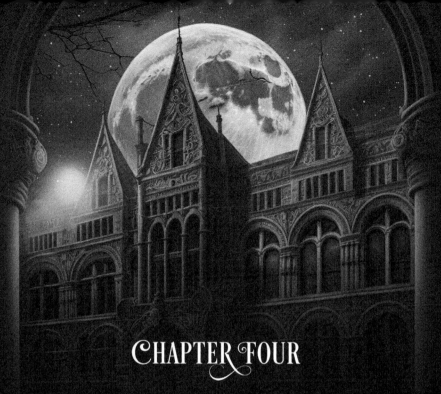

CHAPTER FOUR

THE HINGES ON THE DOOR SQUEAKED, BUT I COULDN'T move. Just opening my eyes felt like a battle. Everything hurt. From the tips of my toes to the ends of my hair.

Footsteps sounded, and I took in the sneakers on the stairs. A little of the tension in me eased. Sneakers usually meant Caspian. He was the lesser of the three evils.

I had no idea how long I'd been in the basement. I'd given up on trying to track time. It didn't matter anyway.

Caspian came to a stop in front of me. His brows pinched. "You need to drink."

He crouched beside me, opening a bottle of water. I tried to lift my head, but I couldn't even do that. Caspian cursed, then tilted my head back and poured a little of the water into my mouth.

The cool liquid was a balm to my raw throat.

He repeated the action twice more until the worst of my thirst was gone. But the ache from screaming was still there. Damien's torture had intensified. He'd become obsessed with searching for a way to force the bond, and every time he hit a dead end, he took it out on me.

I turned my head so that I could look up into Caspian's eyes. "Help me. Please."

His muscles locked.

I knew that he didn't agree with what Damien was doing. I could see it every time the three of them descended the basement steps. He could set me free. I knew he could. All it would take was one snip of those bolt cutters that taunted me from the corner.

"Please." My voice was barely audible, more a croak than a word.

"I can't," he whispered. "Damien would slit my throat before I could blink."

I was sure Damien would attempt just that. I didn't blame Caspian for being terrified, but I did blame him for not trying.

"Get a message to Colt." Just getting out those five words had my chest heaving with the effort it took.

Caspian's face went hard. "I won't betray my brethren."

"Even if they're wrong?" I wheezed.

His back molars ground together. "Damien has his reasons. He's been robbed of his birthright."

It was bullshit, and Caspian knew it. In some ways, that made him worse than Damien and Lucien. Those two thought what they were doing was right. That made them psychos with no conscience. Caspian had a conscience. He knew this was wrong. That made him evil.

The door at the top of the steps slammed. "Well, well, well. Isn't this cozy," Damien snarled, Lucien following him down the stairs.

Caspian jerked to standing. "I was just making sure she didn't die on you."

Damien's eyes narrowed on Caspian. "She's mine. If I find out you touched a hair on her head—"

"I didn't," Caspian hurried to say.

Lucien scoffed. "Your loyalty hasn't been all that on point lately."

Caspian's jaw worked back and forth. "I'm here, aren't I? I patrol. I covered for both your asses with The Assembly."

Lucien shoved at Caspian's chest. "I don't need you to do shit for me."

Caspian growled low. "Oh, yeah? Then I can just tell The Assembly that your alibi is nothing but a lie?"

Lucien's eyes flashed red, and he charged, but Damien stepped between the two of them, pushing them apart. "Enough!"

Lucien and Caspian instantly halted. Damien had some sort of hold on both of them, I'd give him that. Whether it was terror or respect, I wasn't entirely sure.

Damien glared at his friends. "The last thing we need is to be at each other's throats. We're almost there. Almost to the finish line."

My heart jerked at that, a million questions filling my mind. None of the answers I came up with were good.

Caspian stiffened. "Did you find someone to help?"

Damien grinned. "A caster who was more than willing to share knowledge for a price."

A fresh wave of nausea rolled through me. I had no idea what a completed bond would feel like when it was one of free will and destiny, but I knew that whatever Damien was trying to force me into would be dark and twisted. Everything surrounding him was nothing but pain and destruction.

"They can bond you?" Caspian pressed.

"He needs to gather some supplies for the spell, but on the full moon tomorrow night, it'll be done," Damien assured him.

Hot tears leaked from my eyes, spilling down my face. I thought it was impossible for me to cry any more. I'd spent hours while I was alone, letting the tears free. My only respite was imagining those few blissful moments when I'd thought I was wanted. When I'd thought I had a home. Before I realized everything was a lie.

Caspian shifted on his feet. "Are you sure this is a good idea?

It might be an act of war. The Assembly could have you sentenced to death."

Damien's jaw hardened to granite. "You doubt me?" he growled.

"N-no. I just don't want you to have more trouble," Caspian defended.

"The Crescents won't have a choice. They won't be willing to lose Leighton, so they'll have to live with me as a part of their bond."

Caspian snapped his mouth closed, but I could tell there was something about Damien's plan he didn't think would work.

The red in Damien's eyes glowed brighter. "I can smell your disbelief. I won't have your insolence in my den," he snarled.

Damien's arm shot out, claw-like talons lengthening from his fingers. They slashed across Caspian's throat so fast he didn't have a prayer of stopping it. His hand flew to his neck as blood gushed from the wounds.

Caspian collapsed to the ground, a gurgling sound emanating from him. Damien just watched, a blissful smile on his face.

Lucien laughed. "Thank God. He was getting fucking annoying."

Caspian's hand loosened around his throat, his eyes going wide before the life left them altogether. Bile surged up my throat, but I forced it down.

"Clean up this mess," Damien snapped.

Lucien's eyes flashed, but he nodded. Just as he reached the bottom step, a series of beeps sounded. Lucien froze, then he yanked out his phone, tapping on the screen. His face paled as his head jerked up.

"The Crescents. They're here."

CHAPTER FIVE

DAMIEN CURSED. "WE CAN ESCAPE THROUGH THE TUNNELS. Help me get her unlocked."

"Are you fucking kidding? Leave her. I heard Trace has gone feral. He'll burn us alive," Lucien snapped.

Just the sound of Trace's name had a war of emotions taking flight inside me. Hope, hurt, longing. It all mixed together in a complicated stew I didn't have a prayer of untangling.

"I'm not going to lose her," Damien growled. "She's my one hope to get my birthright back."

"I'm not getting dead for your damn birthright," Lucien shot back. But he was already moving toward the door in the far corner of the basement.

"Lucien!" Damien ordered.

He ignored Damien and jerked open the door, disappearing inside.

Damien let loose a slew of curses and hurried over to me. "I'll kill him for this."

I hoped he did. Then Damien would be all alone when the guys came for him.

Damien dug in his pocket, pulling out a set of keys. He shoved one into the lock, the shackle digging deeper into my ankle. I couldn't hold in my whimper as fresh pain bloomed.

"Shut up," he snapped.

I bit the inside of my cheek to keep from crying out again. I squeezed my eyes closed, praying that the guys moved quickly, that maybe I would get my freedom after all.

Damien twisted the key, and the cuff fell away. I stared down at my ankle. Blood seeped from an angry wound that looked infected, and bruises surrounded it.

"Get up," Damien ordered.

"Can't," my voice was barely a whisper.

"Now!"

Even if he'd threatened me with death, I wouldn't have been able to obey. My body had simply given up. I didn't blame it. It had been through far too much.

More curses slipped from Damien's lips, and he bent, hauling me up and over his shoulder.

I couldn't hold in my cry this time. My body was too broken to keep quiet.

"Shut your mouth, or I'll cut out your tongue," Damien gritted out.

My breaths came in quick pants, a mixture of fear and trying to manage the pain.

Damien straightened and headed for the door to the tunnels.

I couldn't let him get me in there, couldn't let him escape. This was my one chance, and I had to take it.

Just as we reached the mouth of the entryway, I grabbed on to the doorjamb. My fingers grasped as hard as they could while my muscles trembled with the effort.

"Enough!" Damien yelled.

I still held on, praying I could just take enough time so that the guys would make it to me.

Damien's arm came down in a swift move across mine, breaking my hold in a vicious strike.

Hot tears streamed down my face as Damien picked up his pace again. I couldn't give up, though. I had to fight.

I bounced against his back as he entered the tunnel, and I did the one thing I could. I went for where he was most vulnerable. I reached between his legs, grabbed his balls, and squeezed as hard as I could.

The scream that filled the air was more animal than human. Damien dropped me from his shoulder, and I landed on the stone floor with a thud. Agony washed through me in a steady pulse as the world flickered around me.

Damien howled, cupping himself as he bent over and struggled to breathe.

Footsteps sounded above me. I tried to scream. To yell for help, but my voice was too ravaged.

I heard the telltale sound of the hinges on the door. Then footsteps on the stairs.

Damien snapped straight, his gaze jumping to me and then to the basement. For a second, I thought he might try to take me again, but instead, he ran down the tunnels.

"Leighton!" Dash called.

I tried to yell for him, but I couldn't get my voice to cooperate.

"Holy hell," Declan muttered. "That's Caspian."

"Or what's left of him," Ronan echoed.

"I smell her, but it's too mixed with other things. Death. Urine," Colt muttered.

"Where. Is. She?" Trace gritted out.

"She has to be close," Dash urged.

I put everything I could into screaming. All that came out was a wheezing squeak. But it was enough.

"There!" Declan shouted.

Footsteps thundered against the stone.

"Get a light," Colt ordered.

A second later, I squeezed my eyes closed at the assaulting brightness.

A litany of curses filled the air.

"Leighton?" Dash whispered as he crouched next to me.

"She's covered in fucking bite marks," Ronan snarled.

Dash touched a light hand to my shoulder, and I couldn't hold in my whimper. He snatched his hand back. "I don't know where to touch her to lift her."

Trace's ragged breathing was audible. "She's in too much pain. I feel it fucking everywhere."

"LeeLee…"

I almost broke at that familiar nickname. The one I'd always loved. Fresh tears spilled over now.

"Open your eyes. Please," Colt begged.

My eyelids fluttered, bringing their faces into focus in a series of snapshots.

"Hurts," I croaked.

Agony filled Colt's expression. "I know. We're gonna help you, okay?"

But I couldn't say another word.

Ronan stepped into view, his face completely closed down. "Dash, you need to knock her out."

His eyes flared. "It's too risky with all these injuries. We could lose her."

"I don't want to hurt her," Ronan growled.

"Out," I whispered. "Get me out."

Dash's gaze jumped to me. "It's going to hurt," he warned.

I tipped my head up and down in what I hoped resembled a nod.

Dash looked at Trace. "You won't be able to take all of it, but you can take the worst."

Trace didn't hesitate. He crouched and linked his tattooed fingers with mine. A second later, a faint buzz took root in my muscles, easing a bit of the agony.

Dash's jaw locked, and he slid his arms under me, lifting.

A new wave of pain coursed through me. If I'd had any voice left, I would've screamed. But I didn't. Then blessed darkness took me.

CHAPTER SIX

A FAINT BEEPING SOUND GRATED AT MY SUBCONSCIOUS, but I just wanted to slip back into the nothingness. I loved the nothingness. There was no pain or grief or terror. There was simply an endless sea of black where I could float for the rest of time.

"It's been too long. We should call the doctor again," Declan said.

"He said she needs time," Dash assured him. "We've done everything we can. My herbs and potions. Human medicine. Your blood."

"It's not enough," Trace growled.

"Breathe," Colt told him.

"I don't want to fucking breathe. I want Leighton to wake up, and then I want to hunt down Lucien and Damien and peel the flesh from their bones."

Ronan grunted. "I'm with the psycho for once."

"I can stay with Leighton if you guys want to go hunting," Dash offered.

"Not leaving her," Trace muttered.

I pulled away from the darkness at that. It was so unlike Trace. He usually wanted nothing to do with me.

Colt pitched his voice low. "The more time you spend with her, the harder it's going to be for your demon to walk away."

"Don't care," he snapped.

"All right, then," Colt mumbled.

"Any updates from your team?" Declan asked.

Colt blew out a breath. "They're still searching. Nothing yet. It's like the two of them just vanished."

"And The Assembly still has their thumbs up their asses," Ronan groused.

"They have to make sure it doesn't appear they're rushing to judgment," Dash argued.

"Rushing?" Ronan growled. "We gave them the tapes from those damned cameras. She was fucking tortured for fourteen days. I lost count of the number of times he bit her. She's covered in scars. What more proof do they need?"

Something smashed against the wall, and Briar let out a hiss.

"Let's not get Trace any more riled up," Declan said in a low tone. "He already torched three cars and a building."

"I just need to know she's safe," Ronan defended.

"I know," Declan said in a low tone.

"She won't be safe until Lucien and Damien are dead." Barely restrained rage pulsed through each of Trace's words.

"We know," Colt agreed, sounding exhausted. "And one way or another, we'll make them that way. I promise."

Breath hissed from between Trace's teeth. "I need the killing blow. I don't know if my demon will be satiated without it."

There was silence for a moment before Colt agreed. "We can give him that for at least one of them."

Trace grunted again but didn't say another word.

I had the most bizarre urge to comfort him. Even with as much of an asshole as he'd been. Even with how I knew they didn't want me. I still hated the idea of him hurting, of him being at odds with his demon.

I tried to pull out of the nothingness, but it was like quicksand, wanting me to stay. My fingers fluttered against the mattress.

"Guys…" Declan said.

"What?" Colt asked.

"I think Leighton's starting to wake up."

Shuffling sounded, and I could sense bodies pushing closer.

I fought against the tug of the darkness.

"Open those eyes, LeeLee," Colt whispered.

I wanted to so badly. I wanted to know that I was free. Away from Damien and his torture. But I was so scared that if I opened my eyes, this would all just be a dream.

"You're safe, Mon Coeur," Dash whispered. "Come back to us."

My heart clenched. I didn't want to let those words in, couldn't trust them. But still, I tried to force my eyes open.

My eyelids fluttered, letting in a burst of sunlight. The first true daylight I'd seen in weeks. I squinted against it, giving my eyes a moment to adjust.

Slowly, I took in the guys surrounding my bed. They looked rough. All of them had scruff on their jaws and dark circles under their eyes. Their clothes were rumpled, and their hair was in disarray.

"How do you feel?" Dash asked.

I did a mental survey, bracing for that familiar residue of burning pain that Damien's bites left behind. Instead, all I felt was a low-level ache in my muscles. "Okay." My voice was a husky rasp. Apparently, all the screaming had done some damage there.

His mouth thinned. "Do you want a sip of water?"

I nodded slowly.

Dash took a cup from the nightstand and placed a straw between my lips.

I took a long pull. The cool water was heaven on my throat.

He tugged it away. "We don't want to give you too much. Your stomach's been empty for a while."

That was when I caught sight of all the wires. I was in my bedroom at The Nest, but there was a slew of medical equipment around it. There was a heart monitor and an IV pole that housed a bag of clear liquid and one with red liquid.

My heart hammered against my ribs, my breaths coming quicker as I stared at the bags. Blood. Memories of being bitten slammed into me. Memories of Caspian's throat being slit.

"It's okay," Declan hurried to say. "It's just fluids and some of my blood. Dragon blood heals better than anything else we have."

I struggled to get my breathing under control, but it wouldn't obey.

All I could see was Damien's twisted face, his fangs elongating as I braced for agony.

"She's having a panic attack," Ronan snapped.

"It's okay, Leighton. You're safe," Dash comforted. He reached out, resting a hand on my shoulder.

I scrambled away from him. "Don't touch me!" The tears came then, a mixture of panic and grief. I couldn't let him be a comfort. Not when that would be ripped away again. Not when it was a lie.

Dash snapped his hand back as I hugged my knees to my chest and rocked back and forth. "Don't want me." I whispered it over and over again as I rocked.

I caught flashes of the guys' faces. Each one wore a different expression, a mixture of emotions. Pain. Rage. Regret.

Ronan's throat worked as he swallowed. "Will you let Declan stay with you? He didn't know where you were. Never knew. We hid it from him."

Declan's head snapped in Ronan's direction, his jaw going hard. "Ronan..."

"It's true. I swear it on my life."

I kept rocking but studied Ronan. I read nothing but truth in his eyes.

"O-okay."

Ronan jerked his head in a nod. "Let's leave them."

"No," Trace snarled.

Colt caught him by the tee. "Now's not the time. Let's hunt those that would hurt her. Then we can make amends."

Trace's teeth ground together. "Hunt." It was all he seemed to be able to say, but it allowed Colt to shove him out of my bedroom. Ronan followed him without a backward glance. But Dash's gaze cut to me. So much hurt there.

"I know you won't believe me, but I love you, Leighton. I always will. And one day, you'll see."

His words hurt worse than any tear of my flesh inflicted by Damien. Because I wanted so badly for them to be true, but I knew they weren't.

CHAPTER SEVEN

MY THROAT CONSTRICTED AS THE DOOR CLOSED BEHIND Dash. I dug my fingernails into my palms to keep from crying, but it was no use. The tears came anyway.

Declan's expression twisted in pain. He sat next to me on the bed, leaning against the pillows. "Come here."

I could barely make him out through my blurred vision. "You didn't know?"

He shook his head. "I didn't even know they had found our mate at all."

I blinked rapidly, trying to clear my tears. "Would you have come for me?"

Declan's eyes went silver. "Leighton. I've been searching for you every day of my life."

The sobs came then. I let myself collapse against Declan's chest, and his arms went gently around me. "I just—I wanted to be wanted."

The words sounded so juvenile, but I couldn't find any better ones. For so many years, I'd been so casually discarded, kicked around, and so very alone. I lived my life in a constant state of terror. Colt had been the piece of hope I'd held on to. This little bit of light I could escape into.

To learn that he'd known where I was all this time and hadn't even sent an email? It shattered my heart into pieces so small, I knew it would never be put back together right.

Declan's hand stroked up and down my back. "Trust me when I say I was pissed as all hell when I found out." He paused. "I broke Colt's nose."

I tipped my head back so I could see Declan's face. "You did?"

He nodded. "Colt didn't even try to stop me. He knows he fucked up."

I let my head drop back to Declan's chest. I didn't want to hear the excuses.

"They thought they were doing the right thing."

"Don't, Dec."

He tensed beneath me.

"I can't right now. It hurts too much."

His hand picked up his ministrations again. "Okay. Just rest. You're safe now."

But I wasn't so sure that was true.

⌣

I didn't wake to voices this time. I woke to purrs. Briar was curled into my side, vibrating with her joy at being reunited.

My fingers sifted through her fur as I blinked against the low light in the room. It came from a lamp on my nightstand, the sky outside having gone dark. Sometime during my unconscious state, my heart monitor and IV had been removed.

My hand trembled as I reached for the glass on the bedside table. I took a couple of sips of water and waited to see how my stomach would handle it. No nausea greeted me, but I didn't want to push it.

I shoved myself up on the pillows, and Briar let out a grumble of protest.

"Sorry, girl." I picked her up and cuddled her to my chest. "I missed you."

She licked my chin as if to echo the statement.

I listened carefully as I stroked Briar's fur. I didn't hear a sound. Something about the quiet set me on edge.

I set Briar down on the mattress and swung my legs over the side of the bed. A wave of dizziness swept over me, forcing me to grip the blankets to steady myself. *How long had I been asleep?*

Giving my body a chance to acclimate to the new sitting position, I waited. After a minute or two, I tried standing. The room swam a bit as I did so, but it came into focus more quickly this time.

Briar meowed as if to lecture me for being out of bed.

"I'll be quick," I promised her.

I looked down at myself. Someone had to have cleaned me up and changed me into sweats and a T-shirt at some point, but I didn't want to think about who. I found a pair of slippers near the foot of the bed and slid them on.

Walking to the door, I paused to listen again. Still nothing. I worried the corner of my lip, then took a deep breath and opened the door.

I thought for sure I'd hear strains of voices or video games, but there wasn't a sound to be heard. Slowly, I made my way down the hall to the stairs. My fingers curled around the banister as I took the steps carefully. The last thing I needed was to fall down the stairs.

By the time I reached the bottom, I was winded. I took a second to catch my breath while I planned out my next move. The kitchen. If the guys weren't here, maybe Baldwin would know where they were.

My heart constricted at the thought of the kind man. I'd left without saying goodbye or thank you, and he hadn't deserved that.

I wound my way through the halls and into the massive gourmet space. But it, too, was empty. The entire mansion looked like a ghost town.

A prickle of panic swept through me, and my breaths came quicker. That was when I heard it.

For a second, I thought I'd imagined it, but then I heard it again. The low rumble of a voice. But it sounded like it was coming from below.

My brows pulled together as I turned slowly in a circle. Another muted voice, again, from below.

I walked out of the kitchen and down the hall. As I approached a door, the voices got a bit louder. I stopped in front of it, frowning. The voice sounded again, but I couldn't make out what it said.

I tugged on the corner of my lip with my teeth, then reached out for the handle. Slowly, I turned it.

A dark staircase greeted me, one that had memories slamming against the walls of my mind. Walls that were trying to protect me from the torture of the past few weeks.

My heart beat faster, blood pounding in my ears. I hovered on that top step, trying to hear, but all I could make out were sounds, not actual words.

I forced myself to take one step and then another. The muffled voices got louder. Then one rose above the rest. Trace.

"You think we won't tear you apart? You harmed our fucking mate. Tortured her."

"I-I didn't. It was Damien."

Ice slid through my veins at the sound of Lucien's voice.

"You stood by," Trace growled. "Helped him take her. That makes you worse."

"I-I'm sorry! I didn't have a choice."

"Tell us where he's hiding. If you don't, I'm going to gut you, but first, I'll peel your skin from your flesh, and I'll do it slowly."

CHAPTER EIGHT

MY BREATHS CAME QUICKER AS LUCIEN LET OUT A PANICKED squeak.

"I don't know where Damien is. I swear I'd tell you if I knew."

Fear grabbed hold and wouldn't let go, yet I still continued down the stairs. Some part of me needed to see. To know.

I stopped just as the group came into view. A single fluorescent light illuminated the room, casting it in a bluish light. Lucien was strapped to a chair, his lip bloodied and eye swelling shut. Trace, Colt, Ronan, Dash, and Declan surrounded him. Some of them close, others seeming to be studying the goings-on from further away.

Trace pulled something from his waistband so fast, the only thing I could register was a flash of silver before he was slamming it into Lucien's hand.

Lucien howled in pain, bucking against the constraints, but it did no good.

Trace stepped back, and it was then that I could see he'd stabbed a knife clean through Lucien's hand and into the wooden arm of the chair. My stomach roiled, and I had to force down the surge of bile in my throat.

"You know something. Not telling us just means you're giving my demon a chance to play. Really, I should thank you."

"H-he's obsessed with you. The Crescents," Lucien stammered, sweat beading on his brow.

The guys shared a look of confusion at the name.

"That's what he calls you," Lucien explained. "Because of your marks."

The little crescent moons that resembled a tattoo or a dark birthmark.

Ronan bared his teeth at Lucien. "I don't give a damn what cute little nickname he's given us."

Lucien shook his head back and forth in a rapid, staccato movement. "No, you don't get it. He's *obsessed*."

Colt pushed off the table he was leaning against, stalking toward Lucien. "Explain."

Lucien gulped. "He thinks he should be in your bond. Thinks that you're going to take over and cast the vamps out of Emerald Bay. You've already acted against us."

Colt's eyes narrowed. "The Assembly punished the vamps because members of your den attacked unprovoked. That carries consequences. It has nothing to do with us."

"But it showed Damien that the vamps don't have as much control as he thought," Lucien explained. "He thinks that when you guys take power, you'll cut us out completely."

Declan studied Lucien carefully. "It's more than that. He thinks the vamps should have complete rule, doesn't he?"

Lucien paled. "N-no."

Trace moved in a flash, taking the handle of the knife and twisting it in Lucien's hand. "Don't lie to us."

Lucien screamed.

I sank to the step, covering my ears. It was too much like my own screams from the past weeks.

"He wants us to seize power!" The words tumbled from Lucien's mouth as if he had no control over them.

"Why did he take Leighton?" Dash asked. His voice carried a tone I'd never heard from him before, empty, cold.

Lucien swallowed hard, eyeing Trace.

Trace pulled another knife from his waistband and used it to begin cleaning his fingernails. "The truth, vermin."

Lucien's eyes flared red for a moment, and I knew that if he could've killed Trace, he would've in a heartbeat.

"He wanted to find out what you were up to, and then he got the idea that he could bond with her. Then you would have no choice but to accept him."

The room went eerily silent. The only thing I could hear was the beating of my own heart.

"What. Did. You. Say?" Trace snarled.

Lucien paled. "He wanted to force the bond with Leighton, said that you'd have to let him in if he was connected to her."

Colt's jaw was hard as granite. "Even if he could find someone to do it, Leighton never manifested as an anchor, bonding with her could kill her."

Tremors rocked my body as Damien's determined face filled my memory.

"He found a caster who said he could do it."

Dash cursed, charging forward. "Who?"

"H-he didn't say." Lucien's gaze jumped around the room. "He won't stop. He thinks she's the way to get his power back."

"Where is he?" Trace said, his voice low with a feral edge.

"I don't know! I took off when I saw you on the cameras. I have no idea where he went. But he'll be close. He wants her."

"I don't believe you." Trace moved to the corner of the room and grabbed a rolling tray, guiding it over to Lucien.

I couldn't make out its contents at first, but when it reached the light, I sucked in a breath. Blades. Pliers. Hammers. It was a torture kit.

"W-what are you doing?" Lucien squeaked.

Trace picked up a pair of pliers, examining them in the light. "I'm going to get the answers I need from you. I think we'll start by taking some teeth. It'll make it harder for you to talk, but if you're motivated properly, you'll find a way."

My breaths came quicker, short, little pants instead of full inhales and exhales, as the memory of Damien's bites filled my mind.

Dash crossed his arms over his chest. "The root of the tooth is one of the most sensitive parts of the human body. It's a good choice, T."

Lucien's head jerked back and forth. "Y-you can't do that."

Trace prowled toward him. "Watch me."

Black dots danced in front of my vision as fear pulsed deep. The softest sound escaped me, but five heads jerked in my direction.

Colt cursed and then was striding toward me. I wanted to get up, to run. But I couldn't move.

"LeeLee. It's okay. He can't hurt you."

As Colt reached out, I scrambled back. "No!"

Agony ripped across his expression, but he stopped.

Declan hurried around him as I struggled to breathe. "Leighton, look at me. You're safe."

"I'm not. He'll never stop." The words were barely discernable through my pants, but the guys got the gist.

Declan lifted me into his arms. "We'll stop him. We've got you."

I couldn't get any more words out. I was lost to the memories now, the pain, as if I were living it all over again.

"She's having another fucking panic attack," Ronan growled.

"We need a sedative," Colt barked.

"I've got one," Dash said.

Footsteps pounded on the stairs. The sound only sent a fresh wave of memories over me, and I thrashed in Declan's arms.

"Shit! She's losing it," he called.

More hands held me, but I couldn't stop fighting. I had to get away.

"Dash! Fucking hurry!" Colt yelled.

More footsteps and then a prick in my arm. I cried out, but a second later, the pain eased, and I was drifting away. I welcomed the nothingness again.

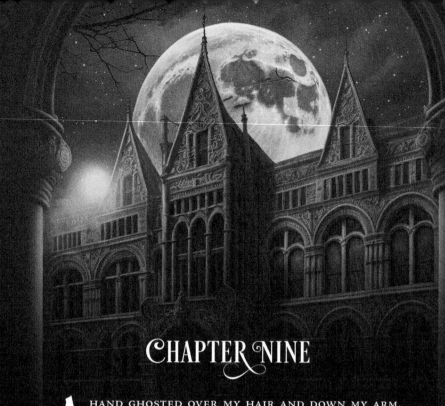

CHAPTER NINE

AHAND GHOSTED OVER MY HAIR AND DOWN MY ARM. Something about the tenderness of the action eased me. That and the peace of the nothingness. Floating in that sea of black. But something was pulling me back.

The voices. They were tugging me toward consciousness again, but I didn't want to go. I wanted to stay where I didn't have to feel a thing.

"Trace got a list of Damien's hangouts," Ronan said.

"Lucien still breathing?" Dash asked.

"Breathing, but not exactly in one piece," Ronan grumbled.

"Drop him somewhere and call it into The Assembly," Colt ordered. "They can deal with him now."

"Think we'll get blowback for this?" Declan asked.

His voice was closer, and the scent of fresh rain and mint that surrounded me told me it was him who was stroking me.

There was quiet for a moment before Colt answered. "We

could, but it's on record that Leighton's our mate. I don't think even The Assembly would try to punish us for doing what we need to protect her."

Declan's finger traced a spot on my arm. "I lost count at fifty."

"Fifty what?" Dash asked.

"Bite marks. He scarred her. Did it intentionally. She'll never be able to forget what he did to her because of it. Every time she looks down, the reminder will be right there," Declan gritted out.

"He's going to pay," Ronan snarled.

"There's not enough pain in this world to even the score," Declan shot back.

Everyone was quiet for a few beats, and then it was Dash who spoke.

"Where's Trace?"

"Cleaning up," Ronan answered. "He was a mess."

"We should check on him. Then deal with Lucien so he doesn't have to," Dash said.

Ronan grunted in affirmation, and then there was the sound of a door closing.

The ministrations on my hair and arm continued, pulling me closer to consciousness. My eyelids fluttered. The barest hint of rising sun came through the windows as I opened my eyes.

Declan brushed the hair out of my face. "How are you feeling?"

My mouth felt dry as a desert. "Okay."

"Think you could handle some broth and crackers?" he asked.

I nodded.

"Okay, I'm going to go get that for you. Be right back."

Declan shifted off the bed and started for the door.

It was then I realized that not all the guys had left. Colt sat in a chair next to my bed, his face a blank mask.

My stomach pitched, and I pushed up higher on the pillows.

"I'm so sorry, LeeLee."

Each word hurt. A fresh burn on already scarred skin.

"Please don't," I whispered.

Pain streaked across Colt's expression before he could hide it. "Give me five minutes. If you never want to hear another word from me, I'll accept that."

Pressure built inside of me. Everywhere. My chest. My eyes. My throat.

I couldn't speak, but I managed to nod.

Colt leaned forward in his chair, leaning his elbows against his knees. The move made the muscles in his forearms flex, veins popping. "All my life, my father warned me that my mate would be at risk. He drilled it into my head practically before I could speak. Do you know why?"

I stayed quiet but shook my head.

Colt swallowed, his Adam's apple bobbing. "My mom didn't die in a car accident. She was murdered."

Everything in me strung tight at the admission.

"She took me out to the beach one day when I was just two years old. Had security with her. But not enough." Colt's words were strangled, as if he had to force each one out of his throat.

"What happened?" I whispered.

"Rival pack. One hoping to encroach on our territory. They were smart, though. Waited until my father was out of town on business. Our pack enforcers didn't stand a chance. They had to choose between me and my mom. She was an alpha female who ordered them to protect me while those monsters dragged her away."

A choked sound came from my throat.

"It's my first memory. Watching her being taken by those bastards while tears streamed down her face."

"Colt…"

"They took her. Tortured her. Raped her. Left her body at our gates when they were done."

Silent tears tracked down my cheeks.

"My father always warned me that my mate would be at risk of the same thing. If she happened to be an anchor, she'd have a prayer of protecting herself. If she wasn't, I'd need to hide her away so that no one could ever find her."

My chest constricted, making it hard to breathe.

Colt traced a design on his hand with his thumb. "Dad saw the connection between us and knew what it might mean. He told me I had to wait. I begged him to go get you after your mom took you away, and he said we couldn't, that we needed to know if you were meant to be a part of this world."

"And when you didn't feel me manifest?" I asked.

Colt swallowed hard. "I made him send someone to check. They didn't sense any anchor abilities in you."

My heart cracked.

"I still begged him, told him that we could protect you. He refused. I fought him on it practically every day, even though I *knew* what had happened to my mom. Knew what a risk it would be, but I missed you with every breath. You haunted my dreams every damn night."

That pressure inside built. Colt had lived his own kind of torture over the years we'd been apart, his own waking nightmare.

"It was never that we didn't want you," Colt said in a harsh whisper. "We always wanted you." His gaze lifted to the window. "Then Dad died. He left me a letter, telling me to leave you be, that it was for the best. I should've listened."

A pained sound escaped my throat, and Colt's eyes jerked to me.

"But I didn't. Because I felt like I was dying, being away from you. It never mattered to me if you had no magic or enough to set the world on fire. I just wanted *you*. My LeeLee. My best friend. My soulmate."

Tears spilled over quicker now, and I didn't do a damned thing to brush them away.

"I've always been selfish when it comes to you. So, I went and got you. Ronan and Trace thought I was being reckless, but I did it anyway." Colt shoved to his feet. "And because I was selfish, you got hurt. Hell, LeeLee, you could've died."

"Colt—"

"Every night since you've been back, you scream in your sleep. I'll hear those screams until the day I die. And I'll never forgive myself." Colt's gaze met mine. "But don't you think for a damn minute that I didn't love you. I will until the last breath leaves my lungs."

Colt didn't wait for my response, he turned on his heel and left.

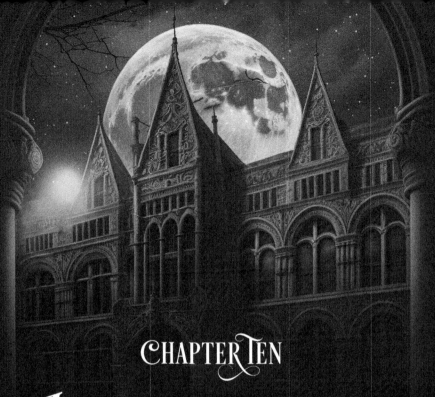

CHAPTER TEN

I STARED AT THE DOOR, FROZEN. I HAD NO IDEA HOW MUCH time passed, but I couldn't have moved if the house was on fire and I was about to go up in flames. I was a fool. So caught up in my own pain I hadn't stopped to consider the agony of those around me, what they were living with each and every day.

My heart cracked at the knowledge Colt had left me with. I'd seen photos of his mom. He got his wild, multi-colored hair from her. God, she'd been beautiful. Even just in the pictures I'd seen, I knew she loved him with everything she had. And now, I knew it for a fact. She'd given up everything for him.

I understood his father never being the same. I understood Andrew wanting to protect me because of what had happened to his wife. And now, Colt was carrying that same guilt because he'd brought me here and I'd been hurt.

The door I was staring at opened. I had to blink a few times to bring the figure into focus.

Declan took one look at me and picked up his pace. He sank to the mattress, hands framing my face. "Hey, what's going on?"

"I'm a monster."

His brows pulled together. "What are you talking about?"

"All I could see was my own hurt, but Colt's been dying inside."

Declan pulled me against his chest, arms wrapping around me. "Leighton."

"I didn't stop to think that he might have had his reasons. That they all did. I just thought they didn't want me."

My voice broke on my last words, the pain breaking through them and into the air around us.

"Colt gets it. We all do. You were alone for so long. No one knew how bad it was, or they would've intervened."

I swallowed hard. "I let Chloe get in my head."

Declan pulled back, frowning. "What do you mean?"

"It was her and Damien that told me. She said that the only reason Colt and Ronan came when they did was that they were worried the abuse was so bad the cops might get involved, and they didn't trust what my mom would say."

Declan's teeth ground together. "That fucking bitch. She lied. No one knew about the abuse. I swear to you."

I nodded. "I know." All it had taken was one moment of seeing Colt completely vulnerable to know that. We'd all made mistakes, but I knew with everything I had that he loved me. That he always had. Because I felt the same. I just didn't have the first clue about how to fix it all. Too much was broken. There was too much to overcome.

Declan reached out and tucked a strand of hair behind my ear. "We're going to figure this out. I promise."

Before I could say a word, a soft knock sounded on the open door.

Dash stood in the entryway, a tray balanced in one hand. "I've got soup. Is it okay if I come in?"

My heart twisted as if someone were wringing it out. There

was still a glimmer of hope in Dash's blue eyes, but there was hurt in them, too. Hurt that I had put there.

I nodded. "Thank you."

Dash strode across the expansive space, Briar greeting him with a hiss. He set the tray on my bed. "Just text me if she needs anything else," he murmured to Declan.

Dash turned to leave, and there was a sharp tug in my chest.

"Dash?" His name slipped from my lips with a desperate edge.

He froze, slowly turning around.

"Do you want to stay?" I asked hesitantly.

The corners of his lips tipped up. "Sure."

I scooted back against the pillows, pulling the tray closer to me so that he could sit on the end of the bed.

Dash lowered himself to the mattress, studying me. "How are you feeling?"

My stomach rumbled as if to answer.

He chuckled. "Hungry, I guess."

I nodded, looking down at the tray. There was what looked like a simple broth and then bread that was still steaming. He'd also brought water, ginger ale, and apple juice.

Declan pushed the tray even closer. "Baldwin made the bread fresh."

"It smells amazing." I broke off a piece and popped it into my mouth. I closed my eyes, unable to help the moan that escaped my lips.

When my eyes opened, it was to find both Declan and Dash staring at my mouth. My cheeks heated.

"Sorry," I mumbled.

Declan grinned. "Never have to apologize for enjoying your meals."

"Amen to that," Dash muttered.

I looked up at him. "Did everything, uh, get dealt with?"

A shadow passed over Dash's expression, but he nodded. "Lucien's gone. The Assembly has him in custody now."

"What will they do with him?" I still didn't quite understand The Assembly's role in the supernatural world.

Dash seemed to understand that my question held more than I'd given voice to. "They are responsible for trying every supernatural who violates the terms of our peace treaty."

"So, like a court for supernaturals?"

"Pretty much," Dash agreed.

"They also play the role of advisors," Declan explained. "They are supposed to help guide the leaders of our kind so that we can continue in a time of peace."

"That's why they have a say in the anchor you bond with?" The question slipped free before I could stop myself.

Dash's expression gentled. "They can share their opinion, but they can't force us to do anything."

"But if you don't have an anchor that's powerful enough, you could go insane."

Declan's fingers wove through mine. "We're going to find a way. The most stable bonds are when your anchor is also your true mate. We'll figure this out."

I stared down at my soup. Even if we could heal the rift we'd all created, I still didn't have the power they needed.

Dash's fingers slid beneath my chin, lifting my face so that I had to meet his eyes. "The fates gave us you as a mate. A gift I'll be forever grateful for. The fates are going to show us the path to be together. I believe it with everything I have. You just have to have a little faith."

But every time I'd held on to that faith before, it had been ripped out from under me.

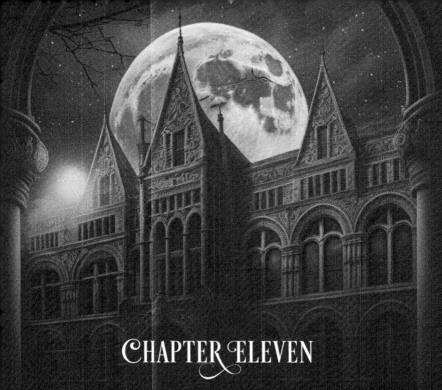

CHAPTER ELEVEN

I FLIPPED OVER, THE BLANKETS TWISTING AROUND ME, AND Briar let out a grumble from her cat tower. She'd left me hours ago, my tossing and turning disrupting her beauty sleep. I lifted my head and let it fall back against the pillow.

I'd tried everything I could think of. Counting down from one hundred. Picturing myself on a relaxing beach somewhere. A meditation exercise I'd found online. Nothing worked.

The moment I closed my eyes, I'd see things I didn't want to see. Memories I feared I'd never be rid of.

I turned on my side so that I could see out the big window in my room. The moon was full, and a shiver skated over my skin. While I was grateful for the comfort its light brought, I was reminded that the full moon was what Damien and his caster had been waiting for to do that dark magic they had planned.

I shoved those memories from my mind and focused on the moonlight reflecting on the water. The tide sent ripples through the surface, and I watched the glow dance as it did so. I let the image lull me into a trance, and before I knew it, sleep was pulling me under.

Cold, hard floor. The scent of mildew. Darkness everywhere.

My eyes flew open as I took in the basement. No, no, no. This wasn't happening. Couldn't be.

I clambered to my feet, trying to run for the tunnel I knew would take me to freedom, but something caught on my ankle. I tripped, slamming into the ground with a painful thud. My gaze snapped to my feet. The shackle.

This wasn't real. Couldn't be. I needed to wake up. I'd read somewhere that to stop a dream, you had to call it out. "This is a dream. Wake up."

It did no use.

Pressure built behind my eyes, and my nose stung.

The hinges on the door above squeaked, and I jerked upright. Footsteps sounded on the stairs. Each one dug terror deeper into my bones.

Damien stepped into the low light of the basement. "There you are, Little Lamb. I've missed you."

I couldn't help the tremor that racked my body. "You aren't real."

He arched a brow. "I'm not?"

Damien strode forward and gripped me by the hair, hauling me up. "Tell me how I'm not real."

White-hot pain flared in my scalp, a whimper escaping my lips.

"I love those noises you make," Damien purred. "But I want to hear you scream."

He hauled his head back, fangs elongating, and he sank his teeth into my flesh.

The fiery burn swept through me with a ferocity that stole my breath. And then he got my scream.

"Leighton, you're dreaming." The smooth, hypnotic voice tugged me toward consciousness.

"You're safe, Little Bird. I've got you."

My eyes flew open to meet swirling violet orbs.

There was no hesitation. I threw myself at Trace.

His arms encircled me, holding me tight. "You're safe. Just breathe."

There were no tears this time, but my entire body shook. Trace tried to keep me steady, but I only shook harder. "It was so real."

He brushed the hair out of my face, his lips ghosting over the top of my head. "Just a dream."

It was, but it wasn't. My mind melded my worst memory with my greatest fears of what might come.

"He had me again," I whispered.

Trace gripped me tighter. "That's never going to happen."

The words were rough, angry. A solemn vow.

"You can't know that. We have no idea where he is. Or what he's planning."

"We're going to find him," Trace gritted out. "And then I'm going to gut him, nice and slow."

I shivered in Trace's arms.

He shifted so that he was lying against my pillows, bringing me with him. His fingers skimmed up and down my spine, a faint buzz lighting in my muscles.

"How did you know?" I whispered. He'd been in here before I'd opened my mouth to scream.

Trace's fingers halted for the briefest moment and then continued on their journey. "I felt it."

"What does that mean?" I remembered the guys explaining a little about imprinting and how it could make Trace unstable in the process.

"It can be undone with distance."

I froze, a whole different kind of pain taking root in my chest. "Because you don't want to be linked to me."

It wasn't a question, but Trace answered anyway. "I don't want to be linked to anyone. Even the guys."

"Why?"

"Because I hurt people, Little Bird. Even when it's the last thing I want to do. Look what I've done to you."

I lifted my head so that I could see those violet eyes. There was so much pain and grief in them. I would've given anything to take it all away. "I think you try to push people away so that they won't see the amazing person beneath the mask. I think you want people to hate you so that they won't see just how worth loving you are."

Trace's muscles went hard beneath me. "I'm an asshole."

"Yeah, you are," I agreed.

His eyes flared with surprise.

"But you're also loyal, protective, and fierce. You're always there for the people you care about when they need you."

"I don't care about anyone," he snapped.

"Bullshit," I clipped. "You care about every damn person in this house."

Trace's jaw worked back and forth. "We keep each other alive."

I laughed then.

"Stop laughing," he growled.

"Trace…" My gaze swept over his beautiful face, all perfect symmetry and gorgeous angles. It caught on those violet eyes and tempting mouth, his lip ring glinting in the moonlight. "If all you cared about was keeping me alive, you wouldn't have woken me up from a nightmare."

Trace grunted. "I feel your fear. It's annoying."

I grinned. "You like me."

"Shut up."

My grin only widened. "You *really* like me."

Trace moved in a flash. He rolled us, pinning me to the mattress with his powerful form. "I need you to hear me, Little Bird. The greatest act of love I'll ever give you is staying the hell away."

CHAPTER TWELVE

"I'M LOSING MY MIND!" I MOANED AS I FLOPPED BACK ON the recliner in the screening room. "If I watch one more movie, my brain is going to turn to mush."

A week had passed since the guys had rescued me from Damien's torture chamber. He was still in the wind, but I was healing. Scratch that, I was healed. Whatever magical properties were in Declan's blood, I felt the best I had in my life.

The nightmares had eased, too. But I knew why. Each night, I would wake up to realize I wasn't alone. Trace always snuck in after I had fallen asleep and was gone before I woke up. He never mentioned his nightly visits, and I didn't either. I was simply grateful that he gave me the gift of sleep.

Things with Colt were still strained. I understood where he'd been coming from, but I couldn't magically erase the hurt, either. But we were both trying. This took the form of daily games of gin rummy. I knew we were making progress when he stopped letting me win and started getting competitive.

Ronan was physically present, but his walls were back to being sky-high. Not just with me, but with Declan, too. And I knew it hurt Dec. He was so incredibly strong, but his brother shutting him out again killed him.

Things were easiest with Dash. Maybe it was his gentleness or his ease. I was comfortable simply being with him. But I was over the daily movie marathons.

He lifted the remote and switched off the screen. "What do you want to do?"

I straightened in my seat. "Can we go somewhere?"

Dash's lips pursed. "I'm not sure that's a good idea."

"Damien's a douche canoe who ruins everything," I grumbled.

Dash chuckled. "Not arguing with you there."

"I want to move. Go for a walk. Stretch my muscles. I'm going stir-crazy."

Dash stood, holding out a hand to me. "Come on."

I let him pull me to my feet and tug me out of the screening room. "Where are we going?"

"You'll see."

Dash didn't lead me up the stairs. Instead, he turned down a hall I'd never been to.

"How big is this freaking house?" I muttered.

"It's perfect for hide-and-seek, that's for sure."

A second later, he stopped at a door. He opened it and flicked on a light. Scratch that, at least a dozen lights.

My jaw dropped as I took in the massive space. It looked like a training facility for Olympic athletes. "*This* is your gym?"

Dash grinned. "It doesn't suck."

It definitely did not. There were at least a dozen cardio machines, including treadmills, stair climbers, ellipticals, and rowers. I couldn't count the number of weight machines. A rope dangled from the ceiling, and in the middle of all of it was a massive mat that looked as if it were a makeshift fight ring.

I glanced at Dash. "Is this where you do your martial arts training?"

"Sometimes. I work with a trainer who owns a gym about thirty minutes away, but I spar with the guys down here a lot to keep in shape between sessions."

I brightened as an idea took hold. "Train me."

Dash's brow furrowed. "What?"

"I want you to train me. Teach me how to defend myself. To fight back." I'd felt powerless for so long. Maybe something like this would change that.

"I'm not sure that's such a good idea. You're still healing. You—"

I pressed a finger to Dash's lips to stop him. "I'm 100 percent healthy. The doctor agreed. *This* will help my mind get there. I might not ever have anchor abilities, but I can learn to protect myself."

Dash didn't move or say anything for a moment. Then he snagged my wrist and pressed a kiss to the center of my palm.

The guys had been cautious about their displays of affection since I'd run. Trace only touched me when he held me at night. Ronan didn't touch me at all.

Colt would drop a kiss to the top of my head or on my temple. Declan would brush chaste kisses across my lips. And Dash was big on hugs.

Just the faintest feel of his mouth against my hand had my body shivering with longing. I missed the way the guys had made me come alive with their touch. I knew we had a lot to figure out before we went there again. But it didn't stop me from missing it.

"Okay," Dash said.

My eyes went wide. "Okay?"

He chuckled. "It's not a bad idea to get some training." His gaze raked over me. "You should be okay in that for today."

I looked down at myself. I was barefoot, wearing sweats and

a tank top that had a built-in bra. It wasn't a ton of support, but that was probably all right.

"We need to warm up first. Let's jog around the mat."

I wrinkled my nose. "Jogging? I thought I was going to learn to be a badass."

Dash laughed. "Badasses need cardiovascular and muscle strength. You want me to train you? I'll be putting you on a strict regime. Running at least three days a week. Weight training another three. Fight training six."

My jaw went slack. "Seriously?"

He shrugged. "You said you were bored."

"I might be regretting that," I mumbled, following Dash as he picked up to a jog.

He didn't make me run for long. Maybe five minutes, but I was panting by the end. Then he led me in a series of stretches. Finally, Dash came to stand in the center of the ring.

"First things first. You need to know the human body's strengths and weaknesses."

I joined him in the ring.

"Strongest places on you." Dash brushed his fingers across my elbows and then my knees.

A pleasant shiver skated across my skin.

"Weakest spots on an opponent." Dash pointed to his nose, throat, below his ribs, and then his groin.

I nodded.

"Where you hit depends on the hold you're in. But no matter how you get out, the first thing you do is run. Do *not* stay and fight."

He didn't have to tell me twice. I wasn't about to give Damien a second shot at me. "I have a feeling all your *training* is going to make me a faster runner."

Dash grinned. "You'll curse me at first, but then you'll start to feel really powerful."

My lips curved in a smile. "I'd like that."

"Okay." Dash moved in a flash. He was in front of me one

second and behind me the next. He pulled me into a hold where he had both my wrists in his grip and my body pinned against his. "How would you get out of this?"

Heat rolled through me. It had been so long since I'd felt the pressure of Dash's body against mine. Every thought flew out of my head. I didn't remember why we were here or what I wanted to learn. There was only Dash and me and the pulsing need between my legs.

My hips rolled of their own volition, pressing my ass against Dash.

He growled as he hardened. "Leighton…"

I couldn't stop myself. I pressed harder, needing to feel more. A whimper escaped my lips, and Dash froze.

"Mon Coeur… are you hurting?"

My eyes closed at the endearment, and I nodded.

"Are you missing us?"

I nodded again.

"What do you need?" he whispered, his lips skimming the column of my neck.

My head tipped back, giving him better access. "To let go…" I needed to release all of this pent-up fear, anger, and hurt. I needed to feel free.

Dash's hand slipped under the waistband of my sweats but not beneath my underwear. Instead, he stroked me through the thin cotton. "So wet. You have missed us."

My eyes stung. I had missed them. So much it hurt.

He nipped my ear with his teeth. "When you fully let us back in, you'll get your reward."

I stiffened at that, but Dash trailed his lips down my neck.

"But I'll give you a little something to take the edge off."

Dash teased my throat with kisses and nips as his fingers stroked me through my panties. My hips moved against them, seeking more. My core cried out to be filled.

"Please, Dash."

"I know, Mon Coeur. But not until we have *all* of you. Mind, body, and soul."

I whimpered as he spread me wider through the cotton. His finger rubbed against my clit, and my body bucked as I panted.

"Dash…"

"Come for me, Mon Coeur. Let me hear you break."

Dash dropped a hand to pinch my nipple as he pressed down on my clit.

I fractured in his arms, releasing some of all that had been building. But I knew it was only a glimmer of what I truly needed. But to get it, I'd have to take the most terrifying leap of all. Trusting the guys with my heart.

CHAPTER THIRTEEN

"WHAT ARE YOU WEARING?" Trace clipped as I sank into the chair between Dash and Colt at the dining table.

I ignored the snap in his tone as I surveyed the breakfast options. "I'm pretty sure it's my school uniform."

"Why?" he gritted out.

"Because I'm going back to classes."

It had been over a week since I'd been rescued, and while I was getting my homework assignments via email, I knew I was falling behind.

Colt cleared his throat. "I don't think that's a good idea."

I turned toward him, feeling that awkward tension between us. I hated everything about it. I'd always been comfortable around Colt, even when he'd shown up out of the blue after almost a decade apart. Now, I wasn't sure where we stood. It was as if we were both trying to make our way back to each other, but not exactly sure what the path was to get there.

"If I stay cooped up in this house for another day, I'm going to lose my mind."

Colt frowned. "We've got the screening room and gym. The pool and library. The—"

I reached over and squeezed his hand. Colt froze, staring down at the contact. Heat bloomed in my palm, spreading up my arm. I swallowed hard as I tugged my hand back, unsure if he wanted me touching him at that moment. "I need some normal, and I don't want to fall even further behind in my classes."

"We still don't know where Damien is," Ronan said, an edge to his voice.

I looked up at him, wanting to drown in those amber-gold eyes. I hated the distance he'd put between us, too. "Do you honestly think Damien is going to show up at school in broad daylight and try to kidnap me?"

A muscle ticked in Ronan's jaw. "We don't know who might be working with him. There are others in his den that go to Prep."

The knowledge of that twisted my stomach, but I did my best to keep fear from my expression. "I can't stay locked up in here forever."

"The hell you can't," Trace mumbled.

Dash sighed. "I think what everyone is trying to convey is that we care about you, and we're worried about how exposed you'd be if we all return to classes."

The frustration building in me eased a bit at Dash's words. "I get that." I scanned the table. "I appreciate that you care. I know things haven't been easy lately." Guilt pricked at my skin. "I'm sorry I ran, that I caused all of this…" I wasn't exactly sure how to finish that sentence.

"You didn't cause anything," Declan assured me. "This is on Damien and no one else."

I swallowed, trying to clear the lump in my throat. There were a million other things I wanted to say, to ask. But most of all, I wanted to know if there was any hope for us all. But fear held my tongue hostage. So, I focused on easier topics. "If we don't keep living our lives, Damien wins. He's going to be found eventually, and The Assembly will deal with him, right?"

I forced as much certainty into my voice as possible, even if I didn't quite feel it.

Colt leaned back in his chair. "We've got as many people as possible looking. All the clans are helping."

"All the clans but the vamps," Trace muttered.

I hadn't thought much about how the other vampires felt about Damien. But given what the guys had done to Lucien, they might not be too happy. "Do the vampires think Damien is innocent?"

Ronan grunted. "They were claiming a miscommunication until they were shown the tapes."

Suddenly, my breakfast didn't seem all that appealing. The idea of anyone seeing me in that state had shame washing over me.

Dash reached over and took my hand, weaving his fingers through mine. "Dec's right. The only one this is on is Damien."

I stared down at my plate. "I hate the idea of anyone seeing the tapes."

Declan pushed from his chair, rounding the table and coming to kneel next to me. He pulled me into his arms. "As soon as the trial is done, we'll have them destroyed. But the only one who should be ashamed by those tapes is Damien."

There were grunts of agreement around the table.

I burrowed deeper into Declan's hold, but as my eyes opened, they locked with Colt's. There was such longing in his hazel eyes it stole my breath. I knew my eyes answered with the same. Our gazes held, neither of us pulling away.

Finally, Colt blinked and pushed to his feet. "I need to make a call. Be ready to leave for school in thirty."

Declan released me, his hands coming up to frame my face. "You sure about this?"

I nodded. "I'm sure." But even I could hear the doubt in my voice.

Trace cursed, shoving back from the table. "This is a horrible idea."

I bit the corner of my lip. I guessed, even with him holding me each night to keep my nightmares at bay, some things hadn't changed. Like Trace thinking every move I made was a disaster in the making. And maybe he was right. But I'd do everything I could to prove him wrong.

∽

The ride to school was mostly quiet. Colt drove, with Trace in his typical shotgun position. Dash sat next to me while Declan and Ronan sat in the back seat. The fact that the twins were in the same four-foot radius and not fighting should've been a win, but I was too nervous to think much about it.

"Does everyone know?" I asked softly.

Colt's eyes met mine through the rearview mirror. "Word has gotten around for the most part."

Trace scoffed. "What he means is that no one's been talking about anything else."

My stomach sank. I hated being the focus of attention, and I was about to willingly walk onto center stage.

Dash leaned forward and shoved Trace—hard.

Trace twisted in his seat. "There's no use in lying. She's going to see it firsthand in two minutes."

"You could be a little gentler in your delivery," Dash shot back.

Trace rolled his eyes. "Coddling her isn't going to help."

Said the guy who climbed into my bed every night to keep the nightmares away. I didn't speak those words out loud, even though I wanted to. Because the truth was, I didn't want to risk that Trace would stop showing up. As prickly as he could be, I felt safe in his arms.

Colt turned into campus, and my mouth went dry as he navigated his way into the parking lot. Every student milling around turned in the direction of our vehicle.

"Crap," I muttered.

Declan leaned forward, massaging my shoulders. "You'll be okay. This morning will be the worst of it. It can only get better from here."

I nodded. That would be my mantra for the coming hours.

Colt pulled into his parking spot and turned off the engine. "We stick together as much as possible, and we're always on alert. Frequent check-ins. Got it?"

Everyone nodded.

Doors opened, and we all climbed out of the SUV.

I felt the gazes on us before I even dared lift my head. But the moment Trace, Ronan, and Declan glared in the students' directions, they turned away. All but one.

Chloe stormed toward us, her new bob flying. Her eyes locked on me, and I swore I saw fire in them. "I'm going to *kill* you."

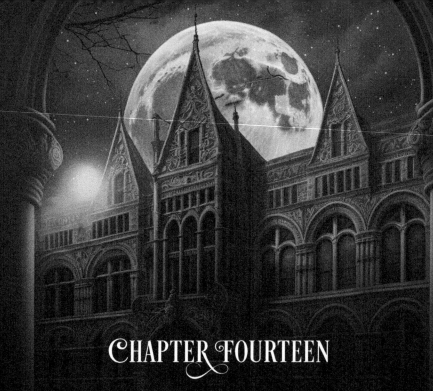

CHAPTER FOURTEEN

ECLAN AND RONAN STEPPED IN FRONT OF ME, BLOCKING Chloe's progress. Her gaze snapped to them. "Seriously?"

Declan glared down at her. "You might want to rethink your words."

Chloe moved to flick her hair over her shoulder, but that didn't work with her missing locks. "This is between me and *Leighton*."

"Anything to do with Leighton will always concern us because she's our *mate*," Ronan snarled.

Chloe winced at the word *mate*. "Then maybe the fates are cursing you with a dud because of all your lies. Who wants a mate that can't anchor them?"

A series of growls filled the air around me.

Chloe paled but didn't give up, zeroing in on me. "It wasn't enough that you're trying to steal them all from me, but you had to take Damien, too?"

I couldn't help it. I laughed. "You don't see the irony in that question?"

Confusion lit in Chloe's expression.

"You're the one trying to steal and manipulate. They aren't your bond. They never have been. And Damien is the last person I would want." I shivered at the thought.

Redness crept up Chloe's throat. "They aren't yours, either. You never manifested."

I shrugged. "I might not be their anchor, but I *am* their mate. You're nothing to them."

Her face fully flamed then. "I'm more than you'll ever be, and when I come into my powers, you'll be sorry you ever crossed me. I'll—"

Trace stepped forward, eyes flashing. "I wouldn't finish that sentence if I were you."

Chloe's gaze snapped to him. "Are you seriously willing to go insane just to keep her around?"

A grin spread across Trace's face, but it had a manic quality to it. "I'm already insane. But that doesn't change the fact that she's mine."

Chloe gaped at him, then turned to the rest of the guys. "This is the road you're willing to go down?"

"Always," Colt said, tone low and menacing.

Chloe's eyes flashed. "You're going to regret that…"

Dash crossed his arms over his chest. "Doubt that. I'd honestly mate with a porcupine if it kept me away from you."

Declan snorted. "I'm with you, man. Good thing Leighton's nice and sweet."

I swore smoke came out of Chloe's ears. "She's going to ruin you, but I won't let you take Damien down with you."

All the guys stiffened at that.

Colt's chest rose and fell in ragged pants. "Damien sealed his own fate. The moment The Assembly finds him, he'll be tried and put to death."

Chloe scoffed. "For her lies? Doubt it."

Ronan bared his teeth at her, and she stumbled back a step. "He fucking tortured her."

Chloe quickly righted herself. "She's *lying*. Damien wouldn't touch her with a ten-foot pole. She probably paid some vamp to put those bite marks on her."

I couldn't help the shiver that skated over me as her words had memories slamming against my mental walls.

Trace stalked forward, sending Chloe skittering back. "If I find out you helped Damien in any way, I won't wait for The Assembly to act. *I'll* end you. But it won't be quick. My demon will feast on each and every scream."

Chloe's face went deathly pale. "Y-you can't say that."

Trace didn't move, didn't blink. "I just did."

Her gaze shot to the guys behind him, as if expecting them to intervene. They didn't lift a finger. She straightened her shoulders, but I didn't miss the tremble in her muscles. "You won't get away with this." Then she fled without another word.

"Well, that was fun," Dash muttered.

My heart still hammered against my ribs. It wasn't because I was scared of Chloe's threats. It was more. In all that had happened over the past few weeks, I'd lost sight of our original problem. I wasn't an anchor. I never would be.

Colt pulled out his phone. "I'm going to have one of our guys start tracking her. She could be feeding information to Damien, might lead us to him."

"That's not a bad idea," Declan agreed. "That chick is batshit. I've never met someone so delusional."

"We need to keep a close eye on her at school. She could do something to Leighton here," Ronan said.

Colt nodded. "We're going to be sticking close."

Dash studied me, a hand squeezing my arm. "You okay?"

I looked up at the five of them. "Has there ever been a bond that had a mate and an anchor that were two different people?"

The guys went still, none of them saying a single word.

Dread pooled in my belly. "No?"

Their gazes shifted, none of them landing on me.

A burn lit behind my eyes. "No more secrets." It was a plea. Secrets were what had almost broken us all.

Colt met my stare. "It's been tried in the past."

"What happened?" I whispered.

Dash swallowed, his Adam's apple bobbing with the movement. "Something about the two competing relationships threw off the balance of the bond."

"What does that mean?" I pushed.

"It made everyone in the bond unstable," Colt said.

"Tell her the truth," Trace snapped.

My gaze shot to him in question.

He didn't look away from me when he spoke. "Everyone in the bond fractured. No one made it out alive."

CHAPTER FIFTEEN

N O ONE MADE IT OUT ALIVE. THE WORDS ECHOED AROUND in my brain as I numbly walked toward the school building.

Dash wove his fingers through mine, squeezing. "We're going to figure this out. We've got time."

I glanced up at him, knowing my face didn't hold the same confidence. "How much?"

Dash shared a look with Colt. "With a bond as powerful as ours?"

I nodded.

"We'll need a tether by the time we all turn twenty-one."

A little of the tension eased. That was still a few years off. But if it wasn't me, they'd need time to find that anchor. The thought made me nauseous.

Dash squeezed my hand again. "We'll figure it out. Keep the faith."

I nodded but didn't truly feel my agreement.

"We're searching for options," Colt assured me. "Talking to people who might be able to find a workaround."

"Okay." My single word was barely audible.

Silence fell on our group as we made our way inside, all of us lost in our own worlds. A heaviness settled in my heart as the knowledge of just how much we were up against took root there. I moved on autopilot, stopping at my locker to deposit books.

The guys stopped with me, surrounding me like my own personal security force. I wasn't going to argue. If it made them feel better, I'd let them. We were all dealing the best we could.

I closed my locker, pressing the key button on the pad to lock it. "Ready."

I got a few nods, and we headed in the direction of my homeroom. I waved as I stepped into the classroom, but Colt followed me inside. The corner of my mouth kicked up. "You don't have to escort me to my desk. I'll be fine."

But even as I said those words, I felt Mimi's glare lock on me.

Colt reached up, squeezing the back of his neck. "We made a few little changes."

I stilled. "What kind of changes?"

"Just some schedule shifts so that you have at least one of us in all your classes."

I gaped at him. "Are you serious?"

He shrugged. "Sometimes it pays to be one of the school's biggest donors."

I blew out a breath, fluttering strands of my hair, but I didn't argue. Instead, I just headed for my desk, shaking my head.

Connor looked up as I sank into my chair. "Hey, Leighton. Glad you're back." His eyes widened as he took in Colt's hulking form. "What are you doing here?"

Colt didn't answer him as he slid into the desk behind me.

"Trust me when I say you don't want to know," I mumbled.

Connor's gaze flicked back and forth between the two of us. "I sense tension…"

"We just got Leighton back from being fucking kidnapped. What do you think?" Colt snapped.

"Colt," I warned low.

Connor winced, his eyes shifting back to me. "You're okay, right?"

I didn't miss how his gaze caught on my bite scars along my neck. I fought the urge to flip up my collar. "I'm good now."

Connor bobbed his head in a nod. "That's good." He glanced at Colt again. "And now you've got a bodyguard."

I wanted to bang my head against the desk. "Pretty sure we're going to be surgically attached at the hip for a while."

Colt grunted, and I knew *a while* was an understatement.

The rest of the students filed in, taking their seats as the bell rang.

"Quiet," the teacher ordered, and I realized I still didn't know his name.

Everyone pretty much obeyed, but I felt their furtive glances and caught snippets of their whispers.

"Did you see her scars?"

"Damien's fucked."

"I heard she made it all up."

I tried my best to focus on my biology textbook but had to reread the same sentence at least ten times. At that rate, it would take me ten hours to make it through the chapter.

A hand slipped beneath my hair, kneading the muscles in my neck. I stiffened for a moment and then melted into Colt's touch.

Something about the tenderness of the action had me fighting tears. I'd missed his touches, even just the innocent ones like this. I'd missed *Colt* in every way I could have him.

"It'll pass," he whispered.

I stole a glance at the teacher who was lost in some game on his cell phone, then turned in my seat so that I could see Colt's face. Those familiar hazel eyes were more comforting than he'd ever know. But even that comfort was painful because it all still felt out of reach.

"I want to believe that," I said softly, my eyes not leaving his.

Colt understood that those words held so much more than concern about gossiping classmates. His fingers kept massaging my neck. "Don't give up on me now, LeeLee. Keep fighting."

The burn behind my eyes intensified.

"Never known anyone who's more of a fighter than you. Don't prove me wrong."

I swallowed hard. "I don't want to be selfish. I don't want to be our downfall."

Colt's jaw went hard. "You could never be our downfall. You're our salvation."

Mimi let out an exaggerated cough. "Slut," she clipped between coughs.

The teacher's head snapped up. "Mimi."

Her eyes went wide with mock innocence. "I had a tickle in my throat. But I think not everyone is focused on their homework, Mr. Canton."

I guessed I was going to learn the teacher's name after all.

His gaze narrowed on me and Colt. "Focus on those textbooks for the short time we're together, please."

The students around us snickered, but Colt didn't drop his hand from my neck. My cheeks flamed as he got into a stare down with Mr. Canton. It was the teacher who dropped his gaze first. Colt let out a low, rumbling growl that almost sounded like a purr.

I reached behind me to squeeze his arm in reassurance. Colt's grip on me eased a fraction, but he didn't disconnect from me all period.

When the bell rang, we stood. Connor shot me a grin as he headed out.

"He needs to stop flirting with you," Colt grumbled.

I smacked his stomach. "It's called being friendly. You should try it sometime."

Colt leaned forward, his lips teasing my ear. "I'm plenty friendly."

Mimi made a gagging noise. "Careful. She's probably going to give you a disease that turns you into a powerless weakling, too."

Colt's eyes went hard. "Watch your step."

Mimi paled but covered her fear by rolling her eyes. "Whatever." That word was diminished by her hightailing it out of the classroom.

I sighed. "Any chance we can get the three of them transferred? Preferably to a school in Antarctica."

Colt chuckled. "Not a bad idea."

We headed out into the hallway, only to be met with Dash and Declan screeching to a halt in front of us.

Declan's eyes flashed silver. "We have a problem."

"What?" Colt growled.

Dash's teeth ground together. "Damien's father is here, and he wants to talk to Leighton."

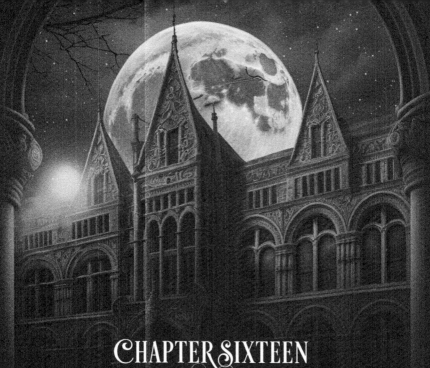

CHAPTER SIXTEEN

ICE SLID THROUGH MY VEINS AT DAMIEN'S NAME. THE thought of his father conjured images of a man harsher and crueler than Damien could ever be. I instinctively pressed into Colt's side.

He wrapped an arm around me, pulling me close. "He's obviously got sources keeping him in the loop."

I looked up at Colt in question.

He tipped his head down to meet my gaze. "Someone had to tell Alister that you were back at school. He knows if he shows up here, on neutral territory, it'll be harder for us to reject a meeting."

A shiver ran through me.

"He can fuck right off," Trace growled as he strode up behind us, Ronan following after him.

Colt's jaw hardened as he glanced in Trace's direction. "You know it's not that simple."

"He knows, but we can't just leave her at his mercy either," Ronan argued.

There was a tension in Ronan's words I'd never heard before. My gaze swept over him, taking stock. A muscle in his cheek fluttered. His jaw was set. A vein pulsed in his neck. Everything about his body was braced.

I slipped from Colt's hold on instinct, crossing to Ronan. I pressed a hand to his chest. "Hey, I'll be fine. He can't hurt me here."

It was the first time I'd touched Ronan since I'd been rescued. Heat bloomed in my palm, snaking up my arm. I'd missed him.

Ronan's eyes went liquid gold as they locked with mine. Then he moved so fast it was a blur. He crushed me to his chest, holding on tight. "You don't know that, Firecracker."

An ache spread along my sternum. It was the first time he'd used my nickname, too. I hadn't realized how much I hated him always calling me Leighton.

I burrowed deeper into his hold, and my hand slipped under his blazer so that I could better feel his heat. "I know because you'll be with me."

Ronan's hold on me didn't loosen, but he pressed his nose into my hair, breathing deeply.

Something wasn't right here. This was more than the leader of the vamps showing up at school to question me. Something had tweaked him.

Dash cleared his throat. "What do you think Alister wants? This is bold, even for him."

Ronan's arms spasmed around me, but he gave me just enough space to turn in his arms so that I could face the group.

"If he wanted to talk to Leighton, he should've gone through official channels, The Assembly," Declan grumbled.

Colt's jaw worked back and forth. "If we deny him, it's an insult. Could point us more toward war."

"Let war come," Trace snarled. "He's been fucking with us for decades. I still think he's the one who leaked information to the shadow demons about our strongholds."

A full-blown shudder racked my body as I remembered the creepy shadow being that had attacked me and Colt. I remembered the guys saying the demons had attacked the clans in ways that said they had inside information.

Colt's expression went stormy, and Ronan shoved Trace. "Not helping."

I glanced at Colt, worry digging in deep. "Colt?"

But it wasn't just him who'd gone dark. It was Dash and Declan, too.

Declan met my gaze across our little huddle. "The shadow demons killed Colt's father and Dash's family. My and Ronan's mother."

I sucked in a breath. Oh, God. An image of that black tar-like substance dripping from the creature's teeth flashed in my head. The article about Colt's father being found drained of blood. I was going to be sick.

"You think it was the vampires who leaked their whereabouts." It wasn't a question, but it still begged for an answer.

"We don't have proof," Dash said quietly.

Trace scoffed. "They're the only ones who want to see us all fall."

"Then why the hell are they in your little peace treaty, Assembly thing?" I asked.

Colt shook his head. "The treaty has been around for generations. There are rules and guidelines in place that don't make it easy to remove clans. There are processes we have to go through."

"Are those processes happening now?" I pressed.

"Kind of," Declan explained. "They've been disciplined for unprovoked attacks, but Alister has played it off as young vamps getting out of hand."

"That's smart," I grumbled.

"He's too smart. Manipulative," Ronan gritted out, his raspy voice skating across my ear.

"But he's also someone we have to play ball with," Colt said. "We don't have a choice."

I took a deep breath. "Let's go, then."

Damien's father probably expected me to cower after what his son had put me through. I wouldn't give him the pleasure.

"Fuck no," Trace snapped.

I turned to him, slipping from Ronan's hold. "I'm not weak, and I won't let this asshole think I am. He wants to play games? I've had to play them my entire life. He thinks he can show up here and intimidate me? He's going to realize I've dealt with far worse than him and his mind games."

Trace's eyes flashed purple. "I know you aren't weak. But that doesn't mean we should drop you into the lion's den."

"I'm not going alone. You'll all be with me. And it's time to show this creep that if you mess with one of us, you mess with all of us."

Colt's lips twitched. "Missed that fire."

My gaze shot to him, liquid heat pooling inside me.

He tugged me toward him and brushed his lips across mine. "Missed *you*."

My heart cracked. "I missed you, too."

Ronan cleared his throat. "As much as I'd love to watch you two make out, I think we need to deal with the bloodsucker first."

Colt glared at him. "Cockblock."

Dash choked on a laugh.

My cheeks heated, but I extricated myself from Colt's hold. "Let's get this over with."

The guys surrounded me as we headed in the direction of the Castle Prep offices. Each step made my insides twist tighter. I focused on my breathing, working to keep it even, knowing that Alister would be able to hear my heartbeat.

As we stepped inside the reception area, we were greeted by a visibly nervous Headmaster Abrams. He wrung his hands as he met Colt's eyes. "I don't want any trouble. Should I call The Assembly?"

Colt clapped the headmaster on his shoulder as if they were old friends. "You won't have any issues today unless Alister starts them."

That didn't seem to reassure Headmaster Abrams, but he stepped aside anyway. "He's in the conference room."

Colt led the way to a set of double doors and opened one, moving inside. The rest of us followed.

My gaze instinctively moved to the man standing at the head of the conference table. I would've instantly known he and Damien were related. Same hair, same dark eyes, but it was the nose and jaw that cemented it.

Alister smiled, and there was nothing authentic about it. He crossed the room, stopping just in front of me. His nostrils flared as he breathed deeply. "Leighton, it's lovely to meet you. I can certainly see what all the fuss was about."

It was the exact wrong thing to say. Snarls sounded from all around me.

Oh, fuck, someone was going to die.

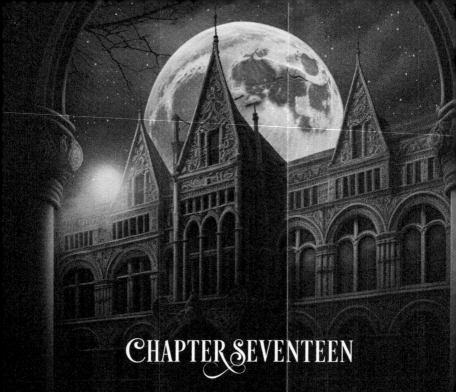

CHAPTER SEVENTEEN

TRACE STALKED FORWARD, THOSE VIOLET EYES FLASHING. "You breathe her air again, and I will slice you from dick to brain."

Alister's two guards stepped forward, their teeth bared.

Alister held up both hands, a placating smile in place. "Now, now, everyone, just calm down. I apologize. I meant no harm."

Ronan growled low and muttered something I couldn't make out under his breath.

"I simply meant it as a compliment," Alister continued, that perfect politician voice in place. "I only came to make amends."

Dash's blue eyes went cold. "Did you consider that your presence might do more harm than good?"

Alister morphed his expression into one of exaggerated empathy. "I hadn't considered that." His gaze slid to me, feeling slimy on my skin. "Do you need me to leave, Leighton?"

I lifted my chin. I knew an unspoken challenge when I heard

it. "Say what you need to, but you'll have to excuse me if I don't believe a word that comes out of your mouth."

Alister's lips twitched, but one of the guards behind him snarled.

"Show the king of the den some respect," the guard snapped.

Alister waved him off. "The girl is allowed to speak her mind." He studied me, his eyes tracking over my body again. They hitched on several of my scars along the way. Something flared in those dark depths, but it was gone too quickly for me to place it.

He focused on my face once more. "I'm incredibly sorry for what my son put you through. I know there's no excuse, but he's been tormented by his exclusion from the bond that he was clearly meant to be a part of."

"If there's anyone to blame for that, it's you," Ronan gritted out.

Alister arched a brow. "Excuse me?"

"Damien didn't come out of the womb evil. Someone made him that way. And it was his darkness that kept the fates from including him in our bond," Ronan said, voice cold.

Red flashed in Alister's eyes for the briefest of moments. "Nature versus nurture. It's a debate as old as time."

"Except, you forget that we knew Damien when he was little," Colt challenged. "We saw him change."

Alister shrugged. "Some bad influences entered my son's life. You know them. I believe you *questioned* one of them."

Lucien's screams filled my mind, and I shoved the memory down.

Declan stepped forward, shoulders squaring. "We did what was necessary."

Alister picked at his thumbnail. "But it didn't get you very far, did it?"

Trace charged forward, but Ronan caught him by the back of his shirt.

Alister laughed. "Now, now, *boy*. You wouldn't want to start a battle you can't finish."

"'That's where you're wrong," Colt said calmly. "We have the alliances on our side. After what your son has done, there isn't a supernatural in Emerald Bay except for the vamps who wouldn't take up arms against you. So, it's *you* who needs to watch your step."

The red was back in Alister's eyes, and this time, it stuck around a little longer. "My son's actions don't speak for my people. The Assembly understands that. I've allowed them to search my lands. My son isn't there."

"Then where is he?" Dash asked, tone flat.

Alister waved his hand in the air. "Your guess is as good as mine."

"Not good enough," Ronan growled.

Alister's eyes narrowed on Ronan. "I have given more than my share of good faith measures."

Ronan scoffed.

"I've cast out Lucien, even though his parents are high-ranking members of my cabinet."

"Oh, boo-hoo," Ronan shot back.

Alister's jaw clamped shut. "I've removed my *son* from the line of succession. The heir that I've trained his entire life."

Trace made a gagging noise. "Maybe that *training* is the reason for him going psycho."

Alister ignored Trace. "Now, I'm forced to start from scratch with my second eldest. He doesn't show the same promise that Damien did."

Did this idiot seriously expect me to feel bad for him? I stared at the man. "I'm sorry if I can't rustle up a whole lot of sympathy for you right now. Because I find it extremely hard to believe you didn't know this was in your son. You could've stopped him, and you didn't."

Again, something flashed in Alister's gaze. It was quick, but I managed to grab hold this time. It was glee. Alister loved that his son was a monster because he was one, too.

"No one can control another's actions, Leighton. I'd think you'd understand that by now."

I bit the inside of my cheek. "Maybe not, but a good parent can guide their child and step in when they're getting out of line."

"And what about you?" Alister asked. "Is your mother guiding you?"

"That's enough," Ronan barked. "You've said what you needed to, and now you can leave."

"Touchy, touchy, touchy. I wonder why," Alister singsonged.

Trace snarled in Alister's direction, purple sparks dancing across his fingertips.

Alister glanced at him with disdain. "Speaking of someone who needs to learn control."

Rage pulsed deep inside me. "Or maybe Trace just knows exactly when he should lose it."

Alister arched a brow at me. "Pot, kettle." He sighed, motioning to his guards. "I hope you'll accept my sincere apology, Leighton. I'd love it if we could be friends."

The man was as nutty as his son.

"Of course, Alister," I cooed. "But be sure to bring your glitter nail polish when I call you for the sleepover."

Dash snorted, and Declan choked on a laugh.

Rage swept through Alister's expression, but it was gone as quickly as it appeared. "I'll be sure to do that."

The door slammed behind him and his men, and no one moved for a few beats.

Finally, it was Declan who spoke. "That was fucked."

Dash exhaled a breath. "It was a test."

I glanced at him in question.

"He wanted to see just how angry we are. Wanted to see our weaknesses. Wanted to see if Leighton was going to break," Dash explained.

I swallowed hard.

Colt squeezed my shoulder. "But now he knows Leighton is stronger than he thought."

Pride swept through me at Colt's words, but it died at the look on Ronan's face.

He shook his head. "Everything Alister said was a carefully crafted lie. He's planning something, and we're in the crosshairs."

CHAPTER EIGHTEEN

THE PISSED-OFF RAGE SWIRLING AROUND THE GUYS DIDN'T abate for the rest of the day. Colt had done what he'd promised. At least one of them was in each of my classes. Whispers of Alister being on campus had spread far and wide, and no one tried messing with us after that, not even Chloe. As if they could all sense that one wrong move would result in the snapping of necks.

Everyone was quiet, stewing in their own thoughts, as we climbed into the Escalade after classes let out. I sighed as I settled into the back seat. Maybe going back to school had been a bad idea. It had certainly been a selfish one.

Declan's fingers wove through mine, and he squeezed, a silent reassurance. That comforting warmth spread through me at his touch.

But Declan's gaze pulled back to his brother, sitting in the row in front of us. Concern swept through his expression, and I knew he was feeling the same thing I was. Worry for Ronan.

Ronan was broody on a good day, but something in the course of the past twelve hours had set him on edge. Even now, he was staring out the window, jaw hard as granite and shadows swirling in his eyes.

I squeezed Declan's fingers, and his gaze came to me. I mouthed the question I wanted to ask. *What's wrong with him?*

Declan shook his head and shrugged, communicating that he didn't have the faintest idea either.

So, I watched Ronan the entire ride home. As if my gaze on him could keep him safe from whatever demons he was battling.

No one spoke a word, and Colt didn't even bother with the radio.

I exhaled a relieved breath when Colt finally pulled to a stop in front of The Nest. The testosterone swirling in the SUV was more than I could take.

The moment Colt put the Escalade into park, Ronan was out the door and rounding the house.

My brows pulled together as I climbed out of the vehicle. I started to follow him, but Colt caught my arm.

He shook his head. "Don't."

"Something's wrong," I argued.

"I know, but he needs time to get his head straight."

"He needs to know he's not alone," I shot back.

These guys had been there for each other through thick and thin, but they made it a habit to leave one another in their heads to stew.

"He knows that," Colt said softly. "He'll come back when he's ready."

I wasn't so sure about that. "What tweaked him?"

Colt's mouth thinned into a hard line.

More secrets.

I pulled my arm from his hold.

Colt's expression turned pleading. "I'm not trying to hide things from you, but it isn't my story to tell."

A little of the tension went out of my shoulders. He had me there. I had my own tender spots that I hadn't taken kindly to others sharing. I had to afford Ronan the same respect. But I also wouldn't leave him alone when I didn't know what he was battling.

I started around the house.

"Little Bird…" Trace warned.

I turned. "Don't."

His expression softened the barest amount. "He's more likely to take your head off than welcome you with a kiss and a cuddle."

"Then I'll just have to sit with him headless."

Dash's lips twitched. "If anyone can reach him, it'd be her."

I caught sight of Declan and didn't miss the hurt in his eyes. He was the only one besides me who didn't know what was going on, and it was his brother who was hurting.

I squeezed his hand. "I'll find him."

Declan jerked his head in a nod and headed inside.

"This is such a fucking bad idea," Trace muttered.

I ignored him and rounded the house. I scanned the massive backyard and didn't see Ronan anywhere. Worrying the corner of my lip, I surveyed my options. Pool house? I didn't think he'd go somewhere that obvious. Gardens on the hillside? Maybe, but there wasn't a ton of cover.

Then my gaze caught on the rocks that led down to the ocean. I remembered how Ronan had found me there my first night in Emerald Bay. Maybe it was a spot he liked, too.

My feet were moving before I made the conscious decision about my destination. But as my brain caught up, my pace quickened. I reached the rocky slope, and there he was, just out of sight.

As massive as Ronan was, he looked so small in that moment. The endless ocean as his backdrop, the huge boulder beneath him. But it was the torture I could just make out in his expression that sliced me open.

The crash of the waves disguised my footfalls as I navigated the rocks. When I was just a few feet away, Ronan spoke without turning around.

"Not now, Firecracker."

My nickname on his lips lessened the bite of his words, but there was no denying Ronan didn't want me anywhere near him right now.

I didn't listen. I crested the final rock and lowered myself to a spot next to him.

"Leighton," he growled. "I don't have a lot of control right now."

"You won't hurt me. You never would."

Ronan's jaw ticked. "You don't know what lives inside me."

For the first time, real fear dug its claws in, not for me but for Ronan. "What lives inside you?"

He stared out at the ocean. "He does."

"Who?"

"My father."

A wave of nausea swept through me. I didn't know much about Ronan and Declan's father, but I knew he wasn't the warm and fuzzy type. I swallowed hard and asked the question I didn't think anyone else had been brave enough to broach.

"What did he do?"

Ronan's gaze didn't falter from its position locked on the water. "He sold me."

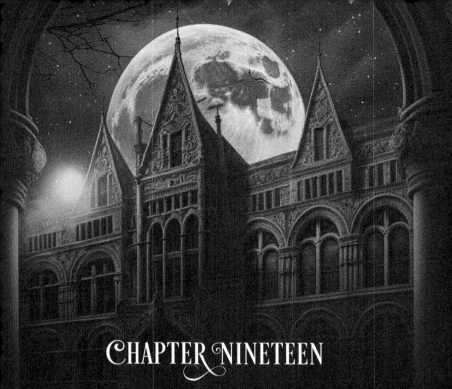

CHAPTER NINETEEN

"**H**E SOLD ME."

Those words echoed around and around in my head. Each one hit with a painful blow against my skull. "Sold you?"

My voice was unrecognizable, even to my own ears. It sounded far away, hollow.

Ronan kept his gaze fixed on the water. "Twins are a complicated thing in our world."

My brow furrowed, not understanding what his being a twin had to do with his father *selling* him. "What do you mean?"

"You know that we're all destined to lead our clans?"

I nodded, but then realized he couldn't see me. "Yes." I didn't know what all that actually entailed, though.

"For demons and casters, leaders are chosen by a test of powers in each generation. For shifters and vamps, it follows a line of succession."

"So, your father is the current dragon ruler?"

A muscle ticked along Ronan's jaw. "The dragon king. And when he had twins, things got a little challenging for him."

"How so?"

"I was born first. By five minutes," Ronan said.

"So, you should be the ruler?"

Ronan's throat worked as he swallowed. "Yes. But my dad wasn't happy about that."

"Why?" I asked the question I needed to but was terrified of the answer.

He shrugged. "My old man is a narcissist. Declan reminds him of himself. An ice dragon. I remind him of our mother. All fire."

Little cracks lit up along my heart. "Didn't he love your mom?"

"Their mating was an arranged one. He wanted strong sons. Her father wanted a strong alliance. And female dragons are incredibly rare."

A lead weight settled in my stomach. I couldn't imagine being forced to marry for strategy.

Ronan's jaw worked back and forth. "He was hard on me and Dec. But we always stuck together, watched each other's back."

A ringing started in my ears. "Hard on you how?"

Ronan sighed. "Shit you don't want in your head."

"Tell me."

He glanced in my direction. "Let's just say you aren't the only one with scars."

Rage burst to life in my chest as my gaze zeroed in on that slice through his brow.

"I knew he wanted Dec to lead. I wouldn't have even cared if he named Dec as heir, but that wasn't enough. My existence in our horde would've called that line of succession into question."

That pit in my stomach was back. "What did he do?"

"When I was ten years old, his guards grabbed me from my bed in the middle of the night. They brought me before my father.

84

He accused me of plotting against him, against Dec. He said I was guilty of treason."

"You were ten!"

Ronan lifted a shoulder, and then it fell. "It didn't matter to him. He said he was showing me *mercy* and selling me to the fighting pits instead of beheading me."

All the blood drained from my head. "The *what?*" I whispered.

"Our world has a dark side. It always has. There are underground fighting rings where supernaturals fight to the death."

I sucked in a sharp breath.

Ronan's gaze met mine. "I've killed more people than I can count." That gaze shifted to his hands. "I never should've touched you. Tainted you."

I took his hands, weaving my fingers through his. "You did what you had to do to stay alive."

His head lifted, eyes blazing that liquid gold. "I'm not a good person."

"You are," I argued. "I've seen it too many times to count."

Ronan swallowed hard. "Colt's dad saved me."

I stilled. "How long were you there?"

"Three years. But Andrew broke me out, got the bosses of the underground to leave me be. Still not sure how he managed that. Then he gave me a home."

I'd be forever grateful to Colt's father for that, but my mind was stuck on the first thing Ronan had said. Three years. That would feel like a lifetime to a little boy. How much torture had he endured?

My fingers tightened around his. "I'm so glad you got out."

"Me, too. Not sure Dec is, though."

I stiffened.

"He never looked for me. He was just relieved to have the power he wanted all along."

That didn't sound like the Declan I knew. "How do you know?"

Ronan's jaw hardened. "I went to find him after I got free. He was happy as a clam in his new role with the horde. He told me he didn't want a damned thing to do with me, that our father had told him what I'd done."

"Your dad lied to him," I argued.

"I know," Ronan growled. "But Declan believed him. Sided with him in casting me out. He didn't give one single fuck that I'd been existing in a living nightmare for three years. Thought I deserved it."

"Ronan…"

"No," he clipped. "Dec might be in this bond, but I'll never trust him. I'll work with him, but that's it."

A vicious ache took root in my chest. There had to be an explanation, a way to heal them both.

"Don't, Firecracker. This is one place you can't meddle." Ronan pinned me with a stare to punctuate his point. "You can't force him on me."

My breath left my lungs in a whoosh of disappointment. "Okay."

Ronan jerked his head in a nod.

"Are those fights still happening?" I asked softly. I couldn't bear the thought of other children, innocents, being left to the same fate.

Something flashed in Ronan's eyes.

"What?" I pressed.

"When we turned sixteen, Colt, Trace, Dash, and I hunted every single soul that had a role in them. We killed each and every one without mercy."

I met those golden-amber eyes and didn't look away. "Good."

Ronan's eyes flared in surprise.

"You expect me to be angry that you ended the lives of people so vile they'll be burning for all eternity?" I asked.

Ronan was silent.

"I'm not. I'm glad you stopped them from hurting others—"

"I didn't just stop them, Leighton. I tortured them. Their ends weren't easy ones."

"Then maybe they felt a millimeter of the pain they inflicted on the world. Maybe you gave them just the barest hint of justice."

I wouldn't allow Ronan to beat himself up for this. Not when he was making this world a safer place. Not when his childhood was *stolen* from him.

"Firecracker," he breathed.

I moved then, climbing into his lap. Ronan's arms came around me, holding me tight. I nuzzled his neck and burrowed deeper into his hold.

Ronan breathed deeply. "How can you stand to have me touch you?"

"These are the hands that made countless people safe. The hands that made me feel cherished. The hands that heal."

A shudder racked through Ronan, and he lifted a hand to my face.

I tipped my head back so I could see those beautiful eyes.

"Leighton." His voice broke on my name.

"I see you. And there's nothing but good."

Ronan's head dipped, his lips a breath away from mine.

"Ronan!" Dash's voice cut through the crashing waves. "You need to move. We found something."

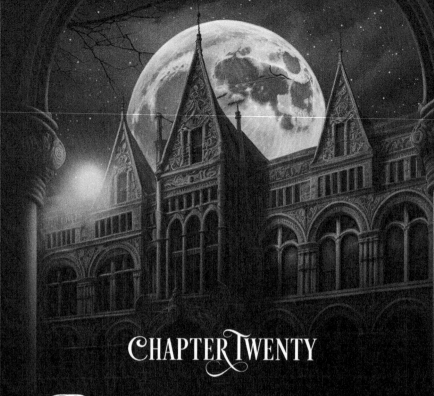

CHAPTER TWENTY

RONAN SCRAMBLED TO HIS FEET, SETTING ME CAREFULLY on the rock. "Come on." He took my hand and helped me navigate the rocks up the hill to the backyard.

Dash took us both in before he focused back in on Ronan. "You okay?"

He jerked his head in a nod. "I'm good. What'd you find?"

Dash glanced at me. "Let's get inside."

My stomach hollowed out as Ronan tugged me forward. I practically had to jog to keep up with his long strides.

The rest of the guys were waiting inside, a tension zinging through the air. I couldn't help but study Declan, so many questions swirling in my head. His eyes locked on my hand in Ronan's, something that looked a lot like longing in his gaze. Was it that he wanted to be in his brother's shoes? Or was it that he missed his closeness with Ronan?

"What?" Ronan clipped the moment the door shut behind us.

"We've got a line on Damien," Colt answered instantly.

My stomach roiled.

"Where?" Ronan demanded.

"The caves just north of Emerald Bay," Dash informed us.

Ronan's jaw ticked. "Gotta be hard up if he's holing up there."

"It's not like he's got a whole lot of allies at this point," Declan muttered.

"We hope he doesn't, you mean," Ronan snapped.

Declan's eyes flared at the bite in Ronan's tone, and I didn't miss the hint of hurt there. *Hell.* There had to be something they were both missing.

"How'd the tip come in?" Trace asked, skepticism lacing his words.

Colt glanced down at his phone. "One of our guards followed a vamp who's been known to run in Damien's circles. Looked like he was dropping off food and other supplies."

"What about Alister?" Ronan asked.

Colt's teeth ground together. "Our team lost him not long after they left the school. He knew we'd have him followed."

"You were tracking the vampire king?" I squeaked. "Can't you get in trouble for that?" I couldn't imagine that going along with their infamous treaty.

Colt shrugged. "He's not playing by the rules. Why should we?"

Anxiety pricked at my skin. "Will you call The Assembly about Damien?"

The guys shared a look, and that anxiety turned to panic.

"Colt?" I pressed.

He met my gaze. "We can't give him the opportunity to get away. The vamp who sits on The Assembly could alert Alister, and Alister could help Damien escape. He could be in Venezuela in a blink of an eye."

"You're going after him…" My voice trailed off, unable to say anything more.

Dash moved in close. "We've hunted more creatures than you can count. We've got this."

But Damien was sly, cunning. And he had an unhinged hatred fueling him.

"It'll be five against one," Colt assured me.

"You don't know that. He could have others helping him."

Ronan squeezed my hand. "We'll be prepared for that."

"How?" I pressed.

"We go armed to the teeth," Trace said nonchalantly.

"And ready to shift," Declan added.

My stomach pitched at the idea of them fighting Damien and anyone else he might've brought over to the dark side. "Please don't," I whispered. "Have your guards watch the caves and call it in."

Colt strode forward, his hands coming up to frame my face. "We need to do this. To make us all safe. And we can't claim to be the future leaders of our people and then sit back and let others take all the risk."

My eyes burned, throat clogging, because I knew he was right. "You'll be careful?"

He bent, pressing a kiss to my forehead. "Of course." He released me and turned to the rest of the guys. "We need a plan."

⌒

The guys poured over the topographical maps spread out on the dining table. The network of caves just north of Emerald Bay was vast. I understood now how easy it would be for Damien to slip through their fingers.

They talked through different approaches and mapped out different exit options.

A hand slipped beneath my T-shirt, tracing circles on my skin. "It's going to be okay," Dash said.

I lifted my gaze to his. "You don't know that."

"We're going to make it so."

There was such confidence in those words that I wanted to believe him. I just couldn't get past the dread building inside me.

Dash bent, his forehead resting against mine. "Mon Coeur, have some faith."

"I have all the faith in *you*. It's the rest of the world I don't trust."

Dash pulled back, his eyes searching. "Are you coming back to us?"

I knew what he meant. Was I finding a way to trust them again? "I'm trying," I whispered.

I wanted to make that final leap, to pull my still-beating heart from my chest and place it in their hands. But I couldn't quite release it. Every time I thought about it, terror gripped me.

Dash brushed my hair away from my face. "You'll get there." His lips brushed mine, a featherlight touch. "I can't wait."

A zing of energy zipped through me, that familiar buzz taking root in my muscles. I leaned forward, seeking more, but Dash retreated.

He grinned down at me. "Uh, uh, uh. Not until we have all of you, remember? We want more than just your body. We need it all."

I swallowed hard, trying not to let that disappointment grab hold.

Colt clapped his hands together, snapping me out of my haze. "Okay, gear up. We need to leave now." He glanced at Declan. "Have we shown you the armory?"

Declan shook his head.

Colt's lips twitched. "You're in for some fun." He led the way down a hall, an excitement humming around him that reminded me of a kid at Christmas.

Colt came to a stop at a door with an electronic pad next to it. He pressed his palm against the pad, and there was a series of unlocking sounds. Colt reached for the doorknob and turned.

The door itself was heavier than it looked. There was a wood façade but then a thick metal beneath it.

Colt glanced at me. "It's also a safe room in case of attack."

Blood roared in my ears at the thought of that ever being necessary.

Colt motioned us into the room, and my jaw dropped. *Armory* was an understatement. This space could equip an army for World War III. And what did that say about what we were up against?

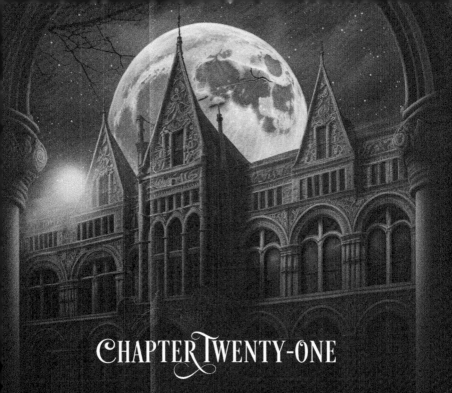

CHAPTER TWENTY-ONE

MY EYES GOT COMICALLY HUGE AS I TOOK IN THE ROOM. No, it was more like rooms, plural. Each one had a different theme of sorts. I wandered deeper as the guys pulled things off walls and stocked duffel bags.

The first area seemed to contain armor of sorts. But it wasn't the stuff from my history textbook. It was techier. I reached out, running my fingers over what looked like a thin, long-sleeved T-shirt. But the material was denser than you would've thought.

"Protects against fire," Dash explained, coming up beside me.

I looked up at him in question.

He shrugged. "Comes in handy if there are ever any issues with dragons or certain demons."

I remembered Trace's purple fire as he fought the shadow demon.

I inclined my head toward the next room. "The guns?"

I wasn't exactly a fan of weapons, but if they were going up against Damien, I wanted them to have everything possible to protect themselves.

Dash glanced to the wall in question as Trace and Ronan loaded a bag full. "There are different kinds of guns that combat different supernaturals."

I nodded, but I felt sick.

Dash wrapped me in a hug. "I know it's a lot to take in, but this stuff keeps us safe."

I'd tell myself that over and over.

I walked further into the room, Dash sticking close. There were shields and crossbows, whips and grappling gear, ropes and blades of every size and shape.

Looking up at Dash, my brow furrowed. "You all know how to use this stuff?"

The corner of his mouth kicked up. "We've been trained in it all since we were very young."

My shoulders straightened. "I want to learn."

Dash's expression softened as he traced a finger down the side of my face. "Heart of a warrior."

"You'll teach me?" I pressed.

He jerked his head in a nod. "*After* you master hand-to-hand."

"Morning runs," I grumbled.

Dash chuckled. "It's the foundation for everything."

"Okay," Colt called. "We got everything we need?"

My blood went cold. I wasn't ready.

The rest of the guys shouted their affirmatives.

"Let's roll out," Colt shot back.

I was swept up in their movements, leaving the armory and heading toward the entryway, then outside. The Escalade was parked in front.

Colt opened the back hatch, and they loaded the bags inside. He crossed to me, pulling me into his arms. "We'll be back in a few hours. Maybe sooner."

My hands fisted in his tee. "Be careful."

"Always am."

I tipped my head back, taking in those hazel eyes I loved so much. I stretched up on my tiptoes and brushed my lips against his. It was barely a touch, there and gone, but I hoped it communicated what I was too scared to say. That I loved Colt, that I wanted to find my way back to him.

A sigh left his lips. "Love you, LeeLee."

My throat tightened, a burn lighting there. "Colt—"

He pressed a finger to my lips. "Tell me when I'm back."

I nodded, and he released me. Then Dash was there. He kissed me, deep and slow. "Make the jump, Mon Coeur," he whispered.

I knew he was right. It was time.

Releasing him, I knew my eyes held that promise because Dash's blazed bright.

Declan moved in, dipping his head and pressing a kiss to my neck. "Don't miss me too much."

I tried to laugh, but it wouldn't come. "Don't be a hero."

He grinned down at me. "I'll try not to." He brushed the hair away from my face. "Stay safe."

As Declan stepped back, he revealed Ronan, who was watching us as if studying a science experiment. But I knew he was trying to understand his brother. I wrapped him in a hug and held on tight.

"I believe in you," I said softly.

Ronan's arms spasmed around me, and he buried his face in my neck, breathing deep. It took a few seconds for him to let go, but he finally did, moving toward the SUV.

My gaze sought out Trace. Shadows swirled in his eyes. Some days, I swore his demons had demons. I moved toward him.

"Don't," he said, voice quiet. "I'm not in control."

I didn't listen. I threw myself at him. Trace had no choice but to catch me. My legs wrapped around his waist, my arms around his neck. "Don't get dead, okay?"

Trace's fingers dug into my ass. "Your life might be simpler if I did."

I grabbed his hair and pulled his head back, hard. "Don't you ever say anything like that ever again. You're a pain in the ass, but you're *my* pain in the ass."

Trace's eyes flashed that bright purple and started swirling.

"Oh, shit," Ronan muttered.

"Dude?" Dash said. "We really don't have time for your incubus to claim Leighton right now. We need to kill a seriously fucked-up vampire."

The purple dimmed to that beautiful violet. "Be a good girl, Little Bird."

A shiver raced through me as Trace lowered me to the ground, my core skating over his rigid cock. I swallowed hard.

"I need to go, *now*," Trace gritted out, making a beeline for the SUV.

Colt motioned to someone, and I looked up to see Baldwin on the front steps. He crossed to Colt.

"You're with her every moment until we get back," Colt demanded.

Baldwin nodded, face serious. "I'll guard her with my life."

Colt glanced down at me. "See you in a bit, LeeLee."

I knew his words were purposely casual, a farewell that could've been cast at any time. But it still killed. Everything burned as I watched them pile into the SUV. The engine started up, and my panic took root.

As the Escalade drove away, pain flashed through me. Everything about this was wrong. And I couldn't shake the fear that I'd never see them again.

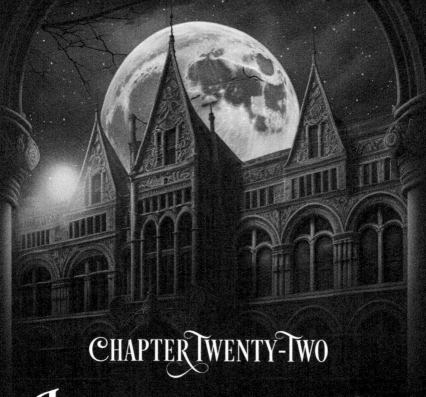

CHAPTER TWENTY-TWO

I SAT AT THE BEND IN THE DRIVE LONG AFTER THE SUV had disappeared. As though if I stayed right there, I could will the guys back to me. I might not have anchor powers, but maybe I could stir up some of my own magic.

An arm slid around my shoulders. "Let's go inside."

"I hate this," I whispered to Baldwin.

"You and me both, cherub. Let's distract ourselves with some baking."

I glanced up at Baldwin, his warm brown eyes full of sympathy and understanding. I swallowed hard and nodded.

He guided me into the house and toward the kitchen. "What do you think we should make?"

The idea of putting anything in my stomach was revolting. "What are some of the guys' favorites?"

Baldwin grinned. "I like the way you think. Colt and Dash are traditionalists. They love chocolate chip cookies. Trace is a sucker for lemon bars. Ronan has loved my peanut butter M&M cookies since the week he moved here. I still don't have Declan pegged."

I glanced at Baldwin. "You were here when Ronan arrived?"

Shadows swirled in Baldwin's eyes. "I've been steering this ship since before Colton was born."

I worried the corner of my lip between my teeth. "How bad was it when he arrived?"

Baldwin instantly understood I was asking about Ronan, but a wary look took over his expression.

"He told me a little of what happened. About the fighting pits." Baldwin's eyes flared. "He did?"

I nodded.

"How a father could do that to their own child, I'll never know," he muttered.

"Me neither."

Baldwin sighed, leaning against the counter. "There are reasons his walls are sky-high. The people he should've been able to trust the most betrayed him."

An ache flared along my sternum. "The Declan I know would never do that. There has to be other factors at play."

"I'm sure there are," Baldwin said gently. "But that doesn't change how it has made Ronan feel. He wouldn't let a single person touch him for over a year."

Pain ricocheted through me. I wanted to grab hold of Ronan and never let go.

"You're good for him," Baldwin whispered. "I've seen him more alive in this past month than ever before."

"I've turned his life upside down," I muttered.

"Maybe that's exactly what he needed."

I hoped, at the very least, he thought all the trouble was worth it in the end.

I looked up at Baldwin. "Let's make peanut butter M&M cookies first."

He grinned.

The kitchen smelled amazing from a blend of half a dozen treats that were now cooling on various racks scattered across the kitchen. I couldn't eat a single thing. Baldwin tried to get me to, offered to make anything under the sun, but my stomach couldn't take it.

I scrubbed the mixing bowl with more force than was necessary. "It's been too long."

Over four hours now.

"Give them time. Things can come up on these sorts of missions."

I was sure they could, but those things were never good.

A trilling ring sounded from Baldwin's direction, and he pulled a phone out of his pocket. "Yes?"

I watched as the blood drained from his face.

"Right away."

He was already moving out of the kitchen.

I dropped the mixing bowl, barely having time to shut off the water as I ran after him.

Baldwin was already halfway down a back hall I hadn't ventured into.

"What is it? What happened?" Panic laced every word.

"I don't know. Just that Colt was hurt."

He shoved open a door, and suddenly, we were in what looked like an infirmary. There were several beds and more medical equipment than I could name.

"How bad?" I whispered.

A muscle in Baldwin's jaw ticked, and he pulled supplies from various cabinets and placed them on a cart. "Bad."

The cramp that grabbed hold of my stomach nearly stole my breath. This wasn't happening, couldn't be.

A door slammed from far away, making me jump.

"That'll be them. Help me strip the bed," Baldwin ordered.

I forced my legs to move, helping him pull back the blankets on the closest bed.

Voices rose, but I couldn't make out the words. A second later, the guys poured into the room.

I stood frozen for a moment as I took them in. Couldn't have moved if you'd given me all the money in the world. They looked as if they'd just done battle with the devil himself. Clothing was torn, their faces and bodies bloody and covered in a black tar-like substance. And they were carrying an unmoving Colt.

That last piece of knowledge had me jerking forward. He was pale, too pale. Eyes closed. And there was a gaping wound in his side.

"Tell me," Baldwin barked as they set Colt on the hospital bed.

"It was a fucking trap," Trace growled. "The caves were crawling with shadow demons. They boxed us in, and we had to fight our way out."

Ronan's face was completely blank, shock settling in. "He stepped in front of me. It should've been me."

My heart cracked.

Dash clapped a hand on his shoulder. "You would've done the same for him."

Baldwin worked quickly, cutting open Colt's shirt.

I gasped. The wound in his side was massive and turning black, as if his flesh was rotting.

Baldwin cursed. "We need to move fast. Cleanse the wound. Dash?"

But Dash was already moving to a farther set of cabinets, pulling out ingredients, then chanting over a bowl.

I moved to Colt's side, slipping my hand into his. It was too cold, not at all the vibrant, fiery Colt I loved so much. Pressure built behind my eyes. "What can I do?"

Baldwin glanced at me. "Talk to him. Keep him here."

I gripped Colt's hand tighter. "Hey…"

I didn't know what to say. What words I could give that would bring him back to me, to us.

Swallowing hard, I let the first thing I thought of tumble out. "This is so much worse than when you fell out of the tree. Your dad was so mad. He told you those higher branches weren't safe, but you just had to see for yourself."

Colt didn't move a muscle.

"Broke your arm in two places. But you let me sign your cast first. Remember what I said?" Tears pricked at my eyes. "Best friends forever, but no more trees."

Fingers twitched in my hand.

I jerked my head up to Baldwin. "I felt something."

"Good. Keep talking," he ordered, as Dash handed him the potion. "This is going to hurt." He glanced at the rest of the guys. "Hold him down."

They moved in around Colt, pressing his limbs and shoulders into the mattress.

"You were out climbing trees the second that cast came off," I remembered. "You'll be doing the same here."

Baldwin poured the concoction into Colt's wound. It bubbled and popped, thick, noxious smoke filling the air. He rushed to open the window, guiding it out.

A low moan slipped from Colt's lips.

"I'm right here. I'm not going anywhere," I promised.

The bubbling intensified, and Colt's eyes flew open. The scream that slipped from his lips was more animal than human as he fought against us.

"Hold him!" Baldwin yelled.

Colt began to seize, his body jerking in staccato movements. Terror gripped me as the guys held strong. Then Colt went limp, and there was nothing at all.

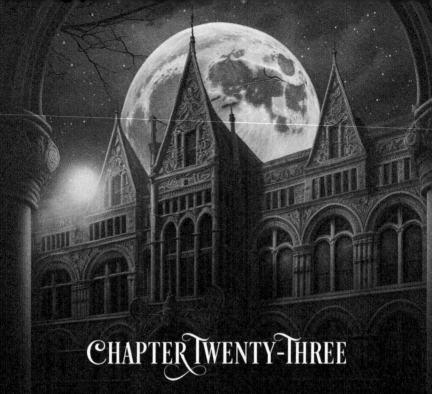

CHAPTER TWENTY-THREE

THE BEEPING OF THE HEART MONITOR GRATED AGAINST my eardrums. My eyes burned, but I refused to close them. I leaned down, pressing my forehead against Colt's and my joined hands. I tried to infuse all the life I had in me into Colt. I would've given him the very last breath in my lungs if I could've.

Someone squeezed my shoulder. "You need to get some rest," Dash said.

I straightened, shaking my head. "I'm good."

"It's been over twenty-four hours," Declan told me something I already knew.

Each second of that time was carved into my damned soul, but Colt still showed no signs of waking. I'd watched as Colt's wound miraculously knit itself back together with his shifter healing and the help of some of Ronan's blood. But he still hadn't woken.

I looked at the guys positioned around the room. They'd all

been treated for their injuries. Some had been worse than others, but none nearly as bad as Colt's. "Why isn't he waking up?"

Ronan squeezed the back of his neck, picking up his pacing for the millionth time.

It was Trace who spoke. "Sometimes demon venom can cause a sort of sepsis in the body."

"What does that mean?" My voice took on a high-pitched quality as fresh panic hit.

Trace winced. "Colt's trying to fight it off. It's just a matter of time to see if he's able to."

"We need to do something! Give him medicine. Help him." My words tumbled out faster and faster.

Dash squeezed my shoulder again. "We've done everything we can."

"There has to be something else." The burn in my eyes intensified, feeling as if they'd been dunked in acid.

Ronan looked at me, grief ravaging him. I wanted to comfort him, but I couldn't let go of Colt to do it.

There was a knock on the door, and then it swung open.

I twisted in my seat to see our newcomer, then stiffened as Darius stepped into the space. The temporary alpha of Colt's pack until he was ready to take over. The person who'd never wanted me in any of their lives.

His face was a mask of fury. "Why the hell didn't you call me?"

Trace, Ronan, and Declan stepped between us in a flash, while Dash stayed at my side.

"It didn't concern you," Declan said calmly.

"Didn't concern me?" Darius bellowed. "He's *my* wolf. *My* responsibility."

"No," Trace said drolly. "You're *his* wolf."

A muscle fluttered in Darius's cheek. "Not yet. I'm still the alpha of this pack."

"In name only," Ronan snarled. "And you've proven time and

time again that you don't have Colt's back. He wouldn't want you around when he's in this state."

I read between the lines. Colt wouldn't want Darius around when he was vulnerable. Everything in me twisted. Would Darius try to use this opportunity to seize power? To take what was Colt's for himself?

Darius let out a low growl. "You insult my honor?"

"I speak the truth," Ronan shot back.

"The Assembly won't stand for this. He's of my clan. My *pack*. I'd be within my rights to take him back to our territory."

I was on my feet in a flash, shoving through the guys. "Get out."

Darius's eyes flared. "Excuse me?"

"Get. Out." Rage pulsed through each word.

"You don't control me, little girl. Hell, you're the reason he's in this mess."

Pain streaked through me, but it quickly morphed into fury. "GET OUT!"

My voice boomed so loud I swore the walls shook.

Darius stumbled back a step in surprise, then anger lit his expression. "You don't—"

I charged forward, shoving all my weight against the man's chest. "No! You don't! You don't get to come in here and pretend you care. Pretend that you have Colt's best interest at heart. If you want to get to him, you'll have to come through me!"

An arm went around my waist, tugging me back.

I fought against Trace's hold, but he just gripped me tighter. "Be still, Little Bird."

My tears came hot, fast. "He doesn't get to be here. He's against Colt. I have to keep Colt safe. I have to." Sobs wracked my body as more gibberish left my lips.

Darius's face paled at my state.

Ronan and Declan glowered at him.

"You need to leave, now," Declan snarled.

104

Darius's eyes flashed, but he jerked his head in a nod. "Text me updates, or I'll be back."

Ronan just grunted, but Darius must've taken that as agreement because he disappeared out the door.

"Little Bird…" Trace held me as I sobbed.

"Need to keep him safe," I mumbled.

"Should we sedate her?" Dash asked quietly.

"No!" I screeched. "Colt," I begged.

Trace carried me over to the hospital bed and placed me gently on it, next to Colt.

I burrowed into his uninjured side, breathing him in. That sandalwood scent wrapped around me. I nuzzled his neck, needing more.

My tears fell onto his skin. "I'm so sorry."

I pressed closer, my body melting against Colt's.

"She's losing it," Ronan hissed.

"She needs him," Trace said quietly. "I think this will help. It's what eases my demon."

The guys shared a look. It was Declan who finally spoke.

"What happens if he doesn't wake up?"

Silence descended.

Trace's eyes flashed purple. "Then we'll lose her, too."

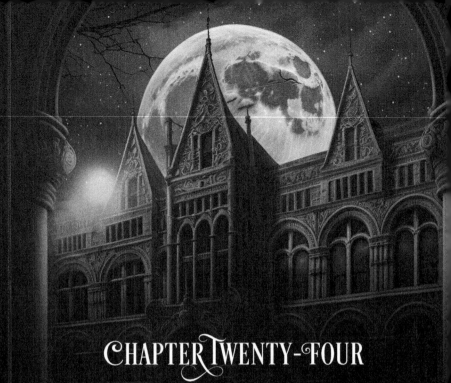

Chapter Twenty-Four

A HAND TRAILED UP AND DOWN MY SPINE IN TEASING, comforting movements. It felt as if I were lying against a giant heating pad. I wanted more of that warmth, wanted to dive into it and bury myself deep.

Then the quiet hit me. The beeping of the heart monitor that had been my constant companion was gone.

I jerked upright, panic slicing through me. The room swam as I blinked. It took a few tries to bring everything back into focus.

That was when I saw him. His multi-colored hair mussed, scruff dotting his jaw, hazel eyes full of concern.

"Colt."

His name came out on a choked sob.

"Come here, LeeLee." He tugged me against his chest.

"Is this real?"

He chuckled, the sound vibrating through me. "Very real."

"Are you sure?" I didn't trust my own senses.

"I'm okay. I promise."

The tears came in earnest then, sweeping through me in vicious waves. Colt just held me tight, whispering sweet nothings over and over until the sobs subsided.

"I'm right here, LeeLee."

"I thought I was going to lose you," I choked out.

"Never gonna happen." Colt's words were a vow. I felt it in every syllable.

I tipped my head back so that I could take in his face. "Are you okay? Where is everyone? The doctor needs to check you over."

"Already done. Clean bill of health. I'm almost fully recovered."

My eyes flared.

"You slept right through it." Colt's mouth dipped to a frown. "You pushed too hard. The guys told me you were up for over twenty-four hours and that you almost got into a fistfight with Darius. What were you thinking?"

I frowned right back. "He didn't get to be here. Not when he's not on your side."

Colt brushed my hair from my face. "So fierce."

"I'm sorry," I whispered.

His brows pinched. "About what?"

"Locking you out. Thinking that you might not want me in your life…it hurt so bad—"

"I'll always want you. Nothing I've ever wanted more."

I swallowed hard. "I didn't think about what might've been keeping you away. I let my hurt get the best of me."

Colt's fingers tangled in my hair. "That's natural. You've been through a lot." Darkness filled his eyes. "If I'd known what you were going through, I'd have come so much sooner, consequences be damned."

"Colt—"

"I'll never forgive myself for not being there when you needed me."

"Don't."

His fingers slid down the column of my neck. "It's true."

I lifted a hand to Colt's face, his scruff pricking my palm. "What if we decided to start over?"

Hope flared in those gorgeous hazel eyes. "You willing to give this bond a shot? Fully and completely?"

There were no half measures when it came to this bond. I couldn't give pieces of myself here and there. I had to give myself completely or not at all.

I shifted up, brushing my lips across Colt's. "I love you, Colt. I always have, and I always will."

Colt moved on a growl, flipping us so that I was beneath him, and he was hovering above me. "Say it again."

"I love you."

He nipped at my bottom lip. "Again."

"I love you."

Colt took my mouth in a powerful kiss. His tongue stroked in, demanding and comforting all at once. Colt was earthy heat I could sink into for the rest of my days.

I lost myself in the tangle of tongues. Each twist and flip had my belly dipping, then tightening, my core crying out for more.

"Colt," I whispered against his lips.

He pulled back a fraction, searching my eyes. "Tell me what you need."

My fingers trembled against his muscled back, the skin so incredibly smooth. "I need all of you."

Those hazel eyes flared wide. "LeeLee…"

"Please."

He searched my face for any hint of indecision. "You're sure?"

I nodded. "Never been more sure of anything in my life."

Colt's fingers dipped beneath my T-shirt, skimming against my stomach. It was such a gentle gesture, the barest of touches, but it had my body waking up and standing at attention.

"Need to see you. Been dreaming about it ever since that day in the attic."

I blushed as I remembered coming alive beneath his and Dash's touches.

Colt fisted the hem of my shirt, pausing as if expecting me to protest. I didn't. And a second later, my shirt was flying to the floor.

Colt leaned against his elbow, gazing down. He traced the edge of my lace bralette with his finger. "So pretty. So perfect." His lips spread into a grin. "Love how you flush everywhere."

"The curse of being a redhead," I muttered.

Colt chuckled, his head dipping low and lips skimming across my skin. "Could make a game of getting that pretty pink to spread."

He pulled down one strap of my bra, then the other. His tongue flicked out, lashing against my nipple.

My core pulled tight, wanting, needing.

"Colt," I whispered.

"Need to prepare you, LeeLee. Can't rush it."

But I wanted to. Wanted him, *all* of him. And couldn't wait.

Colt's lips closed around my nipple, and he sucked deep.

I nearly bowed off the bed, a whimper leaving my lips.

His hand slipped beneath my sweats and under my panties. "I'll ease the ache."

My legs fell open on instinct, begging for anything he'd give me.

Colt slid two fingers inside, his thumb circling my clit.

My breaths came faster.

"So tight. Can't wait to feel you milking my cock. God, LeeLee, I could come just thinking about it."

A pleading mewl left my lips.

Colt's teeth grazed my nipple, and my hips bucked.

"Be a good girl and stay still," he commanded.

I tried with all my might to keep still as Colt teased and toyed, but soon, my hips were moving again, rising up to meet the thrusts of his fingers. Wetness spread between my legs, and Colt inhaled deeply.

"God, your scent. Nothing like it."

My face flamed.

Colt's eyes locked with mine. "Never be embarrassed. I love knowing I turn you on. That this scent is just for us."

Another rush of wetness pooled between my thighs.

Colt grinned. "I have to see that pretty pink between your thighs."

He moved so fast I barely saw it, tugging my sweats and panties off and sending them to the floor. He spread my thighs, settling between them.

I squirmed, wanting to cover myself.

Colt gripped my thighs, his eyes going hard. "Never seen anything more beautiful. Glistening. Pink. So ready and wanting."

My core spasmed at his words.

Colt's tongue flicked out across my clit, and all embarrassment fled. I just wanted more. He teased and toyed but always stopped shy of where I needed him.

Another whimper slipped free, and Colt's gaze shot to mine. "Ready, LeeLee?"

I swallowed and nodded.

"Need the words."

"Ready," I whispered.

Colt stood, and my breath hitched.

"Condom?" I squeaked.

His fingers trailed up my leg. "You can't get pregnant unless we're fully mated. We have to claim you."

"Claim me?" I asked.

Colt's fingers traced designs along my skin. "It's a different process for each supernatural, but there's always a mark. For me, it means my teeth sinking into that sweet skin with a mating bite."

My heart picked up speed, some deep part of me craving that bite.

His lips twitched. "And we aren't susceptible to human diseases."

"Oh."

A smile stretched across Colt's face as he stepped back and shucked the joggers he wore.

My eyes went wide. There he was. *All* of him. His dick standing tall and thick, pressed against his belly.

"You keep looking at me like that and this'll be over before it's begun."

My eyes flew to his face.

Colt smiled, stalking back toward me and climbing onto the bed. He hovered over me. "Legs around me."

My limbs moved on instinct, and his tip bumped against my entrance.

"Colt," I whispered.

"Love you with everything I have," he said against my lips.

Then he slid in. My mouth dropped open. Everything was sensation. A bite of pain, but so much more. Heat and delicious pressure.

"Fucking heaven," he muttered, his face pressing into my neck as he struggled to breathe.

A moan escaped me.

"You okay?" he gritted out.

I tried to get words out, but I was feeling so much. Instead, I just made a nonsensical sound.

Colt pulled back. "LeeLee?"

"More," I whimpered.

His lips met mine in a soul-stealing kiss, and Colt began to move. Slow, easy thrusts at first, those hints of pain melting into nothing but heat.

My heels dug into Colt's ass, and he arched deeper into me, making my eyelids flutter.

"Eyes on me, LeeLee. Want to see those stars when you come."

My inner walls spasmed, and Colt cursed.

He picked up speed, my own hips rising up to meet him. We found a rhythm that turned a flicker into a flame.

"Not gonna last," he ground out. "Too fucking good."

My muscles began to tremble, and my legs shook.

Colt's hand dipped between us, finding my clit. He pressed down, and everything around me shattered in a spiral of light.

Colt shouted something undiscernible, thrusting impossibly deeper.

Wave after wave pulsed through me as my fingernails dug into Colt's back. All I could do was hold on because I knew nothing would be the same.

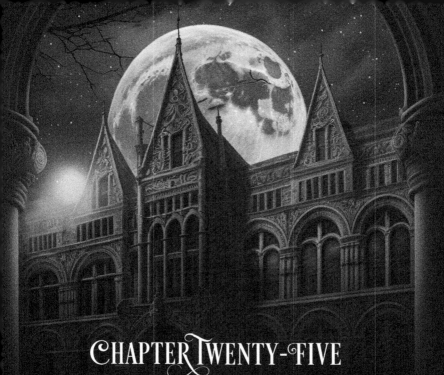

CHAPTER TWENTY-FIVE

"HOW DO YOU FEEL?" COLT ASKED AS I PULLED MY discarded shirt over my head.

My cheeks heated. "Good."

He moved in close, wrapping his arms around me. "Truth."

I buried my face in his chest. "Happier than I've ever been."

Colt's hold tightened. "Love hearing that. Love *you*."

Everything in me warmed. "I love you, too."

"How are you feeling physically?" he pressed.

"A little tender," I confessed.

"Warm bath for you tonight. Need to make sure I'm taking good care of you."

I pulled back, searching Colt's face. "What about you? I'm not sure what we just did was wise, given your injuries."

Colt's lips twitched. "LeeLee…I would've given a kidney for what we just had."

I scowled at him. "Not funny."

He brushed the hair back from my face. "I'm fine. No pain at all. I'm just going to have lower energy for a few days."

I watched for any sign that he wasn't being truthful, but I didn't see anything. "Is that your shifter healing?"

Colt nodded. "That, Ronan's blood, and, I think, having you close."

My eyes flared. "Me?"

"You're my mate. After we're bonded, we'll be able to help each other heal, but even just having you close can increase health and well-being."

"That's incredible," I whispered.

Colt brushed his lips over mine. "You're incredible."

I jerked back. "Wait, if you had this magical healing all this time, what about your broken arm when you fell out of the tree? You were in a cast for six weeks."

He gave me a sheepish smile. "Dad was so pissed. He'd always told me I had to be careful not to get hurt around people who didn't know."

"But you were so determined to climb that damn tree."

Colt chuckled. "My punishment was having to stay in the cast even though I didn't need it."

I shook my head. "No wonder you were cranky."

He pressed a kiss to my temple. "At least I had you to keep me sane."

"Always." My fingers twisted in Colt's T-shirt. "Did anyone see Damien in the caves?"

In the hours we'd sat vigil at Colt's bedside, the guys had spoken in low tones about the vampire and the trap, but I honestly hadn't been able to take much in.

Colt stiffened, and I instantly regretted my question.

"You don't have to talk about it," I hurried to assure him.

Colt ran a hand up and down my back. "It's okay. I'm just pissed as all hell that we didn't see this possibility."

"The trap?" I asked.

"That he might've been working with the shadow demons."

A chill ran down my spine. "I thought they were after all supernaturals. Wouldn't they want to kill Damien, too?"

"They usually are. But Damien must have some sort of deal with them. Information in exchange for giving them a targeted hit list."

Anger bubbled down deep. "I'd like to castrate him with a rusty butter knife."

A startled laugh burst out of Colt. "I had no idea you could be so vicious."

"He tried to kill you. He almost succeeded. I would do anything to stop that."

Colt wrapped his arms around me. "I'm good, LeeLee. I'm not going anywhere."

I burrowed deeper into his hold, relishing the feel of his strength and the beat of his heart against my cheek. "Promise me."

"I promise."

I pulled those two words deep inside, holding them close.

Colt gave me one more squeeze and then released me. "Let's get out of here. It smells like a hospital."

I shook my head. "It basically is a hospital, which only a billionaire like you would have."

He shot me a cocky smile as he led us to the door. "Comes in handy sometimes."

"Let's not have any more need for this room, okay?"

"Sounds like a good plan to me."

Colt guided us down the hall toward the lounge room. Each step made my stomach churn.

Colt's steps faltered, and he glanced down at me. "What's wrong?"

"How do you know anything's wrong?"

"I can smell your anxiety."

My jaw dropped. "You can *smell* it?"

"Shifters have a keen sense of smell, and every emotion has a unique scent."

"I really can't have secrets around here, can I?" I grumbled.

Colt laughed. "You'll get used to it." He sobered. "What's wrong?"

I worried the corner of my lip. "Are they going to be mad? That we...you know?"

Colt's hands came up to frame my face. "We've known we would share a mate our whole lives. We want you to be close to all of us. It's not the same as being with you ourselves, but there's a comfort in knowing you've been with one of our bond mates."

I wanted to believe him. I just wasn't sure how that was possible.

"Come on. You'll feel better after you see everyone."

Colt gently pushed me forward and toward the sound of explosions coming from the TV in the lounge. The moment we stepped inside, four sets of eyes swung toward us.

Declan's and Ronan's nostrils flared as they breathed deep, and my face turned fire-engine red. Damn that shifter smell. Trace's eyes went molten purple, and I knew his incubus sensed it, too. It took Dash a second longer.

He scanned me up and down, then grinned. "Looks like you gave Sleeping Beauty a hell of a wake-up call."

Ronan threw a remote at Dash. "Grow up."

Dash just smiled wider. "Does this mean the band's back together?"

Colt wrapped his arm around me, pulling me close. "What do you think, LeeLee? Ready to give this a real shot?"

I swallowed hard, forcing myself to look around the room. Each of the guys wore a different expression, but there was an element of hope in all of them. "Do you want this?"

Dash was the first to answer. "You know I do."

Declan gave me that warm, reassuring smile. "I'll always want this. Always want you."

My stomach gave a flip.

Ronan took a deep breath. "Never felt more grounded than when I'm with you. Yes, I want this."

My gaze shifted to Trace. His hands were fisted tight, a battle raging in his eyes.

Dash turned to him. "This is it. All of us. We'll have your back."

Trace's Adam's apple bobbed as he swallowed. He shook his head as he pushed to his feet. His eyes locked with mine. "I'll do everything I can to keep you safe. I'd give my life for yours. But I can't give you this."

And then he was simply gone.

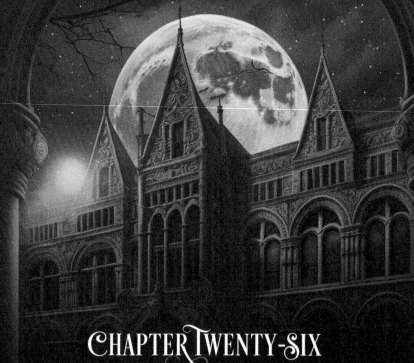

CHAPTER TWENTY-SIX

TRACE HADN'T COME TO MY ROOM LAST NIGHT. THE knowledge burned deep in my chest, leaving behind an ache I wasn't sure would ever lessen. The ache of having someone your soul craved within touching distance, yet impossibly out of reach.

"Hey, you okay?" Dash asked gently.

I gave myself a mental shake as I pulled on knee-high socks. "I'm good."

Colt didn't look convinced. "You don't need to go to school today."

When Trace hadn't miraculously appeared last night, the nightmares had come again. The ones where Damien had me locked away where no one could find me, and the agony of his bites never ended.

My own screams hadn't woken me. It was Dash shaking my shoulders, the guys behind him. Only Trace had been missing.

My mouth went dry as I thought about where he might've been. Or with *who*.

I shook myself out of it. I needed to be grateful for what I had. Colt and Dash had slept the rest of the night with me, making me feel secure and safe.

I shoved off the bed. "I'm good, really. I need school and normal." At least the hope of normalcy, because who knew if Alister would show up again.

Dash grabbed my backpack for me. "Then we'll do normal." His eyes twinkled. "Wanna make out under the bleachers?"

A laugh burst out of me. "Are we gonna get detention for that?"

Dash pulled me into his arms, his face getting close. "I don't know, Mon Coeur. But it would be worth it."

Colt rolled his eyes. "We're all gonna get detention if we're late, so let's get some breakfast."

Dash kissed the tip of my nose. "Later."

There was a world of promise in that one word, and a shiver ran through me.

"You're killing me, Mon Coeur."

I bit my lip.

He tugged it free. "You should come with a warning label. So dangerous."

I blushed, slipping from his hold.

"Can't wait to see all the places you blush," Dash called.

My face only got hotter. I hurried down the hall to the stairs, Colt and Dash quickly catching up with me.

Muted voices came from the dining room, and I moved in that direction, bracing myself. As I stepped inside, two pairs of eyes lifted to me. Declan had gone home late last night, saying he needed to make an appearance on horde lands. That had sent Ronan storming off. Now it was just Ronan and Trace at the dining table.

My gaze instantly sought out Trace. He looked rough, with

119

dark circles under his eyes and hair disheveled. His skin was a shade paler, making the tattoos on his hands and neck stand out more. The moment our gazes locked, he averted his. My stomach dropped.

"Morning," Ronan greeted. "How are you feeling?"

"Good," I said, forcing cheer into my voice as I sat.

I opted for fruit and yogurt this morning, unsure if I could handle more.

Dash frowned at me. "That's all you're having?"

"It's a healthy breakfast."

"You need more protein, fat." He inclined his head to his plate piled high with eggs, bacon, and biscuits.

"I don't need that *every* morning," I argued.

"You should bring a snack to school with you in case you get hungry later," Colt said. "This might not hold you over."

"I think I'll survive," I muttered.

Ronan covered a laugh with a cough.

I pinned him with a glare.

He only laughed harder. "Love watching them turn into mother hens with you."

"It's not funny," I grumbled.

One corner of Ronan's mouth kicked up. "It's a little funny."

Conversation stayed light as we ate, but when we finished, Colt disappeared into the kitchen, reappearing with two protein bars that he shoved into my backpack. I just rolled my eyes. If it made him feel better, I could live with it.

We made our way outside to the SUV, and my gaze kept pulling to Trace. I couldn't help but worry about him. I moved a little closer. "Are you okay?"

His eyes snapped to me. "Fine."

"You don't look it."

Trace's back molars ground together. "Don't need you worrying about me, Leighton."

The use of my name hurt. I longed for that lilting of his

voice when he called me *Little Bird*. But I swallowed down the pain. "You can't stop me from worrying. That's what happens when you care about someone."

Panic flared to life in Trace's violet eyes. "Haven't you learned by now? You should never care about monsters."

He climbed into the front seat of the Escalade and slammed the door.

Dash moved in behind me, squeezing my neck. "Give him time."

I didn't respond. There were no words to say. Not when I wasn't sure that this was a rift that would ever heal.

The ride to school was quiet. But Dash held tight to my hand the whole way, tracing comforting circles on my skin. When Colt parked, Trace shot out of the SUV like his ass was on fire.

Colt frowned at his disappearing back.

Ronan climbed out of the back seat. "I'll make sure he's okay."

My chest cracked. I wanted to do that. To soothe Trace's demons. But he didn't want that from me.

Instead, I followed Colt and Dash into the school. We wound our way through the sea of students to my locker. I deposited books and then shut the door.

"Ready," I said, glancing up at Colt and Dash.

"Here's to a normal fucking day," Dash said. "Maybe a little teen pregnancy scare."

I snorted.

As we headed down the hall, I caught sight of Chloe. Mimi and Grace were back at her sides. I guessed she'd forgiven them for going after what she considered *hers*.

The smile that spread across Chloe's face set me on edge. It had an evil glint that matched her black heart. She flipped the strands of her bob as she came to a stop in front of us, her eyes going to Colt. "Heard you ran into a little trouble in the caves."

I stiffened, my spine snapping straight.

Colt's face stayed carefully blank. "Not sure what you're talking about."

Confusion filled her expression for a moment, and then her face reddened. "They should've gutted you when they had the chance."

Rage, hot and dark, blasted through me. I didn't think. I simply lunged.

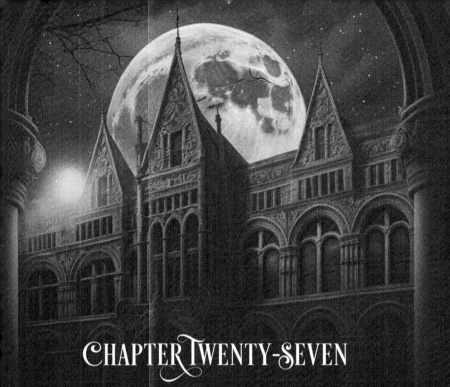

CHAPTER TWENTY-SEVEN

I FLEW AT CHLOE, KNOCKING HER TO THE FLOOR.

She shrieked, but quickly began to fight back, her knee going to my ribs.

Pain pricked, but the rage pulsing through me dulled the worst of it. My fist struck out in a blow to her torso as we rolled.

Chloe cursed, her palm slapping across my face in a stinging blow. The metallic taste of blood filled my mouth, and I bit back a yelp.

Students shouted and catcalled while Dash and Colt tried to grab hold of both of us. But we were too fast. Chloe rolled me over, her hands fisting in my hair and yanking hard.

"You'll never be stronger than me. I've been training to rule my whole life," she growled.

"Then why are you pulling my hair like a kindergartner?" I got off a punch to her ribs that had her wheezing.

But Chloe quickly recovered, scratching her nails down the side of my face. "I'm going to make your life a living hell."

"Enough!" Colt yelled, but we ignored him.

My leg came up with a blow to Chloe's pelvis that had her loosening her grip on my hair.

Rage bloomed in her eyes. "He should be rotting in the ground. You all need to learn your lesson."

Chloe's hand fisted, and she got off a punch that had me seeing stars.

Dash's lessons flashed in my mind, and my hand came up in a palm strike to her nose. There was a satisfying crunch, and then Chloe was screaming.

Colt caught hold of me, pulling me off Chloe as I kicked and bucked, trying to get free.

"You broke my fucking nose!" she shrieked. But her voice didn't sound right. There was too much blood gushing down her face.

"It should've been your neck!" I yelled back.

Suddenly, Ronan was in front of me, breathing hard from obviously running in the direction of the ruckus. "Firecracker…" He couldn't disguise the amusement in his voice. "You broke her nose?"

I kicked out, trying to get free from Colt's hold. "I'm going to *kill* her."

Colt cursed. "Help me, would you?" He scowled in Dash's direction, who was trying to help Chloe up. "You just had to start teaching her martial arts."

Dash shrugged. "She wanted to learn how to protect herself."

Ronan grabbed hold of my arms. "I'd say she's an A-plus student."

"You're going to pay for this," Chloe sneered.

Dash dropped his hold on her, and Chloe tumbled to the floor again. "Suddenly don't feel much like helping you."

Chloe gasped and spluttered, blood going everywhere. "My father won't stand for this. He'll have you brought before The Assembly."

Dash's eyes went cold behind his glasses. "And what do you think The Assembly will have to say about the death threats you've been leveling that everyone in this hallway heard? Or about your knowledge of Damien's plans?"

Chloe paled. "I don't know what you're talking about. Everyone heard about what happened."

Dash's gaze narrowed on her. "But no one knew it was Damien who set it up."

"I-I just assumed," Chloe stammered.

Mimi and Grace took a large step back from their so-called friend.

"What the hell is going on here?" Headmaster Abrams snapped as he strode through the crowd.

Chloe burst into loud, fake sobs. "She attacked me. She's crazy."

The headmaster's gaze jerked to me, then back to Chloe. "Both of you, in my office, now."

"Oh, shit," Ronan muttered.

This was not good.

⌐

My foot tapped against the wood floor as I held an ice pack to my face. I could already feel the shiner coming on. The only relief I had was that Chloe was in worse shape.

She sat in a chair on the opposite side of the room, an ice pack pressed to her face, as well. But there was also rolled-up cotton in her nostrils that made it look as if she'd shoved two tampons up her nose. She glared at me.

Colt reached over and squeezed my hand. "You sure you don't want to go home?"

"She can't go home," Chloe snapped. "She has to be expelled first."

"Chloe," Mimi whispered from her spot next to her friend.

Chloe's eyes flashed with rage. "You don't think she deserves at least that?"

"It doesn't matter what I think. I just don't want you getting your throat ripped out by a rabid wolf," Mimi hissed.

Chloe jutted out her chin. "He can't touch me."

Colt's gaze lifted slowly until it locked in on Chloe. "I wouldn't be so sure about that…"

She paled a fraction but kept up her bravado. "You wouldn't dare."

"Test me," Colt snarled.

The door to the headmaster's office opened, and he stepped inside. Taking us all in, he sighed. "I can see you haven't sorted this out."

"I want her expelled," Chloe demanded.

Headmaster Abrams sank into his leather desk chair. "That isn't your decision."

Her eyes narrowed on the school official. "My father will be livid."

"I'm sure that's true, but I've gone over the camera footage and talked to the students in the hall. You baited them."

Chloe flushed. "I'm not allowed to speak my mind anymore?"

"Not if that mind is full of death threats," the headmaster said.

"She attacked me!" Chloe shrilled.

Abrams winced. "I'm aware." He shifted his gaze to me. "We have a no-violence policy on this campus. That's in place for a reason. We can't risk exposing our kind to the human authorities."

I swallowed hard. "I'm sorry. I shouldn't have done it, no matter how much she deserved it."

Headmaster Abrams pressed his lips together as if to keep from laughing. "Since both of you were in the wrong, you'll both be serving detention today."

"You've got to be kidding me," Chloe snapped.

The headmaster arched a brow at her. "Would you like to turn that into a suspension?"

She snapped her mouth closed.

"That's what I thought," he said. "I would also like you two to keep your distance from one another for the rest of the month."

"My pleasure," I muttered, and Colt choked on a laugh.

Headmaster Abrams turned to Chloe. "Am I understood?"

"Yes," she clipped.

"All right, then. All of you, get to class," he said.

Chloe launched to her feet, charging out of the office, Mimi on her heels.

Colt and I stood, moving at a more reasonable pace.

Headmaster Abrams looked up from his desk. "Colt?"

He turned to face the man. "Yes?"

The headmaster glanced out the open door. "You need to watch your back around that one. I don't have a good feeling. But right now, my hands are tied."

Colt's expression darkened. "I don't have a good feeling, either. But her father's gotten her a lot of protection."

"I'm aware," Headmaster Abrams agreed. "I wouldn't trust that man, either. He's grasping for power, and he's doing it through his daughter."

"We'll keep eyes on her," Colt promised.

"Good," the headmaster said.

But Chloe was sly and the worst kind of vindictive. Simply having eyes on her would never be enough.

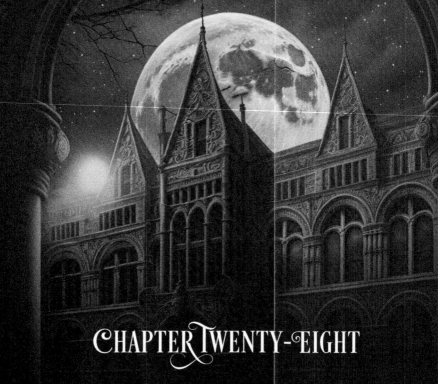

CHAPTER TWENTY-EIGHT

THE ONLY SOUND IN THE CLASSROOM WAS THE TICKING OF a wall clock and the occasional flip of a paper or textbook page. But the side of my face burned as if someone were shooting laser beams at me. Instead, it was just hatred coming at me in waves.

I didn't bother lifting my head or acknowledging Chloe's presence in detention at all. She wasn't exactly following the headmaster's dictates. There were snide comments from Chloe, her friends, and random students I didn't even know.

I tried my best to focus on my AP Bio textbook, but the words and diagrams swam on the page. That just pissed me off. Every time I thought I was catching a little bit of a break, something else would hit.

A buzzer went off, and Ms. Piper, my English Lit teacher and detention warden, looked up from her grading. "That's it for today. Just remember, crime never pays."

That had my lips twitching as a few other students laughed. I shoved my textbook into my backpack and got to my feet, heading for the front of the classroom.

Someone shoulder-checked me from behind, and I almost went sprawling.

"Watch where you're going," Chloe snarled.

"Chloe…" Ms. Piper warned.

"She cut me off," Chloe shot back.

Ms. Piper arched a brow. "It's a classroom, not an LA freeway. I think you could've avoided her."

I stepped to the side, knowing the ensuing fight would never be worth it.

Chloe stomped by me, leveling me with a glare.

Definitely not keeping her distance.

Ms. Piper shook her head, letting out a low whistle. "And that's what happens when Daddy never tells you *no*."

A laugh burst out of me.

She gave me a gentle smile. "Take care of yourself, and watch your back around that one."

"Thank you. I will."

Declan popped his head into the classroom, worry creasing his face. The moment he caught sight of me, the anxiety eased a bit. "You all done?"

I nodded, glancing at my English teacher. "Have a good night."

"You, too." Her mouth curved. "But somehow, I don't doubt you will."

My face heated as I swallowed back a laugh.

Declan looked puzzled as he moved toward me, taking my backpack. "What's going on?"

"Ms. Piper's funny."

She began putting her things in a bag. "I do try."

Declan's confusion didn't lessen, but he dipped his head toward my teacher. "See you tomorrow, Ms. P."

"See you."

We headed out of the classroom and down the hall, Declan slipping his hand in mine as a couple of Colt's security guys trailed behind us. Declan glanced down at me. "You have everything you need?"

I nodded. "Good to go. Where are the guys?"

"They had a meeting with Darius to go over a few things."

My lips thinned.

Declan squeezed my hand. "Colt won't be alone, and he's back to full strength."

"He said it would take a few days to get his energy back."

"Meaning he shouldn't go run back-to-back marathons. He can handle a meeting with a less-dominant wolf."

I grunted some choice words about Darius, and Declan grinned.

He released my hand and wrapped an arm around me. "So protective."

"Well, I clearly need to be. You guys get yourselves into all sorts of dangerous situations."

"Says the girl tackling someone in the hallway today."

My cheeks heated as we stepped outside and into the afternoon sunshine. "She deserved it."

Declan opened the passenger door of his G-wagon for me. "Not arguing with you there."

I climbed inside, buckling my belt as Declan rounded the vehicle and the security guards got in their Range Rover. Declan slid behind the wheel and started the engine.

"Thanks for waiting for me. You didn't have to," I said.

"No problem." An unnamed emotion passed over Declan's eyes, something shadowy that had my stomach twisting.

"What's wrong?"

He shot me a quick glance as he backed out of the parking space. "Nothing."

"Don't lie to me. We don't do that anymore, remember?"

A muscle in Declan's cheek jumped. "Sometimes it's better for me not to be in on those meetings."

"Why?"

"They don't trust me."

An ache settled in my chest. "They've fought alongside you. They've welcomed you into their home."

"I think *welcomed* might be too strong a word."

"Declan…" I reached out, weaving my fingers through his.

"I'm not the one who bailed, but they all look at me like I'm a traitor."

I stiffened, my fingers tightening around his. "What happened?"

Declan's hand tightened on the wheel, making the leather creak. "Ronan ran off when we were ten. We'd always been close. Life might've been shit, but we had each other. Then he just took off. Hid out for a few years and then just reappeared, living the high life with Colt and his dad. I dunno…maybe he was with them all along."

My mouth went dry. "How do you know he ran away? That something didn't happen to him?"

Declan shot a look in my direction, those eyes of his a molten silver. "He left a damned note. Said he was done and didn't want to be a part of our family anymore."

My heart hammered against my chest. It didn't add up with anything Ronan had told me.

"I get wanting to leave. Our dad…he's not a good man. But I would've gone with him. Instead, he just bailed. On me. On our bond. And then he acts like I betrayed him. I'm the one who had to live with the monster alone."

A sourness took root in my belly. "Monster?"

Declan's fingers twitched in my hold. "He's a hard man. He never accepts anything less than perfection."

"No one's perfect."

Declan scoffed. "He thinks I should be."

"And if you're not?"

Declan was quiet for a long moment. "He'll make sure I know that it isn't acceptable."

That sourness rooted itself deeper, spreading. What hell had Declan been living in all these years? He thought he was alone, that his brother had abandoned him, but in reality, they'd been ripped apart.

Ronan's words echoed in my ears. Ones that warned me against meddling. But I had to. I couldn't watch them both live in agony, hating each other, when that hate should be focused on someone else entirely.

"He didn't run away, Dec."

Declan glanced my way. "What are you talking about?"

I swallowed hard. "Ronan didn't run away. Your father sold him to some underground fighting pits."

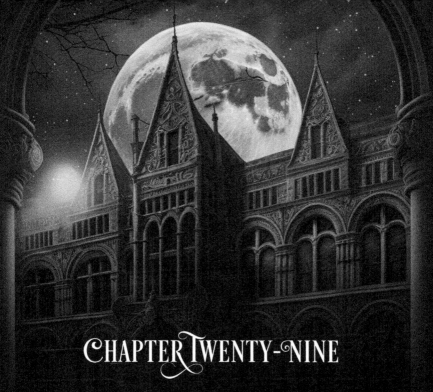

CHAPTER TWENTY-NINE

"Talk to me," I begged, as Declan's foot pressed down on the accelerator.

But he didn't. He hadn't said a word since demanding to know more.

I'd told him what I knew, which wasn't much, and Declan had gone cold.

I squeezed his hand as hard as I could, hoping the bite of pain would bring him back to me somehow.

"I thought he left," Declan said in a hoarse whisper.

"I know," I said softly.

"He was living in hell, and I was pissed at him."

"You didn't know."

Declan's Adam's apple bobbed as he swallowed. "He thought I knew?"

"Your father is clearly a master manipulator."

Declan shook his head as he swung into the drive of The Nest.

As soon as the guard saw it was us, he opened the gates. Declan didn't hesitate. He gunned it up the cobblestone road. Screeching to a halt, he threw the SUV into park and pulled out his keys.

"Dec, wait. You need to be calmer—"

But he was already gone.

I cursed, jumping out of the G-wagon and running after Declan.

Voices came from the dining room, and I moved in that direction.

Declan skidded to a stop in the space, and the guys looked up. Declan only saw Ronan, his twin. "Dad sold you?" he croaked.

Ronan's gaze shot to me. "What the fuck did you tell him?"

I paled, never having seen such anger pointed at me from Ronan. "I'm sorry. I—"

"Did. He. Sell. You?" Declan's voice bellowed so loudly I swore the walls trembled.

Dash and Colt were on their feet, moving toward Declan. Trace stood, staying near Ronan.

Ronan shoved back from the table. "Like you didn't fucking know."

"I didn't," Declan snapped. "He told me you ran away."

Ronan scoffed. "And you just believed him."

"He had a note. It was in your handwriting."

Ronan's footsteps faltered for a moment, then he shook his head. "You should've known me better than that."

Declan shoved Ronan hard. "And you should've known me better. You think I would've been okay with sending you into that nightmare? I know what those pits are. Know they're hell on Earth."

Ronan whirled on Declan. "You don't have a first fucking clue. Hell would be a vacation compared to them."

Declan paled. "I didn't know."

Ronan's eyes flashed. "You wanted the crown."

"Because you didn't. I didn't want you to have to rule when you didn't want it. I wanted to change things!"

A muscle ticked wildly along Ronan's jaw, his hands fisting. "Bullshit!"

Declan got right up in his face, grabbing his shirt and shaking him. "Look at me and tell me you think I'd betray you like that."

Ronan brought his arms up, breaking Declan's hold. "You never came looking for me. Not once. I lived in blood and death for three goddamned years, and you were just living the dream." Ronan jerked his head in a shake. "Get the hell away from me."

He stormed out of the room without another word.

The only sound was Declan's heavy, ragged breathing.

No one moved. No one spoke. But my heart broke into a million tiny pieces.

That pain was nothing compared to what Ronan had endured. The thought jerked me into motion. I started for the door, but Colt caught my elbow. "Don't, LeeLee."

I pulled my arm from his grasp. "I have to."

"He was different after the pits," Colt said, his voice low. "He's not always himself when he's triggered. He could hurt you."

"He won't." My voice held more confidence than I truly felt. But I wouldn't leave Ronan alone in this, even if it put me at risk.

"Little Bird…" Trace warned.

I shook my head. "He needs to know he's not alone."

I moved without waiting for an answer. I jogged down the hall and listened. There was nothing. I went for the stairs first. Ronan's room was his fortress, his sanctuary. If he hadn't gone for the beach, this was where he'd be.

Making my way down the hall, I stopped in front of his door. The keypad lock taunted me. I worried the corner of my lip as I grabbed hold of the knob.

I didn't let myself think too hard. I simply twisted. The door opened.

Maybe Ronan hadn't thought anyone would dare follow him while he was in this dark a mood. Maybe he'd been too distracted to lock the door behind him. Whatever the reason, I was grateful for it because I didn't have the first clue as to how to pick a lock. Especially one as high-tech as this.

"You shouldn't be here," Ronan growled as he paced the floor of his bedroom.

"Maybe not, but I'm here anyway."

His head jerked up, that gold in his eyes flashing. "This is none of your damned business."

Pain carved a home in my chest. "I care about you. Both of you. Your dad fucked with both your lives, and you needed to know it so you can stop blaming each other."

"He should've known," Ronan growled.

"If this happened now? Sure. But he was ten years old. He saw a note in your handwriting."

Ronan picked up a porcelain pen holder on his desk and chucked it against the wall. "He knew me better than that. He wanted the power!"

I took two steps in Ronan's direction. "And shouldn't you have known Declan better than that? Shouldn't you have known that your father would mess with Dec's head?"

Ronan grabbed a picture frame and threw that against the wall next. Glass flew in every direction. "He left me to rot!"

I grabbed hold of Ronan's tee and held on. "He didn't. And deep down, you know it."

That gold went molten as Ronan growled low. "You need to leave. I'm not in control."

My breath hitched as Ronan's hand closed around my throat.

"You stay, and I'll take it out on this tight little body. I'll break you. Destroy you."

My eyes flared, but I didn't look away. "Do it."

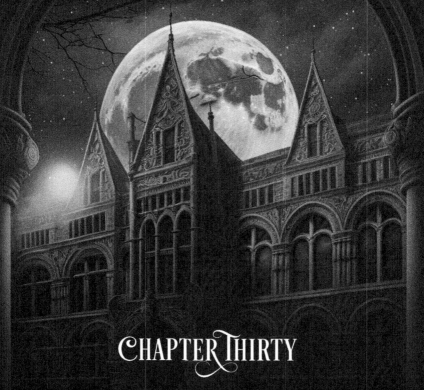

CHAPTER THIRTY

RONAN'S NOSTRILS FLARED, AND HIS FINGERS FLEXED around my neck. "You're not ready for this."

Blood roared in my ears. "Take what you need."

Ronan's free hand traced up my thigh, underneath my kilt. "My little firecracker. So fierce. So brave."

My breath hitched as heat pooled low.

His fingers swept higher, skating featherlight across my skin. "You don't know what I could do to you."

Maybe not, but I wanted to find out.

My fingers fisted tighter in Ronan's tee, pulling him closer.

That gold in his amber eyes flamed brighter. "You don't know what you're doing."

"Then maybe you should teach me a lesson," I challenged.

A low growl left Ronan's throat as his fingers ghosted along the apex of my thighs. "Does this turn you on? Knowing I'm riding the edge? That I could flip and hurt you?"

"*You* turn me on. Whatever form you come in."

Ronan's hold on my neck loosened, his hand dropping away. He leaned forward, skimming his nose down the column of my throat and breathing deep. "Your smell taunts me."

A shiver skated over my skin, sending echoes to the deepest parts of me.

"Tell me you're sure."

I swallowed hard. "I'm sure."

Ronan moved in a flash. He grasped the sides of my shirt and ripped it down the center, sending buttons flying.

A gasp escaped my lips.

The corner of Ronan's mouth kicked up. "Changing your mind, Firecracker?"

I shook my head. "Never."

Ronan's gaze went hooded as it skated over my chest, lingering on the swell of my breasts encased in pale pink lace. A finger skimmed the line of the bra. "So delicate. So fragile."

Another shiver coursed through me, taking root in my core.

"Scared, my little firecracker?"

"No," I breathed.

"I almost believe you."

Ronan's hand shot behind me, unhooking my bra. It fell to the floor along with my ruined shirt. He stared at me as if committing the image to memory. "So sweet and innocent, standing in the lion's den."

I arched a brow, forcing a look of challenge onto my face. "I thought you were a dragon."

A low, rumbling laugh escaped him. "So much worse than a lion."

"Prove it."

Ronan threw a hand out, and talons grew from his fingers. My eyes went wide as those talons shot toward me. He shredded the side of my skirt in a single second, leaving me in nothing but my lace panties, knee-highs, and shoes.

"Scared now?" he growled low.

Anger flared deep. He was trying to frighten me. To get me to leave so he could stew in his fury alone.

I jutted out my chin. "You'll have to try a little harder."

Those golden eyes flashed. A claw trailed up the center of my panties, and wetness pooled between my legs.

I couldn't hold in my whimper.

Ronan's teeth ground together as his finger hooked on the side of my underwear. There was one flash of a talon, and the lace fluttered to the floor.

Ronan knelt, lifting one of my legs and pulling my shoe free, then the other. He gazed up at me. "I'm keeping the knee-highs on."

Heat flared, sweeping through me like a wildfire only he could extinguish. But I knew Ronan would only want me to burn hotter.

He leaned forward, pressing his nose to my core and breathing deep. "Heaven and hell, right here."

A soft mewl escaped me.

Ronan's tongue lashed out, a sharp swipe to my clit.

My legs shook.

"So sweet."

Ronan stood. "Turn around."

His voice was gruff, commanding.

I did as he instructed, my heart hammering against my ribs.

"Grab the desk."

I bit the inside of my cheek as my hands hit the dark wood. The cool surface warred with the heat pulsing through me.

Ronan's hand dipped between my legs, teasing my entrance. Each pass of his fingers stretched me wider, making me ache to be filled.

"Be very sure, Firecracker."

"Please," I begged. I was no longer just wanting to comfort Ronan. I needed him just as much. To lose myself in whatever demons he needed to shed.

Ronan's fingers were gone. Then there was the sound of a

zipper. Each tine of metal was like a mini gunshot going off in the silent room.

He grabbed hold of my hips, fingers tightening as he battled for control. He thrust inside on one long glide.

My mouth fell open on a silent plea.

Ronan didn't wait. He took. Each arch of his hips hit a spot I didn't know existed. Each time he bottomed out, my eyelids fluttered.

His fingers gripped me tighter, digging in to the point of pain, but I didn't care. The pain only drove the pleasure higher.

I met Ronan thrust for thrust, my hips pushing back and seeking more.

My entire body trembled. My core squeezed him tight. "Take what you need," I breathed.

Ronan cursed, and then he truly let go. He pounded into me, letting his animal nature bleed into taking me. Thrust after thrust.

Tears leaked from my eyes. It was too much. I felt him everywhere. Yet it was everything I could ever want.

I tipped over the edge, lighting a fuse that rocked through me. Light danced in front of my eyes as I clamped down around Ronan.

He cursed, thrusting once more as he emptied himself into me.

I felt it all in the deepest parts of myself.

Ronan bit down on my shoulder, teeth digging into my skin, holding me in place as he wrung out every ounce of my pleasure.

As my legs collapsed, he caught me, lowering us both to a chair. Chests heaving, bodies slick with sweat, Ronan held on. He breathed me in over and over, as if only my scent was a balm to those most savage parts of himself.

He pressed his lips to my neck. "Thank you."

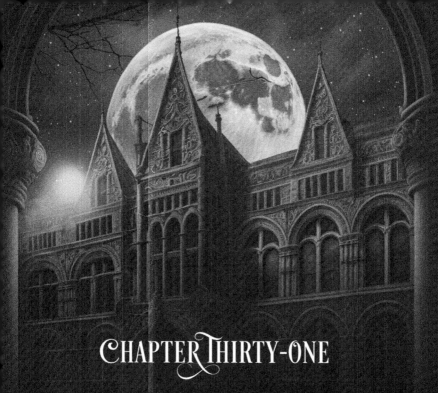

Chapter Thirty-One

THE WATER RAINED DOWN ON US AS RONAN GENTLY ghosted a washcloth over my skin. He dipped his hand between my legs. His amber eyes locked with mine. "Tender?"

My cheeks heated. "Maybe a little." But it was a tender I relished. As if I'd be carrying the memory of Ronan in my muscles.

His other hand lifted to cup my cheek. "I'm sorry."

My face scrunched in annoyance. "I enjoyed every second of that, so don't you dare take it away."

Ronan's lips twitched. "I just should've been more mindful. You're new to this."

My fingers gripped his hips. "You needed to let things go. I wanted to help you do that."

A shadow of grief passed over his expression.

"Ronan…"

His throat worked as he swallowed. "He didn't know."

I pressed my lips to the underside of Ronan's jaw. "He didn't."

"I don't know if I can take that."

My brows pulled together. "What do you mean?"

"So many years lost. So much anger and hatred. And for what?"

An ache took root at the very core of me. Coming to terms with hating the person you'd once loved the most, for all the wrong reasons? It could tear you up inside if you let it.

My fingers dug into Ronan's hips harder.

He looked down at me in question.

"You can't let your dad win. The guilt of this? It could destroy you both if you let it. Don't let him win."

Something flashed in Ronan's eyes. A determination that had hope flaring to life inside me. He searched my face. "I don't know where to start."

"You start with getting to know your brother again."

Pain etched itself into Ronan's face.

I pressed a kiss to his chest, right over his heart. "You can do this. I'll be there with you if you want."

Ronan's arms went around me, pulling me close as the warm water cascaded over us. "Didn't realize how much I was missing, not having you in my life."

My heart squeezed. "Well, you're stuck with me now."

I hoped he was anyway. But fear crept into the warm fuzzies I was feeling at Ronan's nearness, his walls coming down. Terror that we wouldn't find a way to save us all from madness, from death.

Ronan brushed my wet hair away from my face. "No one I'd rather be stuck with."

He reached behind me and turned off the water. As I wrung the excess water out of my hair, Ronan stepped out of the shower and grabbed towels. He wrapped one around me with a tenderness that had a sweet ache taking root in my chest. Then he handed me another for my hair.

We toweled off in the quiet of the bathroom. Ronan seemed

lost in his thoughts. I was sure he was replaying a million moments from the past and worrying about what was to come.

I followed Ronan out into his bedroom and stopped short, catching sight of my mangled clothes on the floor. I glared at him.

His brows lifted. "What?"

"You ruined my uniform. What the hell am I supposed to wear?"

A wolfish grin spread across Ronan's face. "I'm keeping that uniform for memory's sake."

"Boys," I huffed.

He chuckled. "I'll get you a tee and some sweats."

"Or you could go get me some clothes from my room."

Ronan pulled open drawers, grabbing an array of items. "I like the idea of you in my clothes."

My insides went warm and squishy at that.

He crossed to me, handing me a tee, boxer briefs, and a pair of sweats.

I couldn't resist. I lifted the T-shirt and pressed it to my face, inhaling deeply.

Ronan arched a brow.

My face heated. "I like the way you smell."

He grinned again. "What do I smell like?"

"Like a dewy morning after a thunderstorm."

Ronan's face went soft. "Now I want to fuck you nice and slow."

My core spasmed.

"Don't look at me like that, Firecracker. You're too sore."

"Maybe—" I began.

Ronan kissed the tip of my nose. "Later."

I huffed out a breath. "Fine."

He laughed, and the sound held me hostage. I'd heard plenty of Ronan's chuckles, but never his full-out laughter. The sound was rich and smoky, and I wanted to live in it forever.

He shook his head. "I've created a monster."

I shrugged and dropped my towel. "It's your own fault, then."

Ronan's gaze went hooded as it tracked over my body. "I've got zero regrets."

I pulled on the boxer briefs, which were far too big. But the sweats had a drawstring, so when I pulled that tight, everything stayed up. Then I slipped on the T-shirt. "I'm stealing this." The cotton was that perfectly worn softness.

"A firecracker and a klepto. What a combination."

I laughed and leaned into Ronan, pressing my lips to his. "Your klepto."

Gold flashed in Ronan's eyes. "My everything."

My heart thudded against my ribs so hard it hurt. This little glimpse of true happiness was almost more than I could take. "Are you ready?"

Ronan swallowed hard. "As ready as I'll ever be."

I wove my fingers through his. "I'm with you."

"I know."

Still, we stayed there for a beat. Just waiting. I'd give Ronan all the time in the world. This wasn't something I could force. He needed to take that first step.

Ronan squeezed my hand. "Let's do this."

I returned the grip and started for the door. Ronan opened it, then locked it behind us after we left. His steps were even, not fast or slow, but I felt the heaviness in them. The weight of coming to terms with all he and Declan had lost.

I looked up at Ronan as we descended the stairs. "It might take time. But you can't give up."

I couldn't imagine that the road Ronan and Declan had to walk down would be an easy one. There would be a fair share of bumps and potholes. But if neither of them quit walking, they'd get there. To a place they'd been missing for over seven years.

Ronan's jaw set. "I won't."

"This is when your stubbornness pays off."

His lips twitched. "I guess so."

The guys weren't in the lounge or the dining room, but I caught movement out the back windows. "There." I pointed.

The four of them were scattered on chairs outside by the pool. Ronan gripped my hand tighter as he led me in that direction. Four heads lifted as the door opened.

Ronan released my hand and walked in the direction of his brother. I held my breath as he came to a stop. He swallowed hard. "Can we talk?"

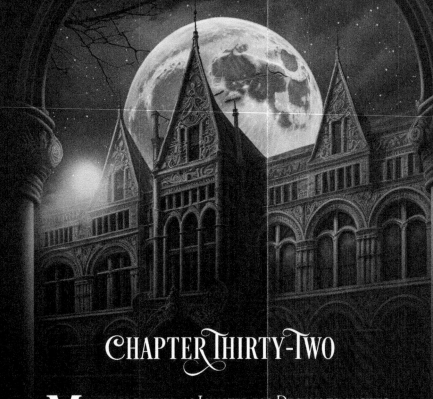

Chapter Thirty-Two

MY LUNGS BURNED AS I WAITED FOR DECLAN TO ANSWER. He stared up at Ronan, a glint of silver in his gaze. Then he jerked his chin in a nod and stood.

Air whooshed out of my lungs on one giant exhale. I didn't take my eyes off them as they walked across the lawn.

They didn't speak at first, but then I saw Ronan's lips begin to move. A little more of the pressure in my chest released.

An arm slid around my shoulders, pulling me against a muscled chest. Dash's lips pressed to my temple.

"Never thought I'd see the day," Colt muttered as he joined us.

"Me neither," Trace echoed.

Dash glanced down at me. "It's Leighton. She's a miracle worker."

I shook my head. "They just needed to get it all out in the open. The truth is what will set them free."

Dash shook his head. "But you're the one who got the truth out of them both."

Colt's jaw hardened. "Should've known Patrick O'Connor was behind this."

"Fucker," Trace muttered.

There was an extra bite to Trace's words, and as I glanced over at him, I didn't miss the anger and almost frenetic energy that pulsed through him.

Concern washed through me as I took in the dark circles under his eyes.

"He's a piece of work," Dash muttered.

"Understatement," Colt agreed.

Declan and Ronan's father didn't even deserve to be called that. "I wouldn't mind junk-punching him," I mumbled.

Colt's brow arched. "Getting vicious on us now?"

Dash chuckled. "I think that already began. She *is* the one who tackled Chloe in the hallway today."

Had that been today? It felt like a million lifetimes ago.

I glanced at Colt. "Their dad. What's his deal?"

Any amusement fled his face. "Power hungry. Control freak. And he's incredibly secretive on top of it. He participates in the treaty and The Assembly but doesn't actually offer a hand to help. I wouldn't trust him as far as I could throw him."

"And Declan is set to take over when he dies?"

Colt nodded. "He said that Ronan defected, so he's ineligible."

"Prick," I mumbled.

I watched as Ronan and Declan turned to face each other. Their heads dipped in such a similar fashion as they talked. A war of emotions played out across both their faces. Grief, anger, hope.

"Can't something be done to hold him accountable for what he did to Ronan?" I asked.

Colt shook his head. "There's no proof. Only Ronan's word."

"Don't need proof to end someone," Trace snarled.

Dash's eyes flared. "Dude, reel it in. You know if we took action against the king of the dragons, it would be an all-out war."

"We could take them," Trace gritted out.

Worry flitted across Colt's expression. "That is the last thing we need. Are you okay, man?"

"Fine," Trace snapped.

But he wasn't. I knew that down to my bones. I just didn't know what to do about it.

Movement caught my attention.

Ronan and Declan walked back toward us. I scanned their faces, trying to read them, but there were so many emotions living just beneath the surface, I couldn't grab hold.

"Well, neither of them is bleeding. That has to be a good sign, right?" Dash asked.

"Hell of a lot better than it's ever been before," Colt agreed.

The twins came to a stop in front of us.

"Well?" Dash pushed. "No one's dead…"

"Their dad could be," Trace grumbled.

Ronan glanced at Declan. "We're starting fresh. As much as we can, anyway."

Tears filled my eyes.

"Oh, crap," Dash muttered. "You made her cry."

Declan's expression softened. "Come here."

I went immediately into his hold, reaching out and grabbing Ronan's shirt as I did so. Ronan moved in behind me, and I was encircled by both of them.

Declan pressed his lips to the top of my head. "Thank you. You just keep giving me more."

Ronan's hand ghosted along my hip. "Don't cry, Firecracker."

"They're happy tears," I sniffed.

"How about no tears?" Dash suggested.

I wiped under my eyes. "Fine. No tears."

Colt surveyed us all. "Well, she ended an almost decade-long feud. I feel like anything else we could do tonight would pale in comparison."

Declan chuckled. "I wouldn't mind eating. Feud-ending works up an appetite."

I lifted my head. "I think we should make dinner together."

Declan grinned. "I like to cook."

The rest of the guys looked extremely wary.

"What?" I asked.

Colt's face heated. "We haven't exactly spent a lot of time in the kitchen."

I rolled my eyes. "So spoiled. Come on, I'll teach you."

⁓

"Shit!" Trace cursed, dropping his knife.

"Did you cut yourself?" I asked, hurrying over to him.

"No. I just—how the hell do you chop it so tiny?"

I tried to hold in my laughter, but it was no use. Other than Declan, the guys were completely helpless in the kitchen. I'd thought a chicken stir-fry would be easy enough to conquer together, but I'd been wrong.

Trace glowered at me. "Stop laughing."

I pressed my lips together, but it didn't work. "I'm sorry. It's just...I had no idea stir-fry could make you crankier than battle."

"It shouldn't be this hard," he grumbled.

"It just takes practice. Like anything else." I started to pat Trace on the back, but he darted away from my touch.

Hurt flared, but I swallowed it down. Trace had made it clear he needed distance from me right now, and as much as that killed, I had to give it to him.

Dash frowned down at a marinade he was mixing. "This doesn't taste right."

Declan moved to his side and dipped a finger into the

concoction. He tasted it and immediately started coughing and spluttering. "What the hell did you put in there?"

Dash's face heated. "I followed the directions. I just added some salt and pepper on top of it."

I grinned at Dash. "How much salt?"

"I dunno, a tablespoon? Salt is supposed to intensify flavors. I read it in a science book."

Ronan handed Declan a glass of water, thumping him on the back.

I grinned at my sexy science nerd. "That might be true, but one of the ingredients in the marinade is soy sauce, and that's already incredibly salty."

"Oh, I didn't know that," Dash mumbled.

Colt slapped him on the shoulder. "Not even you can know everything."

"I think we need to start from scratch there," Declan wheezed.

Dash winced. "I'll follow the directions exactly this time."

"Want me to get you your beakers and test tubes?" Ronan asked with a chuckle.

"Shut up," Dash shot back.

Declan grinned. "Hey, they're all measuring tools. Whatever works."

A beep sounded, and Declan pulled his phone out of his pocket. As he stared down at the screen, his eyes hardened.

My stomach dropped. "What's wrong?"

He shook his head, shoving his phone back into his pants. "Just my dad."

The room went silent as Declan focused back on the cutting board where he was slicing bell peppers.

"Dec…"

He swallowed hard but didn't look up. "I don't think I can go back there. Not knowing what he did."

I moved in close to Declan. "You don't have to."

Colt cleared his throat. "Leighton's right, you can stay here."

Declan's head snapped up. "Seriously?"

Colt nodded, and Declan scanned the room before his gaze stopped on his brother.

Ronan met his stare and didn't look away. "It was where you were always meant to be."

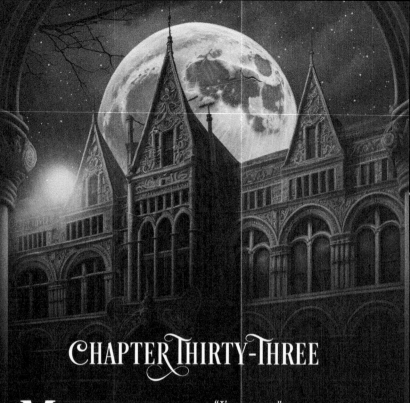

CHAPTER THIRTY-THREE

M Y HANDS WENT TO MY HIPS. "I'M GOING."

"LeeLee…"

"Don't even think about leaving me out of this, Colt," I snapped back.

"We'll be gone for an hour, tops," he assured me.

"You said that last time." Pain lanced through me as I remembered the last time they'd told me they'd be right back.

Colt's arms went around me, pulling me close, as we all stood in the driveway. "This isn't like that. There's a treaty in place. We're just going to get Declan's stuff."

My hands fisted in his T-shirt. "Then there's no reason I can't come with you."

Colt huffed out a breath.

"We're losing daylight," Trace clipped. "Let her come. She's just going to keep arguing."

I glared at him and stuck out my tongue. Not my most mature reaction, but what could you do?

Dash chuckled. "We'll take security, just in case we run into any issues."

A muscle ticked in Ronan's jaw. "No one goes anywhere alone once we're on horde lands. We stick together."

"He's right," Declan agreed. "You never know what Patrick might pull."

I'd noticed over the last several hours that Declan had switched from calling the man his dad or father to calling him by his given name. I didn't blame him.

"Fine," Colt grumbled. He motioned to a handful of guards. "Let's go."

The guys and I piled into the Escalade as the guards got into the Range Rover. Colt and Trace took the front seats, as usual, while the rest of us got in the back.

I tapped my fingers along my thighs as Colt drove.

Dash reached over and took my hand, squeezing it. "We're going to be just fine."

I nodded but worried the corner of my lip.

"It's Leighton we need to worry about," Trace muttered. "One look at Patrick O'Connor and she might tackle him to the ground."

Dash choked on a laugh, but Ronan leaned forward, squeezing my shoulders. "You need to keep it in check, Firecracker."

"I know," I muttered. "But I'm going to give him my death glare."

Declan chuckled. "You'll have him shaking in his boots in no time."

I twisted in my seat. "I can be very intimidating when I want to be."

Declan pressed his lips together to keep from full-out laughing. "I have no doubt."

My eyes hardened on him. "You better watch what you say, or I'll come for you next."

He held up both hands. "I come in peace, swear."

"Whatever," I muttered as I turned back around.

"Everyone needs to be extremely careful with their words and actions," Colt said, his gaze drifting to Trace.

"I already told you that I won't make a move unless he does."

But I could feel the vengeance swirling in the air. Trace wanted Patrick to make that move so he could set his demon free and end Patrick altogether.

Colt sighed, as if worried about my exact thoughts.

We drove in silence for about ten minutes. Then Colt turned off into a forest. A sign read *Private Road, No Trespassing*.

"Welcoming," I muttered.

"Dragons are extremely territorial," Declan explained. "Both of their lands and the air above it."

A shiver coursed through me. I couldn't imagine that Patrick would be thrilled we were here.

Colt pulled to a stop in front of a massive golden gate.

My jaw dropped. "Is that real gold?"

Declan chuckled. "We also have a thing for anything shiny."

"Holy crap," I whispered.

Two guards stepped out, their hands going to weapons at their side.

Colt rolled down his window. "Good evening."

The guard on the driver's side glared at Colt. "What can we do for you, Mr. Carrington?"

"We're here to help Declan with some business."

The guard peeked inside the vehicle, taking stock of everyone inside. His stare stuttered as it passed over Ronan. "One moment, please."

He stepped into the guard house and picked up a phone. I gripped Dash's hand tighter as we waited. A minute later, the guard reemerged. "You're welcome to come inside, but your armed escort and the defector will have to wait outside."

A wall of rage hit me from behind, but Ronan didn't say a word.

"He's my guest," Declan argued.

The guard locked gazes with him. "A decree from your father."

"It's fine," Ronan gritted out. "I'll wait with our guards."

"Ronan…" Colt began.

"I'll be good," he assured.

"Watch your back," Colt warned.

"Always do. Especially around jealous micropenises."

Dash choked on a laugh as the guard's face went beet red.

Ronan opened the back door and slid out, going to the Range Rover and hopping inside. There was a tug deep in my chest. This felt all sorts of wrong.

The guard stepped back, hitting a button in the gatehouse. "Go ahead."

Colt rolled up his window and took his foot off the brake. "Head on a swivel. I don't have a good feeling."

"Me neither," Declan said quietly.

Colt guided the SUV down a winding road until we got to a fork.

"Go to the right," Declan instructed.

Colt obeyed, and soon, small cabins poked out between the trees. I caught sight of children running and playing while adults chatted. It all looked so normal.

Declan seemed to read my thoughts before I spoke them. "There are good people here."

Dash shifted in his seat. "Of course, there are."

"Don't get me wrong, there are bad apples, too. Ones who are as power-hungry as Patrick. And then there are the ones who have just been taken in by his lies." Declan swallowed hard. "I guess I was one of those."

I reached over the seat and grabbed Declan's hand. "But you know the truth now, and you refuse to be blind to it."

Declan leaned forward, pressing his forehead to mine, and breathed me in.

"I'm with you every step of the way," I whispered.

"I know."

Colt slowed, and I looked up, gaping. The house he was stopping in front of looked more like some fancy mountain resort. "This is where you live?"

"Not anymore," Declan clipped.

A hulking man stood on the front steps flanked by two others, only slightly smaller than him.

Declan reached for the door. "Let's get this over with."

We climbed out of the SUV, the guys surrounding me.

The man I assumed was Patrick, with his white-blond hair and gray eyes so similar to Declan's, glared at his son. "Give me one reason why I shouldn't gut you where you stand."

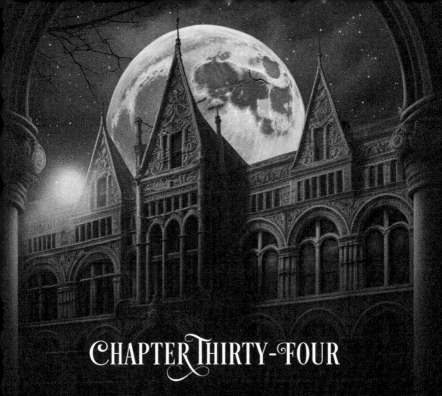

CHAPTER THIRTY-FOUR

ENERGY CRACKLED ALL AROUND ME AS THE GUYS TENSED, going alert in the blink of an eye.

A blank mask slid over Declan's features as he stepped forward. I hated everything about it. It was as if he were draining himself of all kindness and empathy, of any life at all.

"And what would your reasoning be today?" Declan asked casually.

Patrick's nostrils flared. "You *dare* to bring outsiders to our lands?"

Declan arched a brow. "I thought they were allies."

Patrick gritted his teeth. "That may be the case, but they don't belong within our walls. And that traitor doesn't belong anywhere near here."

Declan's eyes melted into a molten silver, the only sign of emotion racing through him. "But he's not a traitor, is he, *Dad?*"

Patrick's spine snapped straight. "Of course, he is."

"He told me the truth. Told me that you fucking sold him into the pits."

The man to Patrick's right shifted uncomfortably. My eyes narrowed on him. He knew. He'd likely stood by while his king had done it, sentenced an innocent boy to hell on Earth.

"He's feeding you lies," Patrick spluttered.

"Not lies when my father pulled Ronan from those pits," Colt shot at the man.

Patrick glared at Colt. "He probably got himself mixed up with the underworld when he ran away."

"Stop lying," Declan gritted out.

Patrick's eyes went the same silver as his son's, but it was darker somehow. "You don't speak to me that way. I am your king."

Declan's jaw worked back and forth. "Not for long."

"What the hell does that mean?" Patrick snapped.

"I'm moving out. Going to live with my bond."

Patrick struggled to keep his breathing under control. "If you leave your horde, you will be dead to me. Cut off. Cast out."

"Not sure you can do that, lizard man," Trace drawled lazily as he cleaned under his fingernails with a large blade.

The man to Patrick's left practically breathed fire. "You insolent little—"

Patrick held up a hand to stop him. "You don't know what I can and cannot do."

Trace arched a brow. "I've made a practice of studying treaty bylaws—everything to do with The Assembly, actually. That's what happens when your parents are dicks of monumental proportions. But I'd say Dec knows just how that feels."

Patrick let out a rumbling growl that shook the ground.

"A future ruler can't be cast out of their clan simply because they wish to live with their bond. It would make for discriminatory practices. If you try to remove Declan from the official line of succession simply because he's choosing to live with us, *you're* the one who'll be cast out," Trace said, his eyes going hard.

Patrick struggled for breath as his face went as red as a tomato. His eyes narrowed on me. "This is your influence. I heard rumblings of a weakling ruining my son's bond. But this is a whole new level of low."

A series of snarls lit the air around me, but I didn't jump. I kept Patrick's stare. "If you think I'm weak because I never manifested, you're wrong. It means I'm stronger than you could ever imagine. I've lived through abuse and torture, and I haven't crumbled. So, you better think twice about coming for me. Or Declan and Ronan."

Declan shifted so that his father's view of me was cut off. "I just need to get my things, and I'll be out of your hair."

Patrick's jaw hardened. "That's where you're wrong. I may not be able to cast you out, but your belongings were bought with *my* money. They'll stay here, waiting for the moment when you return and beg for my forgiveness."

Declan's hands fisted, but he jerked his head in a nod. "They were tainted anyway."

Patrick let loose another growl, but Declan turned on his heel, giving his father his back. It was the ultimate *fuck you*. As if his father wasn't even worth worrying about.

But as Patrick's eyes locked on me, I knew this wasn't over.

〜

I knocked softly on the open door, stepping inside.

Declan looked up from where he was putting away clothes. "Hey."

"Hey," I parroted, unsure of what else to say.

The corner of his mouth kicked up. "They sure work fast around here. Clothes delivered and washed. All in a matter of hours."

"It's Colt's way of caretaking. But it can be a little overwhelming." I sank down on the bed, surveying Declan.

"It's nice," he said, placing another pile of T-shirts in a drawer.

"Are you okay?" It was a dumb question, but I had to ask it anyway.

"Not really." Declan shut the drawer, crossing to me and lowering himself to the mattress.

I twisted so I was facing him and reached up to rub his temples. "Today has been a lot."

Declan dropped his head to my shoulder. "Understatement." He paused. "But you were a little badass. Think you might've made Patrick pause, which is saying something."

"I really, *really* dislike that man."

"That's because you're smart."

I ran my hands through Declan's white-blond hair, digging my fingers into his scalp. "I hate that you've lived your entire life with him."

"But not anymore. We're all making fresh starts."

I kept massaging. "I like the sound of that."

"Me, too." Declan lifted his head, his gray eyes locking with mine. "Don't know how I got so lucky to have you in my corner."

My breath hitched. "I feel the same way."

Declan's hands circled my waist, and he lifted me so I was straddling him, my arms going around his shoulders. His eyes searched mine. "I love you, Leighton."

Everything in me burned, but it was the best kind of pain. "I love you, too."

The corner of his mouth kicked up. "It would've been really awkward if you didn't."

A laugh startled out of me, but Declan stole it right off my tongue as his mouth crashed into mine. His tongue drove inside, not teasing but taking.

"Dec—"

I broke the kiss, jerking back as Ronan walked in.

"Oh, shit. Sorry. The door was open. I'll just go—"

"Wait," Declan cut him off.

Ronan stilled, his stare locking with his brother's.

Declan swallowed. "Stay."

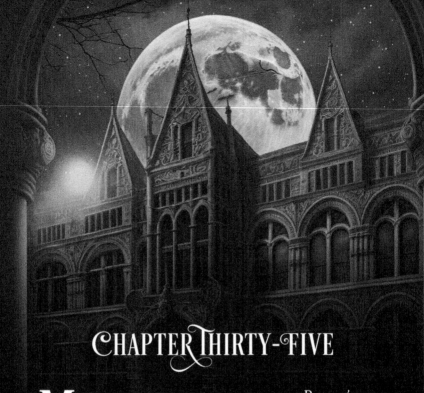

Chapter Thirty-Five

MY BREATH STUTTERED IN MY LUNGS AS RONAN'S EYES sparked gold. He swallowed hard. "You're sure?"

Declan dipped his head to meet my eyes, questioning. I nodded, my heart hammering against my ribs.

"We're sure," Declan said.

Ronan slowly closed the door. The snick of the latch and flip of the lock sounded like cannons in the quiet room. Ronan prowled across the floor. Each step sent my heart fluttering into overdrive.

He came to a stop behind me as I still straddled Declan's lap. He traced a finger up my spine. "She's tender. We need to be gentle with her."

Silver flashed in Declan's eyes, his hand slipping beneath my T-shirt. "Baby, was he rough with you?"

My mouth went dry, words escaping me.

"She likes orders," Ronan purred.

Heat gathered low as my core tightened.

Declan grinned. "Let's see how well she can take them."

"Sounds like a fun game to me," Ronan agreed, his hand dipping beneath my hair and squeezing. His other hand stroked through my strands. "So beautiful, like the richest fire."

My breaths came faster.

Declan's fingers traced designs on my stomach, making me shiver. His hands fisted in my tee. "May I?"

My core clenched. Only Declan could make that simple question a turn-on. I nodded, struggling to breathe normally.

"Lift," Ronan commanded.

My arms went up.

Declan peeled the T-shirt from my body, sending it sailing to the floor. His eyes zeroed in on me, flaring. "Leighton...no bra?"

I bit my lip. "I was in a hurry."

I'd had to change out of Ronan's clothes before we went to dragon lands, and I'd been in a rush.

Declan traced a finger from my chin, down my neck to circle my breast, then my nipple.

Ronan reached from behind, palming my other breast. "Isn't she beautiful?"

Declan's eyes went hooded. "The most beautiful thing I've ever seen."

His head dipped, taking a peak into his mouth and sucking gently.

A whimper left my lips as I rocked against Declan. His hard cock pressed against my center through my joggers. I couldn't stop seeking more.

"So greedy," Ronan purred in my ear, nipping the lobe.

Declan released my nipple. "I think I like her greedy."

He moved in a flash, lifting me off his lap and depositing me onto the bed. His hands went to the waistband of my sweats. "Need to see all of you."

"Yes," I breathed.

Declan shucked my joggers and panties in one swift tug.

Ronan simply watched. He palmed his dick through his sweats as he gazed down at me. "Think I could come just staring at her."

Declan grinned. "But what a waste that would be."

Ronan put a knee to the bed, his fingers tracing over my skin. "Let's take care of our girl."

My heart spasmed at *our girl*. Not just because I loved being claimed by them, but because Ronan was claiming me for the both of them, bringing the brothers together for the first time in years.

"I think she's earned that," Declan agreed as he sank to the carpeted floor.

He pushed my thighs apart, lifting my legs and depositing them on his shoulders.

My back arched, everything in me spinning tight.

Ronan's fingers traced my nipples. "So responsive, just following those beautiful instincts. Perfect."

Wetness gathered between my thighs.

Declan grinned, simply watching. "She loves that praise. Think she might be able to come just from words alone."

I whimpered again.

"She wants *you*, brother," Ronan encouraged.

Declan's eyes went silver. "She has me."

His fingers parted me, and his tongue flicked out. He teased and toyed, circling that spot where I wanted him most but never quite getting there.

My hips bucked, trying to get what I needed.

Ronan tweaked my nipple, sending a spark of sensation coursing through me. "Be still."

My body trembled as I fought the urge to move. "Please."

"Listen to that beautiful begging," Ronan purred. He bent, his tongue laving my nipple.

Declan slid two fingers inside me, and I almost wept with relief. The need to be filled was so intense, I'd never felt anything like it. My hips rocked.

Ronan nipped the peak of my breast. "Still."

I let out a sound that was more animal than human. A sound that begged for release.

Declan's fingers curled inside me, hitting a spot that had black dots dancing across my vision.

"She loves that," Ronan said, his voice going gritty.

Declan hit the spot over and over, fingers twisting and curling.

A pressure built everywhere. Blood roared in my ears.

"Now," Ronan demanded.

Declan's lips closed around my clit, sucking hard as Ronan bit down on my nipple.

I cried out as that pressure released in a flood. My core clamped down on Declan's fingers, but he kept stroking, wringing out wave after wave from my body.

My vision tunneled, and then there was nothing but black.

⌒

"You seriously knocked her unconscious?" Colt clipped.

"I'm fine," I argued from my spot, curled on the couch.

"You need to eat more," Dash ordered. "Your blood sugar got too low."

Ronan's lips twitched as he glanced at his brother. "Not gonna lie, this has to earn us some bragging rights."

I grabbed a pillow and threw it at him. "You're the worst."

Declan's arms tightened around me from behind. "You're sure you're okay?"

"I was out for like two seconds."

Although, passing out from the force of my orgasm was a little embarrassing. Declan and Ronan had freaked. But I would do it all over again.

Ronan lifted my feet and put them in his lap. "We gotta take it easy on our little firecracker. Wouldn't want to break her."

A sound came from the chair across the lounge. Trace's eyes had gone pure bright purple. He shoved up and stalked out of the room.

I bit the inside of my cheek. "Is he okay?"

Dash looked in the direction of the door. "I think his demon's been on edge lately."

My stomach twisted. I knew what that meant. He'd go searching for release. And soon. It made me feel sick.

A ringing sounded, and Colt pulled out his phone. "Carrington," he answered.

He was quiet for a moment, but his face went stormy. "Where?"

More silence.

"How long?"

He began to pace.

"Keep a fucking close eye and report all movements."

Colt jabbed a finger against the screen.

"What now?" Dash asked.

Colt's gaze came to me. "It's your mom. She's here in Emerald Bay."

CHAPTER THIRTY-SIX

ICE SLID THROUGH MY VEINS. I COULDN'T CONTROL THE tremble that took root in my muscles.

Ronan shot forward on the couch. "What the hell are you talking about?"

A muscle in Colt's cheek ticked. "I've had a tail on her since we left Louisiana. Wanted to make sure that she didn't do anything stupid."

"But she did," Ronan growled.

My shaking intensified as memories slammed into the walls I'd erected in my mind. The crack of a slap across my cheek. The shock of a punch to my ribs. The burning fire.

I squeezed my eyes closed as if that would somehow help.

Declan's hold on me tightened. "I've got you. You're safe."

But I wasn't—not if Maryanne was in Emerald Bay.

There was movement, and Colt crouched in front of me. "Nothing's going to happen to you."

"You don't know that," I whispered.

"I do because we're going to make it so," he growled.

My chest ached, a heaviness settling in that was almost too much to bear. "What does she want?"

Colt shook his head. "I don't know. But I've got someone keeping a close eye on her. We'll find out."

Panic lit in my veins, and I jerked upright. "She can't take me, can she?"

I was still seventeen, and my eighteenth birthday had never felt so far away. My rights to live the life I wanted were just out of reach.

Colt and Ronan shared a look.

"What?" I pressed.

Ronan shifted so he was facing me. "She signed a document that gave legal custody to Baldwin."

"But?" I asked, knowing there had to be more.

Dash moved in closer, worry etched in his expression. "Custody isn't that cut and dry. Courts will always want to reunite a family when at all possible."

Family? She and I had never been that. Not even when my father was still alive. She tolerated me because I was a means to an end. To a lifestyle she wanted. And after my father died? It had gotten so much worse.

Nausea swelled, and I shot off the couch, running for the hall bathroom. I made it to the toilet just in time and emptied the meager contents of my stomach into the bowl.

Hands reached out, pulling my hair back. Another rubbed up and down my back.

I heard muted voices but couldn't make out what they said, too lost in the heaving that rocked my body.

Colt kept rubbing my back. "You're okay. Just breathe."

I kept heaving, over and over.

"There's nothing left in her damn stomach," Ronan snarled.

"It's a trauma response," Dash told him.

"Well, how do you fucking stop it?" he shot back.

"Trace?" Dash asked.

There was silence for a moment.

"Fucking fix it," Ronan snapped.

A second later, another set of hands landed on my back. They slipped beneath my T-shirt, and a buzz lit in my muscles. It was like an instant antianxiety pill. Everything in me eased.

The heaving slowed, then it stopped altogether. I could breathe.

"That's it, Little Bird," Trace said softly. "Hold on."

He lifted me in his arms, and it was all I could do to hold my head up.

"Water," I croaked. My mouth tasted like death warmed over.

"Here," Dash said. "This is mouthwash."

He tipped some to my lips, and I swirled it around.

Ronan lifted a cup so I could spit.

"Thank you," I whispered.

My head lolled to the side, into Trace's chest. I couldn't keep my eyes open. Before Trace had reached the stairs, sleep pulled me under.

○

I woke to the most delicious warmth. Surrounded by it. As if I were swimming in pure heat.

I blinked against the light. Colt came into focus first, his eyes locked on mine.

He brushed the hair from my face. "LeeLee."

"Hi," I said, my voice barely audible.

"How do you feel?" he asked.

Declan sat up from his spot behind Colt, waiting for my answer.

"Okay." I wasn't sure that was completely true. My muscles were weak, and my throat was raw from all the vomiting.

"Better than I am, dealing with Dash's hard-on poking into my back all night," Ronan groused.

Dash sat up, hair mussed, and reached for his glasses. "Sleeping surrounded by Leighton's smell is going to do that to me. She's my mate. It's a biological reaction."

"Well, I'm not down with your dick, so let's figure out a way for you to curb that *biological* reaction, science nerd," Ronan clipped.

I shifted, shoving up against the pillows. I was surrounded by four of my guys. They'd all stayed. Then my eyes locked on the fifth.

Trace sat in an overstuffed chair in my sitting area, Briar on his lap, happily purring as his tattooed hands petted her. I took in the designs on those long fingers. For the first time, I realized the designs spelled something. One hand held *love*, the other *hate*. The two parts of Trace that were at war with each other.

I lifted my gaze to his face. "Thank you."

Trace's jaw went tight, but he nodded.

I swallowed against the dryness in my throat, dropping my focus to my laced fingers. "Sorry I freaked out."

Colt wrapped an arm around me, pressing a kiss to my temple. "You never have to apologize about that. I'm just sorry you had to go through it."

Ronan's fingers wove through mine. "Your mom isn't going to be able to hurt you again. We'd run before we let that happen."

My stomach hollowed out. I knew Ronan meant every word. "I can't make you leave your home, your clans."

Ronan reached up to cup my cheek. "Haven't you realized yet? *You* are our home. Our family. You're our everything."

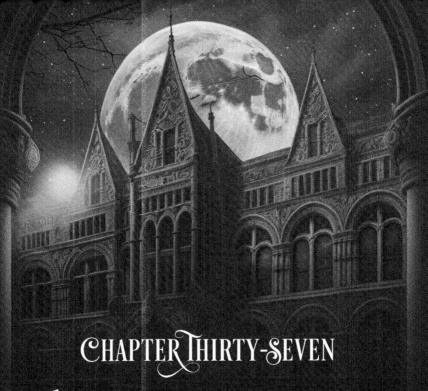

CHAPTER THIRTY-SEVEN

I MOVED THROUGH THE SCHOOL HALL ON AUTOPILOT, Declan on one side and Dash on the other. I didn't even flinch when Chloe glared at me, or her friends dropped snide comments. I had far worse things to worry about than bitchy mean girls.

The guys hadn't wanted me to go to school. And maybe they'd been right. My body felt as if it were weighed down with iron chains by the end of the day. But staying home would've been worse. All I would've had was time to think. To worry. Maryanne's presence taunting me every second. At least school had distractions.

Declan slid my backpack from my shoulder. "How about a movie night tonight?"

I needed to do homework, but cuddling with the guys in the screening room sounded way better. "Sure."

Dash wove his fingers through mine. "I'll text Baldwin on our way home. What do you want for snacks?"

My mouth curved the barest amount. Dash was always trying to feed me. To take care of me. "Tell him to go with whatever mood strikes him."

Dash chuckled. "That's dangerous. We could end up with an eight-course feast in the screening room."

Declan grinned. "I wouldn't hate it."

"Freak," Mimi spat as we passed. "Careful, boys, I hear her disease is catching."

Declan whirled on her. "Careful, Mimi. Your jealousy's showing, and Trace has been on edge lately. Doubt he'd mind taking that out on you. I'll help him bury the body."

She paled but then straightened her shoulders. "You can't touch me. Any of us. The Assembly's watching."

Declan bared his teeth at her. "The Assembly will never know. You'll just go missing one day. Except no one will actually give a damn you're gone."

Her jaw dropped open, but we didn't stop, passing her by and heading for the school's exit.

"I'm getting sick of those bitches," Declan muttered.

"You and me both," Dash agreed. "Might be time for a lesson."

Declan arched a brow in question.

Dash shrugged. "I've got ways to hide the trace of my spells."

Declan chuckled. "I should've known."

We stepped outside, and I caught sight of the rest of the guys waiting at the Escalade. My heart sped up at the vision, a tugging sensation emanating from my chest and almost seeming to pull me toward them. The closer we all got, the harder it was to be apart from them, even if it was just for a few classes.

Colt pushed off the SUV, striding toward me. He took my face in his hand and kissed me long and hard. As he pulled back, he breathed deeply. "Missed you."

I burrowed into his hold. "I missed you, too."

Ronan slipped a hand under my hair and tipped my head back. His lips met mine in a tender kiss. "Hate being away from you."

I pressed my forehead to his. "I know," I whispered.

The only one who kept his distance was Trace.

That wall between us hurt. I knew it wasn't because he wanted to cause me pain. There were scars and fears that kept him separate. I just wished I knew why they were there. Wished I could heal them.

"Let's get home," Colt said.

We climbed into the SUV and headed for The Nest. Dash did his best to keep the conversation light as we drove, but everyone was on edge, not knowing what Maryanne's presence could mean.

Colt pulled to a stop in front of our house, and we all piled out.

"Movies now?" Declan asked.

"I should probably do some homework first," I grumbled.

Dash draped an arm over my shoulders. "We can study in the lounge. Then movie marathon."

I looked up at him. "You gonna help me with bio?"

He grinned. "Always."

Ronan snorted. "Helping you with bio is like foreplay to him."

"Hey, we've all got our kinks," Dash shot back.

I couldn't hold in my laugh. And damn, it felt good to have humor find me again. I patted Dash's chest. "Let's go turn you on."

We filed into the house and headed for the lounge. I flopped onto the couch, and Declan handed me my backpack. I pulled out my bio textbook, handing it to Dash. "Make it make sense."

He snorted. "I'll do my best."

And he did. We spent the next hour going over mitosis and miosis until I actually had somewhat of a handle on the freaky process. I finally had a prayer of getting a good grade on the next test.

"I'm gonna get a soda. Anyone want anything?" Trace asked as he stood. But the moment he straightened, he started to wobble, then crashed back to the chair.

I was on my feet in a flash, but Colt made it to him first.

"Dude, you okay?" Colt asked.

"Yeah, just a little lightheaded."

Dash crouched next to Trace, a worried look on his face. He pressed two fingers to Trace's wrist, checking his pulse. He glanced up at me. "Do me a favor and get some juice and a snack."

I nodded quickly, grateful to have something to do to help. I hurried down the hall and into the kitchen. Baldwin was nowhere to be found, but he'd clearly been busy in preparation for our movie night. There was a massive charcuterie board on the kitchen island and other trays that were covered.

Moving to the fridge, I opened it and grabbed the orange juice. I filled a glass and then took a plate from the stack. Baldwin would just have to forgive me for ruining his perfect display. I took an assortment of crackers, cheese, grapes, and sliced meats, and put them on the plate. Then I hurried back toward the lounge.

Raised voices stopped me in my tracks.

"Have you lost your mind?" Ronan snarled.

"It is what it is," Trace said, voice low.

"You need sexual contact," Dash argued.

"I won't do it," Trace snapped.

"Trace…" Colt began.

"No," Trace cut him off. "I won't betray her like that, but I won't condemn her by touching her, either."

I sucked in a sharp breath as I hovered outside the door.

It was quiet for a moment, and then it was Dash who spoke, his voice even. "Then you're going to die."

Chapter Thirty-Eight

DASH'S WORDS SHOT THROUGH ME, LEAVING A BURNING pain in their wake. But that agony propelled me forward, into the lounge. "He'll die?" I croaked.

Five sets of eyes snapped to me, and Trace cursed.

"I'll be fine," he grumbled.

I shoved the plate and glass at Declan. "That's not what Dash just said."

My heart thudded viciously against my ribs.

Colt sent Dash a scathing look. "You need to watch how you say things."

"No," I snapped. "This isn't something where you try to protect me. I need to know the truth."

"Don't," Trace warned.

I glared at him. "Are you my mate or not?"

A muscle in his cheek ticked.

"Don't be a coward," I pushed. "Answer me."

"I'm your mate," he growled.

"Then tell me the truth."

Trace jerked his head at Dash, who shifted uncomfortably.

He turned to face me. "You know that incubi need sexual contact to survive."

I nodded.

"Well, Trace hasn't exactly been getting that lately," Dash explained.

That thudding in my chest grew fiercer. It was a war of hope and fear. Had he not been with another girl because of his feelings for me? Or was there some other reason?

"Don't mince words," Ronan said in a low voice. "He's starving himself to death."

My eyes flared. "Trace…"

"I'm fine," he gritted out.

But that obviously wasn't true. His color was all wrong. He was too pale, almost gray. Dark circles under his eyes told me he wasn't sleeping. And he'd almost just passed out.

Yet even with how miserable Trace felt, he hadn't come to me. He hadn't made a single move to take us from a tenuous friendship to more. Not even a kiss.

Hurt flared to life somewhere deep, but I shoved it down. Right now, my pain didn't matter. Not when Trace was hurting himself this way.

"You can't keep doing this," I said softly. My next words killed something inside me, but I said them anyway. "If you need it, you should find a willing partner. I won't be mad. I know you don't want me that way—"

Trace shoved to his feet. "You don't know a damn thing."

He stormed out of the lounge, leaving me gaping in his wake. I blinked after him.

"It's not you," Dash assured me quietly.

"It is," I whispered. "I make him miserable."

"No," Colt argued. "He's dealing with a lot of baggage, a lot of hurt. It's tied to relationships for him."

My eyebrows pinched as I studied Colt. They all talked around the demons Trace was wrestling with, but no one would tell me the damned truth.

If they wouldn't tell me, then I'd have to find it for myself. I straightened my shoulders and turned to leave.

"Leighton," Dash called. "Don't."

I shook my head. "I'm not tap dancing around this anymore. Trace and I need to come to an understanding. I'm not going to be his undoing if there's something I can do to help."

Colt opened his mouth to argue, but Ronan held up a hand to stop him. "Let her go."

The guys were quiet for a moment.

Ronan's gaze went soft on me. "She reached me when I didn't think anyone could. It's the mate bond. She's the one that can heal when we think we're too broken."

Warmth spread through me, a balm to those places that were aching so deeply. "Thank you," I whispered.

Ronan crossed the space, leaning down so that his forehead pressed against mine. "You've got this."

I squeezed his hand and pulled away. Taking a deep breath, I headed for the door.

I wandered through the lower level of the house. I hadn't heard Trace on the stairs, so I didn't think he'd gone to his room. But The Nest was massive. It could take me all day to search even just the downstairs.

A tugging sensation in my chest had me turning to the back windows.

I sucked in a breath. There he was, sitting on the rocks overlooking the ocean. He looked so small, almost like a little boy, so lost and alone. My heart cracked.

I forced my feet to move. Heading outside, the wind picked

up, swirling my hair around my face. It didn't take me long to cross the yard.

Trace seemed to sense my presence before I said a word. His muscles tensed, and his jaw went hard. "Go away, Little Bird."

"No," I said, sitting down next to him on the rock.

Trace sighed as if the weight of the world were on his shoulders. And maybe it was.

"Talk to me," I pleaded.

"There's nothing to say."

But he was wrong. There was everything to say.

"Why are you hurting yourself?" I asked. It was the simplest place to start.

Trace's jaw clenched as he stared out at the ocean. "Not going to betray you."

My chest seized.

"It was one thing when I didn't know you, not really. You were just this idea in my head. But then you were here. Real and breathing. You were in my space, and you burned so damn bright I couldn't look away."

My lungs burned, begging for breath, but I couldn't move. "Trace..."

"You're so kind. So quietly strong. Never letting anyone steamroll you, even if they're ten times your size. Never admired someone more."

That burn shifted up my throat to my eyes. "Then why won't you give me a chance? A real one?"

I asked the question I'd been terrified to voice for weeks.

Trace turned to look at me, those violet eyes swirling. "I'll ruin you."

I shook my head. "You won't."

"You don't know that," he gritted out.

"You have to explain why. Tell me," I begged.

Trace's eyes went dead. "Because my love killed someone before."

CHAPTER THIRTY-NINE

PAIN SWEPT THROUGH ME FOR COUNTLESS REASONS, BUT most of all because of the sheer grief that had made a home in Trace. I could feel it like a living, breathing thing. But I couldn't deny the fact that it hurt that he had loved someone else. Killed.

"What happened?" My voice was barely audible, just a faint whisper on the wind. I didn't want the answer, but I needed it. Had to know if I was going to figure out the path to walk with Trace.

A stuttered breath left his lungs. "I was young and dumb."

I waited for him to continue.

"My parents are demons, too, but they're fire demons. When I manifested as an incubus, they didn't want anything to do with me. Incubi aren't honorable in their estimation."

"Then they're idiots," I snapped.

The corner of Trace's mouth kicked up, but it wasn't in actual amusement, just a shadow of the emotion. "I'd been warned that

I could have an extreme effect on romantic partners. But when I hit puberty, I just thought it was cool that all the girls wanted me."

"You're a walking hormone when you're going through puberty. I think that's understandable," I argued.

Trace shrugged, his gaze pulling back to the water. "I met Sarah when we were freshmen. She was a caster and didn't seem to care about me being an incubus. She was funny and a daredevil. Suddenly, I didn't want a dozen different girls. I just wanted her."

My stomach cramped, but I stayed quiet.

"It was that puppy love kind of thing. I don't think we would've lasted, but in that moment, I just wanted more and more time with her. I got reckless, didn't realize she was becoming addicted."

My fingernails dug into my palms. "Addicted?"

Trace nodded. "We never even had sex. I thought that would keep her safe. But she got addicted to my touch. She'd show up at The Nest in the middle of the night, saying she felt like she was crawling out of her skin. She'd beg me to skip class so we wouldn't have to be apart." He swallowed hard. "By the time I realized what was happening, it was too late."

"What happened to her?" I asked softly.

"Colt's dad said we needed distance to break the hold I had on her. He got her parents involved. But no one realized how attached she'd grown."

My mouth went dry as I waited for more.

"She had a psychotic break. Tried to kill her parents just to get to me. Hurt her dad pretty badly. She lives in an institution now and stares at a wall sixteen hours a day."

An ache took root in my chest. "I'm so sorry." I let the silence swirl around us. "But what happened wasn't your fault. You didn't want her to get hurt."

Trace turned to look at me again, a muscle ticking wildly along his jaw. "I was careless. Now, don't you see?"

"Yes and no," I said carefully. "I see why you're terrified, but I also know that we were made to be together. From everything I've learned over the past month, I don't think the Universe would bond us if I couldn't handle you."

Trace surged to his feet. "You don't know that."

I stood quickly. "I know we have to try."

He shook his head vehemently. "I'm not risking it."

Anger pricked at me. "Then what? You'll risk your own death?"

A muscle along Trace's jaw ticked. "You guys might be better off without me."

Everything in me froze, my muscles locking so tight it was physically painful.

"Trace."

His name was sheer pain on my lips.

Then I moved. I threw myself at him with a force that nearly knocked him over.

Trace had no choice but to catch me.

I gripped him with a ferocity that had a rumbling sound escaping his chest.

"Little Bird," he whispered.

"Don't. Don't you ever say something like that ever again. You are important. You are loved. Even when you're an asshole. None of us would ever be the same without you."

"Okay," he soothed, his hand rubbing up and down my back.

"Promise me. Promise you'll fight. That we'll find a way."

"I promise, Little Bird. I promise."

My hands fisted in his button-down shirt. I couldn't let go. Too afraid that he would disappear in front of my eyes.

I swallowed down the sob that wanted to escape, and I forced myself to focus. "You seemed okay before. What changed?"

Trace was quiet for a moment, and then he confessed, "I stopped sleeping with you."

I pulled back. "That contact, it helped?"

He nodded slowly. "It hurts. To be near you and not take what my demon truly wants, but that skin-to-skin contact is enough to keep me surviving."

It killed that being in my presence caused him pain, but we had to find a way to keep Trace alive for now. We'd deal with the rest later.

"Why did you stop?" I asked.

Trace teased his lip ring with his teeth. "I was worried my demon would try to claim you. Mark you as his before I could stop him. He's already imprinting on you. It's a delicate balance."

I frowned. "What does imprinting mean?"

"It means that my demon is starting to think of you as his. It becomes harder and harder to resist the urge to claim you once that happens."

As messed up as things had been between us, I wanted Trace to claim me. Wanted to be wholly his. This beautifully broken boy who would do anything to protect us all. But I wouldn't force him into something he wasn't ready for. I took a deep breath, then lifted my hands.

Trace caught my wrists. "What are you doing?"

My eyes flared, but I didn't look away. "Trust me."

The two words were a plea.

Trace's throat worked as he swallowed, but, eventually, he released my hands.

My fingers went to the buttons on his shirt. I unfastened one, then another, and another. I slid my hand under the fabric and placed it over his heart. The steady beat thudded against my palm, reminding me that Trace was still alive, still breathing.

Trace's eyes went hooded as a buzz took root in my arm. That faint vibration spread throughout my body until I was panting. The urge to wrap myself around him was so strong sweat broke out along my spine.

Trace gritted his teeth and pulled my hand free. "That's enough."

The air left my lungs on a whoosh as I struggled to get my breathing back to normal, but my eyes stayed locked with his. "Promise that you'll come to me if you're hurting."

Already, Trace's coloring was better, the circles not as dark.

He lifted my hand to his mouth, pressing a kiss to the palm. "I promise."

CHAPTER FORTY

As I descended the stairs, I moved in Trace's direction. "How are you feeling this morning?"

A small smile curved his beautiful mouth, gentler than I'd ever seen. "A lot better."

I frowned. "You weren't at breakfast. Did you get something to eat?"

He chuckled. "I actually went for a run this morning. Haven't felt up to that in weeks. And Baldwin gave me a breakfast sandwich. I'm good."

"Do you need, uh, do you need me?" I asked uncertainly.

"I'm okay right now. I'll let you know. I promise."

A flicker of disappointment took root. I wanted that connection with Trace. Craved it. But I also knew I couldn't push. "All right."

Footsteps sounded on the stairs, and I looked up to see the rest of the guys descending. They were all focused on Trace.

Colt strode toward us. "You look better."

"I feel better," Trace admitted.

Dash looked between him and me. "Did you two, uh, figure things out?"

Trace jerked his chin in a nod. "We've got things working for now."

"Good," Ronan said, clapping him on the back. "Because you're a cranky fucker when you stay away from Leighton."

Declan chuckled, draping an arm over my shoulders. "I think we all are."

My cheeks heated.

Colt laughed. "Ain't that the truth."

"Come on, let's hit the road before Leighton turns into a tomato," Trace said.

Dash grinned. "I like making Leighton blush."

My cheeks flushed a deeper shade of red. "Please stop."

Dash ducked his head, his lips skimming my ear. "I love it when you beg."

A shiver racked through me as heat flared between my legs.

The three shifters groaned.

"What?" I asked, panicked.

Declan shook his head. "Shifter senses. We can smell when you're turned on, remember?"

I ducked out of his hold, stalking toward the door. "You guys are all the worst."

Only laughter sounded behind me.

⌒

"Remember, we have a quiz tomorrow," Ms. Carole said as she shut off the projection screen.

The class groaned.

She arched a brow. "If you've been keeping up with your assigned reading, none of you should have a problem."

"Unless all the French syllables swirl in your brain," I grumbled.

Dash leaned over from his desk beside me. "I'll help you study. I might even come up with some *creative* rewards for every answer you get right."

Sam choked on a laugh from her desk on the other side of me. "That's my kind of study buddy. I think I might have to get Seán to do the same thing. I could use a little motivation."

My face flushed. "Shifter hearing," I grumbled.

Sam laughed, her eyes dancing. "Happy for you, Leighton."

"Thanks," I mumbled, shoving my books into my bag.

"See you guys later," she called as she stood and headed for the door.

Dash took hold of my chin, tipping my head back. He took my mouth in a gentle kiss. "You okay?"

I let my forehead fall to his, resting there. "Oh, I don't know. Maryanne is in town, and we have no idea why. We have no clue where Damien is or what he's planning. Trace could die without the touch he needs, but he's damn stubborn. We still have no idea if I'll be able to anchor you or if we'll go insane or get dead. And I'm pretty sure I'm in danger of failing all my classes."

Dash's hands came up to cup my cheeks. "Just a few things swimming in that big, beautiful brain of yours."

"Just a few," I echoed.

He brushed his lips across mine. "Let's take things one step at a time. We can only deal with what's right in front of us. We can start with this French quiz. That's a simple fix."

"Easy for you to say. You're fluent," I groused.

How Dash had managed to transfer into my intermediate French class, I'd never know.

He grinned wide. "That just means I'll be an excellent tutor."

"You better hope so, because it would be a bummer if I had to repeat my senior year."

Dash pushed to his feet, grabbing my backpack and slipping my notebook inside. "You know we'll never let that happen."

My eyes narrowed on him. "You're not allowed to buy me a diploma."

A bark of laughter shot from his mouth. "I'm not buying you a diploma."

"You say that like it's a stretch. Colt basically bought you all into my classes, and he bought the ability to put up cameras all over the school."

Dash's lips twitched. "You've got a point there."

I just shook my head as I stood. "You're all incorrigible."

He wrapped an arm around my shoulders. "But you love us that way."

"Sometimes," I grumbled.

"All the time," Dash argued as we stepped into the hall.

Someone made a gagging sound. "Not sure how he can stand to touch that trash," Chloe said in a voice that she knew would carry.

Students turned in Dash's and my direction, and I fought the urge to duck my head. Instead, I met Chloe's stare. "Doesn't the bitterness ever get old? I guess you're just *that* obsessed with me, you can't help yourself."

A few snickers sounded from the crowd.

Chloe's face went red. "I just hate how you're dragging our future leaders down into the mud with you."

I shrugged. "They say mud's good for the complexion. Must be why we're all glowing."

"No, Mon Coeur," Dash purred. "That's all the sex."

Mimi made a strangled sound while Grace glared, but Chloe looked as if she wanted to murder me on the spot.

I ignored them all and grinned up at Dash. "Good point." I kissed him lightly. "Take me home."

"Thought you'd never ask."

Dash led me away as Chloe spluttered. "You handled that expertly," he whispered.

"She's becoming more like an incessant gnat than anything else," I admitted.

"Good way to think about it."

I stopped at my locker, punching in the code. "I just wish I could squish her."

Dash chuckled. "Pretty sure we all feel that way."

I opened my locker door, and bile surged in my throat.

Blood and things I didn't want to even try to identify coated the entire locker. And a note hung in the center with jagged block lettering.

I'M NOT DONE WITH YOU YET.

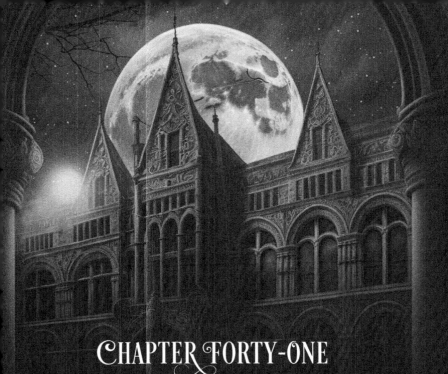

CHAPTER FORTY-ONE

I SWALLOWED DOWN THE BILE BUT COULDN'T KEEP MY entire body from shaking.

"What the fuck?" Dash snarled, quickly turning me away from the carnage in my locker as he slammed the door.

My breaths came in quick pants as he held me.

Dash shifted, pulling out his phone. "Get to Leighton's locker. Now."

Then he was shoving the device back into his pocket. "I've got you. It'll be okay."

"H-how?"

The school was supposed to be safe. Protected. Colt had cameras. There was security.

"I don't know," Dash gritted out.

Footsteps thundered against the floor, but I didn't look up from Dash's chest.

"What happened?" Colt barked.

"Look in her locker," Dash said quietly.

The squeak of hinges sounded, and then a whole series of curses filled the air.

"It's Damien," I croaked. "It has to be."

"He has to have someone helping him," Declan growled.

"More than one person," Ronan said.

A light laugh lit the air, and my head snapped up to see Chloe, Mimi, and Grace walking down the hall. Chloe smirked. "Looks like quite the mess to clean up."

Trace was in front of them in three long strides. Purple sparks shot off him. "What did you do?"

Chloe stumbled back a step. "*I* didn't do anything."

"Back off," Mimi snapped. "You can't threaten us."

Purple fire surged in Trace's hands. "I don't threaten. I promise."

"Y-you can't," Grace stammered. "You'll be expelled."

"Do you think I give a damn?" Trace snarled.

I quickly crossed to him, placing a hand on his back. "Don't. They aren't worth it."

The moment my hand made contact with Trace, the fire in his palms leapt higher.

The girls squealed, scampering back.

"Shit!" I jerked my hand away, and the fire subsided.

Chloe's jaw fell open. "Are you imprinting on her?"

"That's not any of your damn business," Trace barked.

"Trace," Mimi whined. "You can't."

Chloe shot a dark look in his direction. "We'll just have to see what The Assembly has to say about that."

She flounced down the hall, her friends following in her wake.

I looked up at Trace. "Could you get in trouble for you and me?"

He shook his head. "You're my mate. There's nothing The Assembly can do."

But I heard what he didn't say. The Assembly wouldn't be happy about it.

I hugged my knees to my chest. I'd changed into sweats, thinking that would fight off the chill, but there was no luck. I shivered again, and Declan pulled me into his side, grabbing a blanket.

Ronan's fingers flew across the keyboard of his laptop.

"I don't see how it's possible," Dash said. "Someone should've seen something. And we've got a motion detector right above Leighton's locker. That should've alerted while we were in class."

I gaped at him. "There's a motion detector at my locker?"

Dash shrugged. "It's programmed to alert us during times no one should be there. Between classes, after school, at night."

I shook my head. "I don't think I want to know what all you have in place."

Colt patted my thigh. "That's probably for the best."

"Boys and their toys," I huffed.

"Got something," Ronan said, and everyone's gazes moved to him.

A muscle in his cheek jumped. "The feeds were cut for twenty minutes during the last period of the day."

"That should have triggered an alert on all our phones," Trace gritted out.

Ronan nodded. "You're right. I don't know why it didn't. I'm going to have our tech guy dig into it further. But all the cameras in that hallway, along with the motion detectors, went offline at 2:42 and they didn't come back until 3:03."

Dash glared at the computer screen. "Someone would have to know that we put those security measures in place."

Ronan looked up at him. "They were installed at night. The only people who should've known were us and Headmaster Abrams."

Trace let out a low growl. "Sounds like we need to have a little chat with Abrams."

I sat up straight, eyes pinning Trace to the spot. "No torture."

"Little Bird…"

"I said *no*."

He huffed out a breath. "You never want me to have any fun."

Declan choked on a laugh. "Why you gotta be such a buzzkill?"

I glared at him. "Excuse me for not wanting any of you to get expelled."

Colt shifted on the couch. "We are going to have to talk to Abrams. If he's turned, we need to know."

I swallowed hard. I didn't want to know what that could mean. If the headmaster was against us, the school would never be safe.

"Can you have a conversation without bloodshed?"

Trace gave me his best innocent smile. "Of course."

My eyes narrowed on him. "Why do I have my doubts?"

"Because Trace's idea of a conversation ends with us burying bodies in the woods?" Dash suggested helpfully.

I pinched the bridge of my nose. "Somebody help me."

Ronan shot me a grin. "I'll make sure nobody gets dead."

I dropped my hand. "Like you're much better?"

His grin only widened. "I only kill when someone strikes first."

"Except insulting your outfit could be considered striking first," Colt muttered.

"Hey," Ronan shot back. "I have excellent fashion taste."

I stared at him. "You wear nothing but all black."

He shrugged. "It works for me."

Declan choked on a laugh.

"I'm going to have to bail you all out of jail, aren't I?" I groaned.

The sound of a phone ringing cut off any answers.

Colt swiped up his cell and answered. "Carrington."

A pause.

"Go ahead."

As each second ticked by, Colt's features grew harder.

"Don't let her out of your fucking sight," he snarled, then hung up.

Everyone in the room stayed eerily quiet.

Colt's jaw ticked. "We found out who brought Leighton's mom here."

"Who?" I whispered.

His eyes came to me. "The vamps."

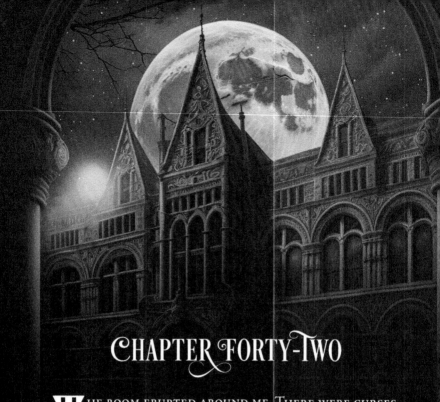

CHAPTER FORTY-TWO

T HE ROOM ERUPTED AROUND ME. THERE WERE CURSES, grumbles, and spat-out oaths. I just stared at Colt.

"How?"

My question was barely audible, but with his shifter hearing, Colt got it just fine. His expression was hard. "I've kept those eyes on your mom since she's been here, trying to figure out what move she was planning. A car picked her up at her hotel this afternoon. Our team reported it took her straight to vamp lands."

Ronan let out a low, rumbling growl. "We knew someone had to have brought her here. She couldn't afford that hotel she's been staying at."

I swallowed, trying to clear the dryness in my throat. "I get that she knows about this world, but how did she find out about the vampires? Or how did they find out about her?"

Dash looked as if he were battling to keep his temper in check, so different from his typical easygoing expression. "I'm guessing

Alister did some checking into you after Damien kidnapped you. He's going to look for any ammunition that might keep you from testifying to what Damien did."

My stomach roiled. The threat of having to return to my mom would do it. I'd endure anything to keep myself out of her grasp.

Declan shifted, rubbing a hand up and down my back. "She's not going to get you."

I nodded numbly. They didn't get how vindictive my mother could be. There was nothing she would hate more in this world than my happiness. And if she knew that the guys around me made me feel the happiest I'd ever been, even in the midst of insane turmoil, she'd do anything to rip them away from me.

⁓

I hugged my knees tighter to my chest as I stared out at the water from my window seat. The moon reflected off the surface as it rippled and danced. The play of light was comforting. If I focused on that and nothing else, I would be okay. The millions of things pressing down on me couldn't grab hold.

My throat burned with the force of me keeping the worries and memories away. My fingers dug into my calves. That bite of pain helped. It kept me in the here and now.

A soft knock sounded on my door.

"Come in."

The answer came automatically, even though I didn't really want the company. I wanted to stay lost in my water and light show. If I saw one of the guys, I'd be forced to confront just how much I had to lose.

Colt opened my door, stepped inside, and closed it behind him. He didn't say anything as he crossed the space and didn't hesitate when he reached me. He lifted me into his arms, then sat, settling me in his lap.

I instantly burrowed into Colt's hold. His heat wrapped around me, reminding me I was safe for now. Yet still, my eyes burned. "It hurts," I whispered.

Colt brushed the hair away from my face. "What does?"

"Loving you all so much and knowing a million different things could rip you away from me."

"LeeLee…"

I couldn't handle any denials he was about to give. "You know it's true. The Assembly. The vamps. Damien. Chloe. The shadow demons. Even me."

Colt's hold on me tightened. "You?"

I tipped my head back to look up at him. "I'm being so selfish. I know that I might not be what you need. That selfishness could end us all."

Colt brushed his lips against mine. "You're always what we need. We may not see the path that's going to get us there, but we have enough light to take the next step."

Everything inside me hurt. Ached and burned with hope and fear. "I want to believe that. I do. But I'm not sure if it's true."

Colt's thumb stroked across my cheek. "Have faith. We just need to take things one step at a time."

"That's hard to do when we're being attacked from all sides."

"Then it's a good thing there's six of us," Colt said with a hint of a smile.

I let out a sigh. "What are we tackling first?"

Any hint of amusement fled Colt's face. "Your mom."

Nausea swept through me. "Don't call her that."

Colt frowned.

"She's never been a mother. She doesn't deserve the term."

Colt's arms spasmed around me. "Okay. We deal with Maryanne first."

I nodded. "And how do we do that?"

"I've got a team digging up all the dirt we can. I can't imagine it'll be difficult to find with the life she's led. Then we tell her what will be delivered to the police if she sticks around. I think she'll come around to our way of thinking."

"It might work."

Maryanne's self-preservation instincts were stronger than anything else. The only thing that rivaled them was her desire to see me suffer. Hopefully, her selfishness would win out.

Colt's hand trailed down my neck. "It will. Trust me."

"I do." It was the greatest gift I could give another human being after all the times I'd been hurt. But Colt had more than earned it.

Sparks of gold flashed in Colt's eyes. His head bent, and he took my mouth. His tongue swept inside, teasing me with long, languid strokes. As if he had all the time in the world and he was going to drown in my taste.

Heat built in my muscles, settling low and growing with each swipe of Colt's tongue.

I shifted, needing better access, needing more. I straddled Colt's lap, his hardening cock pressing against my core. I couldn't help the whimper that escaped me.

Colt's hands tangled in my hair, deepening the kiss.

A sound had me jerking back and realizing we weren't alone.

Dash grinned from the doorway. "Don't you dare stop."

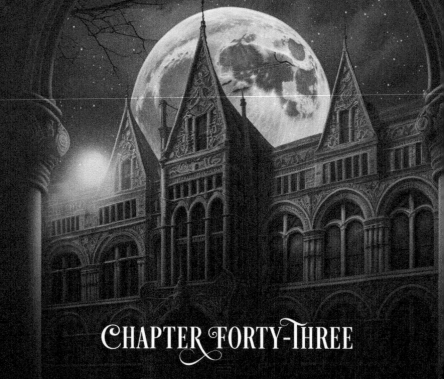

CHAPTER FORTY-THREE

"**D**ASH," COLT GROWLED.

Dash's mischievous grin only widened. But there was a feral edge to it. One that had heat licking up my thighs.

"Love watching you two," he said, his voice going husky.

Colt slid a hand up my neck to cup my jaw. He turned my head so that I had to look at him. He searched my eyes. "Do you want him to leave?"

I squirmed on Colt's lap, and he groaned.

"You're gonna kill me, LeeLee."

"But it'll be a damn good way to go," Dash said as he crossed the room.

"Is that a yes? You want him to stay?" Colt questioned.

"Yes," I breathed.

I wasn't sure what it meant that knowing Dash was watching only turned me on more, but it did.

"Thank fuck," Dash said as he lowered himself to an overstuffed chair opposite us.

I licked my lips.

"Kiss him, Mon Coeur," Dash ordered. "Take what you want. What you need."

My core tightened, searching, aching.

My mouth met Colt's, losing myself in him. I rocked against his hard length, seeking that friction, that release to the building pressure.

"Don't come," Dash ordered, his words cracking out like a whip. "You have to earn that pleasure."

I moaned into Colt's mouth, wetness gathering between my thighs.

"Stand," Dash instructed.

I pulled back, my gaze jerking in his direction.

Dash simply arched an eyebrow as if to ask why I was taking so long.

I glanced at Colt.

His lips twitched. "Better do what he says."

I stood, my legs shaky.

"Undress her," Dash told Colt. "Slowly."

Colt pushed to his feet, circling me like a predator circles prey. His fingers skimmed my waist before getting purchase on my tee. He pulled it up and over my head.

"So beautiful," Dash murmured. "Love that color on you."

I glanced down at my blue lace bra. The color was so similar to Dash's eyes.

Colt stepped behind me, unhooking the bra and letting it fall to the floor.

Dash's eyes went hooded, and he stroked himself through his sweats. "Perfection."

Colt reached from behind and palmed my breasts. He worked my nipples until they were tight peaks, and I was struggling for breath.

"Pants," Dash growled.

Colt dropped to his knees, taking my sweats and panties with him.

"Left leg," Dash ordered.

I lifted it, and Colt pulled the fabric free.

"Right leg."

The routine continued.

Colt's hand glided up my leg to my ass. He palmed one globe, squeezing.

I let out a whimper.

"Such a pretty picture," Dash cooed. "Tell me what she tastes like."

Colt's hand shifted to between my thighs, parting me and dipping inside. He pulled back, sucking his finger clean. "Like heaven and spice."

Dash groaned, pulling his dick free and stroking in earnest.

My eyes zeroed in on his cock. Long and thick, growing with each pass of his hand.

Dash's eyes flared. "Hungry for me, Mon Coeur?"

Wetness pooled, and everything ached. "Yes."

He grinned. "Walk to me."

I moved as if he had control of my limbs. Each step stirred that heat building inside.

"Kneel on the ottoman," Dash instructed.

I swallowed hard and climbed onto the furniture piece in front of him.

"On all fours." Dash's voice was pure liquid heat. "Have you done this before?"

I shook my head.

Desire lit in Dash's blue gaze. "Such a good girl, so eager to learn."

My nipples pebbled.

Colt's hand ghosted over my ass, stroking between my thighs.

My mouth fell open. I was entirely exposed, and I didn't give a damn. I just wanted more.

"Take me in your mouth, Mon Coeur. Careful of your teeth," Dash said as Colt stroked my entrance, fingers tracing and dipping in.

I leaned forward, licking the tip of Dash's cock, then taking him in.

Dash groaned as I started to move up and down, sucking gently. The taste of him had more wetness pooling.

"Take her pussy while I take her mouth," Dash growled.

Colt didn't wait. I heard the rustle of clothes, and then there was pressure at my entrance. He thrust inside on one long glide, and I whimpered around Dash's dick.

His hand fisted in my hair. "That's my girl. Love those sounds around my cock."

I sucked harder, and Dash's hips bucked. Power surged as I felt how much I affected him. My tongue flicked over the ridge around his head.

Dash cursed. "Not gonna last."

Colt thrust harder, deeper. My core trembled around him as pleasure sparked.

I lost myself in the two of them. In this feral rhythm that was the three of us. As I took Dash deeper, to the very limits of what I could take, Colt drove into me. His other hand came around to circle my clit.

Dark spots danced in my vision. Dash's hips lifted on a shout as he emptied himself into me. I swallowed him down, relishing that burst of power. It was almost more than I could take.

Colt pressed down on my clit, and I cried out, Dash slipping from my mouth. I clamped down on Colt as he came. Liquid heat poured into me as I rode every wave.

My legs trembled as the last orgasm coursed through me. Colt caught me around the waist, lifting me up so he could nuzzle my neck, still inside me. "So beautiful."

A strangled sound came from the shadows of my room.

Trace took one step forward. "Worst torture of my life." He pulled on his lip ring. "And the best."

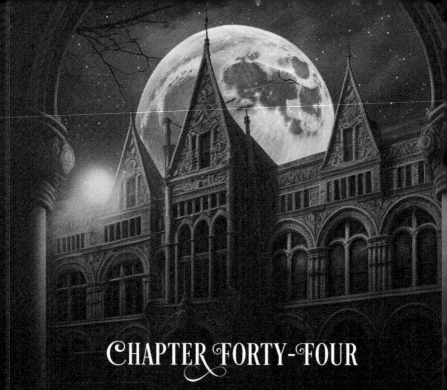

CHAPTER FORTY-FOUR

DASH KEPT TOUCHING ME AS I ATE BREAKFAST. A HAND skated up my spine. Fingers ghosted along my thigh. Heavenly torture.

I twisted in my seat and pinned him with a stare. "Stop it."

He gave me his best innocent smile, but I knew it hid a demanding dom beneath. "What?"

"You know exactly what you're doing."

Trace snorted as he tore off a corner of French toast. "Yeah, he's hoping he turns you on enough that you'll let him spread you out on the table and fuck you in front of all of us."

My cheeks heated.

Ronan smacked Trace upside the head. "Don't be an ass."

He shrugged. "I didn't say it was a bad plan. I wouldn't mind watching."

My blush only deepened at the reminder that Trace had watched me, Colt, and Dash last night. He hadn't stayed after making his presence known, muttering something about going for a run.

Colt cleared his throat. "I think that's enough."

Declan shifted in his seat. "My blue balls would thank you for any subject change."

I buried my face in my hands.

Dash nuzzled my neck. "Don't be embarrassed. We love it."

"Not over breakfast," I grumbled.

"Okay, okay." He squeezed my neck and sat back in his chair. "What should we do today?"

I dropped my hands from my face and scanned the table. "Don't we have various nefarious characters to try to take down this weekend?"

The corner of Trace's mouth kicked up. "I wouldn't mind a little casual murder."

Colt groaned. "*You* are not in charge of activities. Ever."

Trace frowned. "You're always such a buzzkill."

Colt just shook his head and turned to me. "We thought it might be nice to just have a regular weekend."

My brows lifted. "And we can do that?"

He grinned. "Yes. I've got a tail on your mom and people searching for Damien."

I worried the corner of my lip. "A normal Saturday."

I played the words over and over in my mind as if it were a completely novel idea.

Declan chuckled. "We can have them occasionally."

"Not as far as I've seen," I muttered.

Ronan pinned me with a stare. "What do you want to do?"

I really thought about the question for a moment. "Could we go into town? Poke around the stores and walk on the beach?"

"Of course," Ronan said instantly.

Colt looked pained. "Are you sure you don't want to do something at home?"

"Colt…" Ronan warned.

He held up a hand. "Okay. Normal."

The wind caught my red locks, and I spun on the beach. The air was turning cold, but I didn't care. It just meant that the beach was relatively empty and peaceful.

"We should've brought a kite," I yelled.

Trace looked at me as if I'd suggested killing a puppy. "I do not fly *kites*."

I rolled my eyes and stuck my tongue out at him. "Oh, I forgot, you have to brood twenty-three hours a day, and kites are happy."

Trace's lips twitched as the guys laughed. Then he charged.

I squealed as he hoisted me over his shoulder and charged toward the water. "Don't you dare!" I screamed.

"This is what happens when you give me shit," Trace warned.

"If you dunk me, my payback will be brutal." I pinched his side and twisted.

He yelped. "What the hell, woman?"

"Put me down!"

"Okay." Trace moved as if he were going to toss me into the waves and then caught me, slowly lowering me to the wet sand.

My breath caught as our eyes locked. Trace lifted a hand, tucking a strand of hair behind my ear. "Happy looks good on you."

I couldn't move, couldn't breathe. But I so badly wanted to close the distance between us. Wanted to feel that same closeness I'd gotten with the other guys. But I wouldn't take Trace's choice from him. He had to lead. Had to tell me when he was ready.

Trace leaned forward and pressed a kiss to my forehead.

Heat shot through my system in a fiery blaze, and I had to bite my cheek to keep from whimpering.

He released me and stepped back. I nearly collapsed.

Declan stepped in, wrapping an arm around my waist. "Got a little Trace high, there?"

I shook my head, trying to clear it. "I'm good."

Concern and sadness filled Trace's gaze.

I forced my smile brighter. "I think I need ice cream."

Colt's brows rose. "It's freezing."

"It's never too cold for ice cream," I argued.

"I like the way she thinks," Ronan said.

Dash started up the beach toward the shops. "Just don't share with Ronan. He gets competitive."

"Competitive?" I asked, puzzled.

"He'll try to eat it all before you get a second bite."

Ronan picked up some sea kelp and threw it at Dash. "Ass."

Dash narrowly avoided it. "That was uncalled for. You know that stuff freaks me out."

A laugh bubbled out of me. Today had been just what I needed. A reminder that no matter how scary things got, this life was worth fighting for.

We made our way toward downtown and its adorable shops, Ronan and Dash bickering the whole way. Declan dropped a kiss to the top of my head. "Happy?"

I grinned up at him. "The happiest."

We climbed the steps to the street and turned toward the ice cream shop. But a voice stopped me dead in my tracks.

"If it isn't my wayward daughter. Did you miss me, baby?"

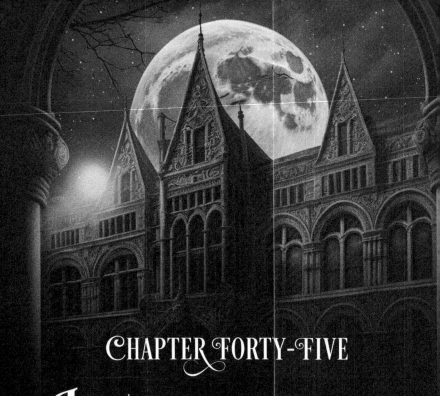

CHAPTER FORTY-FIVE

I COULDN'T STOP THE TREMBLE THAT TOOK ROOT IN MY muscles. Just the sound of Maryanne's voice had a million memories slamming into me, none of them good.

Declan pulled me in tighter to his side. Maryanne's eyes flared, anger burning bright. But she squashed it, an evil grin spreading across her face. "What? No hug? I've been waiting for this family reunion for weeks."

Colt stepped in front of me and Declan. "It would be wise if you went back to your hotel, packed, and returned to Louisiana."

A hint of surprise flashed through her features, as if shocked that he knew where she was staying. Then bravado took over. She rolled her shoulders back, meeting Colt's stare dead-on. "You have no say in what I do."

Trace's eyes flashed violet. "That's where you're wrong."

Maryanne stumbled back a step at the ferocity in Trace's tone and perhaps the violet in his eyes. "W-what are you?"

Trace bared his teeth at her, letting his eyes go full purple. "You wanted to mess with this world? The least you could do is learn your supernaturals. I'm a demon, Maryanne."

"W-what? No. Those—they don't come out in daylight."

Trace's face morphed into a feral grin. "Not all of us have to hide in the shadows. We can find you anytime. Anywhere."

Maryanne began to tremble, but then her hands fisted, and she fought back the fear. "You can't threaten me."

Ronan crossed his arms over his chest. "Watch us."

That anger was back in her eyes. No, it was more than anger. It was pure fury.

"You," she spat. "You think you can get away with murder."

"Been there, done that," Trace singsonged.

A hint of apprehension flickered in her gaze, but she fought it back. "You can't touch me. I have protection."

"We know all about your little vamp lovefest. It won't get you anywhere," Ronan growled.

"Vampires aren't known for their loyalty unless you're one of their kind," Dash informed her. "They'll use you, and then they'll most likely drain you to get rid of the problem."

He spoke as if he were reading my AP Bio textbook. There was no emotion in his voice at all.

"Stop trying to scare me," Maryanne spluttered.

"Dash doesn't lie," Colt informed her. "Never has, never will. He's trying to help you."

She scoffed. "Help me? I'm sure. You're all trying to steal from me. To take what's mine."

Maryanne's eyes landed on me. There was so much rage pulsing in them. Fury she could no longer disguise when her gaze connected with mine. That anger held me captive.

I'd become an expert in reading her cues. Any slight shift in her body language or voice. And everything I was seeing now told me she wanted me dead.

I swallowed hard, pushing deeper into Declan's hold.

"Leighton isn't a possession," Colt gritted out.

Maryanne laughed, but there was nothing pleasant about the sound. "Looks to me like you're using her like one. Not that I blame you; she's not worth much."

Shame washed over me. As much as I didn't want to let her words have any merit, I couldn't help the pain that flared to life as they landed.

Declan let out a low, rumbling growl. The force of it shook the ground beneath us and had people on the street glancing around and mumbling about possible earthquakes.

"Watch. What. You. Say."

Maryanne just laughed harder. "I see she already has her hooks in you. You'll regret that soon enough. Hell, she's completely impotent. No magic in her at all. Why would you even want her?"

Ronan snarled at Maryanne. "She's our mate. There's no one we'll ever value more. It would be wise of you to remember that."

Maryanne straightened her spine. It was then I realized she was wearing nice clothes. Designer ones, if I wasn't mistaken. Her hair looked as if it had been colored by someone who actually knew what they were doing. Someone was making her look presentable.

"I can see that Leighton coming to Emerald Bay has been a grave mistake," Maryanne said with mock concern. "She has fallen in with a bad crowd. I mean, letting herself be passed around by a group of boys like nothing more than a common whore? Any court would put her back in my care."

A series of growls lit the air.

"You signed over your rights," Ronan gritted out.

"And any court will rescind that document when they hear what she's been up to lately," Maryanne said with a triumphant smile.

"You bitch!" Trace started to charge, but Colt caught the back of his shirt.

Maryanne laughed. It had a maniacal quality to it that had

the trembling in my muscles intensifying. If she got me back, I'd be dead. There was no doubt in my mind.

A door slammed, and my gaze shot to some fancy black car on the street. Alister strode toward us, a sly smile on his lips. "I missed the reunion. How unfortunate. I was so looking forward to seeing mother and daughter together again."

Maryanne looked up at the vampire with adoring eyes that had nausea rolling through me. She pouted. "They haven't been very welcoming. They've been quite cruel."

Alister looked at the guys with a hint of disapproval. "Now that doesn't sound like the future leaders I know. The Assembly would be so disappointed."

"This won't work, Alister," Colt warned low.

He gave Colt his most innocent smile. "What won't? I'm simply trying to help."

Dash took a step forward, his blue gaze going hard. "It would be a mistake to make an enemy of us."

Alister's brows rose. "Now, that sounds an awful lot like a threat. Which would be a violation of the truce."

Ronan prowled toward him. "No threat, a warning. If you make a single move against Leighton, we will go to war. And you're outnumbered."

Alister's lips twitched. "No one is threatening Leighton. But the clans believe in family above all else. We'll do whatever we can to reunite them." His eyes flashed. "And your father is helping me."

CHAPTER FORTY-SIX

I STARED OUT THE WINDOW OF THE SUV, ALL THE WARMTH from my *normal day* gone. Even I could read between the lines of Alister's statement. The twins' father had allied himself with Alister. As if I needed another reason to hate the man.

I wrapped my arms tighter around myself as Colt turned into The Nest.

He rolled down his window, and the gate guard stepped forward. "We need to raise the alert level."

The guard's eyes flared. "We're already on yellow."

"We need to move to orange," Colt told him.

The guard nodded. "Right away, sir."

My stomach churned. Maryanne was simply a tool, a weapon for Alister and Patrick to wield, but that didn't mean she couldn't be deadly. I knew the guys would do anything to keep her from getting to me, and that could have disastrous effects if the vamps and dragons were involved.

I struggled to keep my breathing even as Colt pulled to a stop outside the mansion. I was out of the SUV the moment he put it into park. I needed the fresh, clean air. It had become a balm of sorts over the past few weeks.

Dash's hands came to my shoulders. "You okay?"

A laugh bubbled out of me that I couldn't control. "Am I okay? Let's see. My mom showed up out of the blue. And she's working with the two worst people on the planet. Patrick won't stop fucking with Declan's and Ronan's heads. Damien's still on the loose. And I have no idea if we'll all kill ourselves off in the next few years or descend into madness."

"Eh," Trace said as he shut the door. "That's nothing."

I glared at him.

Ronan hit Trace upside the head. "Not helping."

Trace shoved him away. "Would you stop doing that?"

"When you stop saying stupid shit."

"Enough," Colt said quietly. "Let's get inside. We can talk about a plan."

Just the word *plan* had my insides tightening into a painful knot.

"Come on," Dash said, wrapping an arm around me.

I shot a glance at Declan. Emotions warred in his expression. The two fighting for dominance most were guilt and anger.

That just pissed me off. Even with this distance, Patrick was still messing with his son's head.

We all filed inside and headed for the lounge. The guys took seats in chairs and beanbags, while Dash settled me on the couch.

Declan leaned forward in his chair, staring down at his hands. "Maybe I should just go home. Play along. I could be enough to get Patrick to back off."

"Hell no," Ronan snarled.

I gripped the sofa cushion. "Dec, *this* is your home."

"She's right," Colt agreed.

Declan lifted his head. "This is because I left. He wouldn't have been so bold otherwise."

Dash met his gaze. "It's better that he's forced to be bold. Then at least we know where he truly stands."

Trace grunted. "Better to have someone come at you from the front than the back. At least then you can defend yourself."

Declan shook his head. "If I go back, maybe I can change his mind—"

"You're not going back to that monster," Ronan growled.

Declan met his brother's stare. "Ronan—"

"No. We'll chain you up in the basement if you try."

Declan's lips twitched. "Why does that feel like a warm hug?"

Ronan grunted. "Whatever."

Colt leaned back in his chair. "You're not going back there. We stick together. It's the only play."

"But we do need a plan," Dash said.

Colt nodded. "We need to know who's truly on our side."

"And how the hell do we do that?" Trace mumbled.

Dash adjusted his glasses. "We need a series of tests."

Trace dropped his head back against the beanbag. "This isn't the time for brainiac games."

Dash sent him a dirty look. "Scientific experiments are exactly what we need."

Trace opened his mouth to argue, but Colt held up a hand to stop him. "What are you thinking?"

"Tiny, little tests. We give bits of information to leaders in each clan, see what makes it back to Alister," Dash explained.

Ronan shifted. "Could work."

"But it'll take time," Trace argued.

Ronan shot him a look. "And what are you going to do? Torture the truth out of them?"

Trace shrugged. "Whatever works."

Colt groaned. "If they weren't already against us, I think causing them severe bodily harm might change that tune."

Trace's mouth pulled into a frown. "Why does everyone have to be so touchy?"

Dash rolled his eyes. "Losing a finger will do that to a person."

I shivered, and Dash sent me an apologetic look. "Sorry."

"It's okay," I whispered, turning to Colt. "What about your investigator? The one trying to dig up dirt on my mom."

If we could get her to leave, Alister and Patrick would at least lose one of their weapons.

"They're still digging. They've found quite a bit on your mom's ex," Colt said.

I frowned. "Ex?"

Colt winced. "Apparently, the moment vamps showed up to whisk Maryanne away, she kicked ole Chuck to the curb."

"Of course, she did," I muttered. One glimmer of a new meal ticket and he was toast.

"We need to find proof that she was involved in some of his shadier dealings," Colt went on.

A heaviness settled in my stomach. "What kinds of shady things?"

Colt was quiet for a moment. "Did you know he dealt drugs?"

I bit the inside of my cheek as I shook my head. "It shouldn't really be a surprise, though. Maryanne seemed to be imbibing in a variety of substances lately."

Colt shifted.

"What?" I pressed.

He blew out a breath. "There was a charge of rape in the system. It was dropped. The girl was young and scared. Said she didn't want to go through with a court case."

Ice slid through my veins. That poor girl. She must've been terrified. My teeth started to chatter. That so easily could've been me.

Dash pulled me into his side. "Hey, you're safe. He can't touch you."

Ronan stood, grabbing a blanket and draping it over me. "Should've killed that fucker when I had the chance."

Trace ground his teeth together. "Feeling inspired to make a quick trip to Louisiana."

"Trips are going to have to wait until later," Colt clipped. "We need to focus on our enemies here."

A series of alert sounds went off, and the guys stilled. They all pulled out their phones.

My stomach cramped. "What?"

Colt looked up. "It's The Assembly. They're calling you to a meeting."

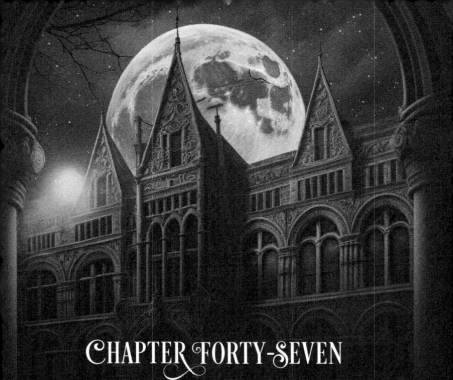

CHAPTER FORTY-SEVEN

BEAUTIFUL SCENERY WHIZZED PAST US AS THE ESCALADE tore down the two-lane highway. The Assembly wasn't kidding when they said they wanted a meeting. They said *jump*, and everyone had no choice but to ask how high.

"Where is the meeting?" I asked.

Ronan wove his fingers through mine and settled our hands on his lap. "It's on our sacred grounds."

My brow furrowed.

"It's where the founding families formed our truce," Dash explained.

There was something enchanting about being able to trace your lineage back that far. If I hadn't been terrified, I would've asked a million different questions.

Ronan squeezed my hand. "There's no reason to be scared. The Assembly won't hurt you."

"How did you—"

"Your scent, remember? I can smell your different emotions. Especially when they're heightened."

"Feels like cheating," I grumbled.

Ronan chuckled, leaning closer to brush his lips across my temple. "I'll take whatever information about you that I can get."

"You could try *asking*. It's slightly less invasive."

Colt's gaze caught mine through the rearview mirror. "Now, where would the fun be in that?"

I stuck my tongue out at him.

I glanced over my shoulder at Declan. He still seemed lost in his thoughts. Or better yet, lost in his father's betrayal.

"Will Patrick be there?" I asked quietly.

Declan's body jerked at his father's name, and I cursed myself for even asking the question.

Ronan's jaw hardened. "He never misses an opportunity to kiss The Assembly's collective ass."

"I don't get that. The Assembly can't control the clans, right?" I asked.

"They only have true control if someone has broken our laws. They are the judge and jury," Dash explained.

"But their influence goes beyond that," Declan said. "They can sway our people. And if enough of your clan turns against you, you can lose power. It's much better to be in The Assembly's good graces."

A memory scratched at the back of my brain. "But they sanctioned the vampires, didn't they?"

Trace scoffed. "Should've excommunicated them."

Colt glanced in the rearview mirror. "Several vamps fed off of humans and other supernaturals without permission. That breaks the treaty, so they were subjected to Assembly law."

My fingers gripped Ronan harder. "What happened?"

"The vampires in question were imprisoned, and the vamps as a whole got a sort of metaphorical slap on the wrist," Colt said.

Dash leaned forward. "It's a dishonor to have your clan as a whole brought before The Assembly."

"It obviously didn't stop Alister from being an asshole," I mumbled.

"No truer words, Little Bird," Trace called from the front seat.

Colt eased off the accelerator and flipped on his blinker. We turned onto a narrow side road that was gravel. The trees that surrounded us almost made it feel as if we were driving through a tunnel. If I hadn't been a nervous wreck, I would've found it beautiful.

"There's no gate or anything?" I asked.

Dash shook his head. "The property is spelled. Humans don't even see the road to turn onto."

"How can I see it?"

He squeezed my shoulders. "You're not human."

"But my powers never manifested." It hurt just to say the words, knowing I could be sentencing everyone in this vehicle to death.

"No, but you're still a supernatural," Dash assured me.

It didn't feel like I was, no matter how much I wished it.

The road opened up into a massive clearing. A few dozen vehicles were parked in a makeshift gravel lot.

My mouth went dry as Colt parked. "There are a lot of people here."

"They all love the drama," Trace grumbled.

Meaning they all wanted to see what The Assembly made of me.

Ronan squeezed my hand again. "It'll be okay."

I nodded numbly, but I didn't believe him.

I forced myself to let go of Ronan's hand and climb out of the SUV. In a matter of seconds, I was surrounded by the guys. That simple action cast doubt on Ronan's words.

We made our way past the lot, and I gasped. The spot was absolutely breathtaking. Lush, green grass that met with a stone amphitheater of sorts. But past it was a steep drop-off to the ocean.

The amphitheater itself looked as if it were carved into the ground, a part of it.

But then I saw the people.

Everyone's eyes were on me as we walked toward the meeting spot. My tongue stuck to the roof of my mouth. They were all watching. Judging.

Trace moved in closer on my right side. "We've got you."

Those words wrapped around me, and I tried my best to hold on to them.

Colt took the lead, Declan at his side. Dash was on my left, Trace on my right. And Ronan brought up the rear. As if he were making sure no one attacked me from behind.

Oh, yeah, all the warm fuzzies about this.

Whispers picked up as we reached the amphitheater. I caught a few choice words.

Never manifested.

Such a shame.

Slut.

What a waste.

The guys glared at those who dared insult me, but I did my best to keep my gaze focused only straight ahead. There was a stage of sorts. With a stone table and bench. It was empty, but I had a feeling that was where The Assembly would sit.

Something caught my attention to the right. A couple. Something about the man was bizarrely familiar. But it was the glare on his face that had me almost stumbling. But the glare wasn't focused on me. It was zeroed in on Trace.

I saw the word *disgrace* form on the man's lips. I glanced up at Trace. "Who is that?"

His jaw ticked. "My parents. Not my biggest fans. To them, having a son who is an incubus is shameful."

Anger flared to life in my chest, and I shoved through the guys, stalking toward the couple.

Their eyes widened at my approach.

"You're pathetic. The fact that you can't see what an incredible son you have is just sad. He's caring and fierce and loyal. It's your loss, your punishment, really, to lose out on truly knowing him. But I hope you have a permanent case of hemorrhoids, too."

Trace's arm came around my waist, pulling me back. "Little Bird…" But there was laughter in his voice.

I let him pull me away, down the aisle. "I do wish it. That or a permanent case of diarrhea."

Trace only laughed harder, and the sound was so sweet it made an ache take root in my chest.

He glanced down at me. "How'd I get so lucky to have you in my corner?"

I grinned up at him. "Well, we know you weren't an angel in a past life."

Ronan choked on a laugh. "That's for damn sure."

A man stepped out onto the stage. "Be seated. This meeting of The Assembly is called to order."

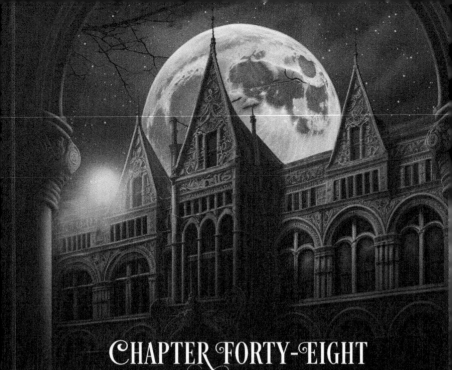

CHAPTER FORTY-EIGHT

MY STOMACH DIPPED AND ROLLED AS THE CROWD WENT silent. Trace pressed his hand against my lower back, guiding me toward the front row of stone benches.

Each step wound my muscles tighter. I caught sight of Alister in the front row on the right. His profile was so similar to Damien's, I fought a shudder. Next to him was Declan and Ronan's father, Patrick. He cast a look in my direction, his eyes going silver. But it wasn't the enchanting silver of Declan's eyes. This was cold, cruel. Beyond him was Darius. Then two women I didn't recognize.

Something prickled the side of my face, and I moved my gaze from Patrick to find the source. My eyes locked with rage-filled ones I recognized. Chloe sat between an older man and woman. She was a mix of their two features, so I knew they must be her parents. She smirked and tossed her hair over her shoulder, which looked ridiculous now that it was cut in a bob.

"Come on," Colt whispered.

We all took a seat in the front row on the left. I hated having my back to the crowd. Hated how exposed I felt.

Colt took my hand, squeezing it. "Everything's going to be all right."

I wished I could've believed those words.

The man on the stage, who looked large enough to be a pro wrestler, scanned the crowd. His eyes narrowed on anyone who dared to even whisper. After several moments, the crowd was deathly silent. The only sounds were the occasional bird call and the wind in the trees behind us.

"The Assembly is called to order," the man boomed.

My mouth went desert dry.

A second later, a line of people formed at the back of the amphitheater. I had no idea where they'd come from. They seemed to simply appear. They all wore robes that were a deep purple velvet, and each one looked elderly, yet somehow, they moved surprisingly spryly.

They filed onto the stage and took a seat. Five in total. Three women and two men.

I knew they were from each of the clans, and I tried to identify who might be from which, but I had no luck. That was until one of the two men's gazes connected with mine. His eyes flashed red for the briefest of moments, and then they were the normal brown again. Vampire.

A chill skated over my skin, and Trace wrapped an arm around me. Even with our shirts preventing skin-to-skin contact, a faint buzz still took flight in my muscles.

"You are all welcome here," a woman with salt-and-pepper hair in a chic pixie cut greeted.

"Thank you for your welcome," the crowd echoed back.

"That's the demon leader," Colt whispered.

"We are here today to discuss the newcomer in our midst." Her gaze found mine, assessing, as if looking for any signs of weakness.

221

I didn't look away. Some part of me knew that doing so would be a mistake I wouldn't recover from.

After a few seconds, the woman gave a slight nod at me and continued. "There are many factors at play, and we must consider all of them."

A slight movement to my left caught my attention. Ronan's hands fisted on his knees as if he could barely restrain his anger. My heart cracked. This had to be hard for him. He hadn't had control of much as he grew up, and this had to trigger that feeling.

"Let's get on with it, Marjorie," the vampire drawled.

Her eyes flashed at him. They weren't purple like Trace's; hers went a burnt orange. "Your disrespect is noted, as usual, Raphaël."

His mouth thinned as his eyes narrowed.

"Let us begin the questioning," another woman said. Her black braids were woven into an intricate bun atop her head, a heavy dose of white interspersed with the black. There were lines in her dark skin that told me she smiled often, and that was a comfort.

"I agree with Delphine," the second man said. "Let's move along."

He sounded incredibly bored with the proceedings.

Delphine rolled her eyes. "Let us call forward the person who demanded these proceedings."

My stomach tightened as I glanced at Colt. We'd thought this was the brainchild of The Assembly itself.

Colt's jaw tightened, a muscle ticking wildly.

"Patrick O'Connor, step forward," Delphine called.

Declan's eyes went glacial as his father stepped up to the stage.

Patrick bowed his head in a show of respect. "Thank you for allowing me to voice my concerns."

None of The Assembly members showed a hint of reaction. But there was something in the third woman's eyes that made me think she saw more than the rest. Those eyes were a warm amber so similar to Ronan's, they were comforting. And the fact that she was the only person who hadn't spoken so far told me she was an expert observer, but there was mischief in those amber eyes that also told me she wouldn't hesitate to raise her voice if needed.

"Speak," the second man commanded.

Patrick's eyes flashed silver, but he quickly squashed it. "As you know, there has been great worry about our future leaders. They have become ensnared by lust and temptation—"

"By our mate," Ronan snarled.

"Quiet, boy," Marjorie snapped. "You'll have your turn."

Ronan snapped his mouth closed.

A small smirk played on Patrick's lips as if he had won a point with that. "They fall prey to this temptation that would lead them down a dangerous road. The girl cannot ground them. She has no magic in her. This will lead to death for all of them. They must be commanded to bond with an anchor of worth. With Chloe."

"Not bloody likely," Trace muttered.

The second man on The Assembly glared at Trace.

Chloe positively beamed.

I felt sick. What was I doing? Maybe I was going to be the source of ruin for us all.

"We already know all of this," Delphine drawled.

Patrick's eyes hardened. "The girl is not yet of age. She is still under the rule of her mother. And her mother does not want her here."

The crowd began to whisper wildly.

"Silence!" Delphine barked. The crowd instantly obeyed. "Do you have proof of this?"

Patrick grinned. "I have her mother."

Sickness swelled in my belly.

"Produce her," the second man demanded.

A second later, Maryanne walked down the aisle, and as her eyes collided with mine, an evil smile spread across her face. And I knew then she'd get what she always wanted. To steal every shred of happiness from me.

CHAPTER FORTY-NINE

MY STOMACH ROILED AS MARYANNE MOVED DOWN THE aisle. Everyone stared at her with blatant curiosity. Everyone except my guys, who glared at her with blatant hatred.

She painted on a look of grief, and I had to give it to her; it was damn believable. Maryanne came to a stop next to Patrick, her hands clasped in front of her.

"You are the mother?" the second man asked.

Studying him more carefully, he had the size that meant he had to be a dragon or a wolf. As I looked more carefully, something told me wolf. He had an earthiness to him that I'd felt around Colt and Darius.

Maryanne bowed her head. "I am."

The third woman narrowed her eyes on Maryanne but didn't speak.

It was the vampire, Raphaël, that did. "Do you wish for your daughter to live among us?"

Maryanne dipped her head further. "I do not. I mean no disrespect, but her father did not wish for her to live in this world if she did not manifest. I must honor his wishes after he has gone."

The crowd murmured amongst themselves.

My fingernails dug into my palm, hard enough to draw blood. The last thing Maryanne cared about was my father's wishes.

Delphine leaned back against the bench. "Yet your daughter is mated to them." She gestured toward us. "To remove her from her mates would be akin to a soul death."

Pain lanced my chest. It was then that I knew she was right. If I was ripped away from the five guys surrounding me, I wouldn't survive.

Maryanne's teeth gnashed together. "But she would be alive."

Delphine shrugged. "Maybe, maybe not."

"I know what's best for my daughter," Maryanne snapped.

Delphine's green eyes went flinty, and Patrick squeezed Maryanne's shoulder, *hard.*

He cleared his throat. "The girl's mother is simply worried for her daughter."

I loved that, to him, we didn't even warrant the use of our names.

Patrick went on. "We understand that concern because we feel the same for our young."

Declan made a strangled sound at that.

Patrick's gaze jerked to him and burned with derision, but by the time he turned back around, his face was a calm mask. "We must respect the mother's wishes."

"This is true," Raphaël agreed. "Family above all else."

"I am just worried for my daughter," Maryanne simpered. "I miss her. I want her back with me."

I couldn't take it. I lurched to my feet. "She's lying!"

The Assembly members turned to stare at me.

"We will not tolerate your disrespect," the vampire snarled.

"Isn't lying to you a greater disrespect than speaking out of turn?" I demanded.

"I would never lie to The Assembly," Maryanne snapped.

I didn't bother looking at her. I kept my eyes on The Assembly. "She has never loved me. Never cared about me. She has beaten and abused me. Her only joy in life has been at my agony."

"I would never!" Maryanne shrieked.

"What proof do you have of this?" Marjorie asked, her voice hard.

I stepped forward, the guys at my back. My heart hammered against my ribs, knowing what I had to do. I first peeled off my sweater, handing it to Dash. His eyes were pained, but he gave me a small, encouraging nod.

I stayed facing my guys, getting strength from all the ways they loved me. Then I lifted up my long-sleeved T-shirt to expose my back.

There was a gasp and several murmurs.

"S-she's lying," Maryanne stuttered. "She was burned in an accident when she was sixteen."

"My so-called mother burned me with boiling water and a pan when I was sixteen. Because she was out of her mind high and looking for my anchor mark. Determined to *burn the Devil out* of me."

"Liar!" Maryanne shrieked. She lunged, but Trace shot forward, shoving her hard. Maryanne stumbled back into Patrick.

Trace bared his teeth at Patrick. "Keep your insane pet in check."

Patrick glared at him but did keep hold of Maryanne, who was still screaming about me lying.

"Silence!" Delphine yelled, and Maryanne had no choice but to obey. "Come forward, child."

I swallowed hard but walked toward the stage. I climbed one step and then another.

Delphine's eyes were kind. "Turn around." I did so. "I have a special gift. I can see the cause of any scar."

Maryanne's face went deathly pale.

Delphine's hand hovered just shy of my burns as she began to chant in that same language that Dash used. Suddenly, she went silent. "You may turn around," she said quietly.

As I did so, my eyes collided with hers.

"I'm so sorry, my child. For what you have endured." Delphine's gaze lifted to the crowd. "She speaks the truth. We will not let her be returned to her abuser."

Maryanne screamed, but two guards appeared and hauled her back toward the parking lot.

Patrick's jaw ticked. "This doesn't change our original issue. She cannot ground them."

"We'll find a way," Colt growled at him.

Patrick scoffed. "Wishful thinking."

"Come to me," a feminine voice crooned. It was so beautiful it almost hurt to hear it.

It was the third woman. The one who hadn't spoken once during the gathering. The one with the amber eyes. Her face was full of deep lines, and her thick, white hair was pulled back into a braid.

"Saoirse," the wolf shifter rebuked.

The woman just cast him a quelling look, and he snapped his mouth closed.

She beckoned me toward her, and it was as if my limbs were under her control. I moved down the table until I was standing in front of her.

"Give me your hand," Saoirse said.

I extended it toward her.

She paused before she took it. "This is going to hurt. But it's the only way."

Then her hands closed around mine.

Hot, burning pain swept through me, and I cried out. The

227

guys shouted from behind me, but then I was released, and relief descended.

Declan caught me around the waist. "What the hell were you thinking?"

Saoirse's mouth curved. "Sometimes, pain is worth it." Her gaze settled on me. "There is magic in her."

CHAPTER FIFTY

THE AMPHITHEATER ERUPTED AROUND US, AND DECLAN hauled me off the stage. The rest of the guys instantly surrounded me, taking up a defensive posture.

"Enough!" Marjorie bellowed. Her voice was so loud it vibrated through me.

The mayhem died down to whispers and murmurs.

"Everyone *sit*," she commanded.

A hush fell over the crowd, and they obeyed.

Her gaze cut to us. "You, too."

We slowly retreated to the stone bench. The guys glanced around, as if taking stock of any potential threats. As I sat, my hands trembled.

Declan covered them with his own and leaned into me. "It's going to be okay."

But I couldn't stop shaking. Maybe it was facing my mother and exposing my scars for the world to see. Maybe it was a simple adrenaline dump. Or maybe it was that flicker of hope at hearing the word *magic*.

"You need to sit, too, Patrick," Marjorie informed him.

He puffed up his chest. "I wasn't done speaking."

"Yes, you are," Delphine snapped.

Patrick's eyes flashed silver again, but Delphine wasn't cowed. She kept his stare until he was seated and turned to Saoirse. "Tell us what you sensed."

Saoirse's warm gaze found me. "There is magic in her. But it is buried deep. Almost as if it were being blocked somehow."

My heart hammered against my ribs. I wanted her to be right so badly that hope hurt.

The wolf shifter scoffed. "That's because she never manifested. I'm sure there's a glimmer of magic in her. But it's not enough for her to ground them."

"We don't know that," Delphine argued. "There may be ways for her to break through her block and fully come into her power."

I glanced at Colt in question.

He grinned. "Told you there was a way."

"This is ridiculous," Alister snapped. "She doesn't have the mark. That tells us all we need to know."

"There is a first time for everything," Saoirse said coolly.

"You would put the fate of all of our clans on the chance of a miracle?" he demanded.

"They will not be whole, fully in their power, unless they have their anchor *and* their mate. We know when that is found in two different people, it can make both bonds unstable." Saoirse's eyes narrowed on Alister. "But maybe that's what you want. Instability so that you can grab power?"

Alister's jaw dropped in affront, but it was forced. "I would never. How dare you even suggest—"

"I was simply asking a question. Remember whose house you are in, Alister."

He snapped his mouth closed and leaned back against the bench, muttering something under his breath.

"I have to agree with him," Patrick said. "It's too risky."

"We need to give them a chance."

I heard the words, but who they belonged to shocked the hell out of me.

Darius stood, dipping his head in respect to The Assembly. "We cannot tear away their happiness without reason. We have time. We risk nothing by giving them a chance."

"If they mate with the girl, claim her, it'll make their bond with another anchor tenuous," the woman next to him said. "They can reject their true mate and bind themselves to their chosen anchor in heart and magic."

My gaze flicked to Colt, pain slicing through my heart. They could choose to be with someone else. Someone who wouldn't mean risking insanity or death.

Not going to happen, he mouthed.

Darius cleared his throat. "This is true. We can ask them to hold off on any mating." He glanced at the crowd, then at The Assembly. "You know that I was doubtful. I thought it was safer to simply bond them to Chloe."

There were murmurs of agreement in the crowd that made me sick to my stomach.

"But I was wrong."

Colt sucked in a breath, his eyes beginning to glow.

Darius took a deep breath. "I saw her when Colt was injured. She threw herself between him and me, a full-grown wolf. She wouldn't let me near him because she doubted my motives. I have no doubt that she would've given her life for his. That is the kind of love and devotion they all deserve."

He turned to face us. "I'm ashamed that Leighton would have any reason to doubt my loyalty to you. It was a wake-up call. I want you to know you have my complete fealty."

Darius sank down on one knee, placing his fist over his heart. "I will serve you for all my days."

Colt pushed to his feet, crossing to Darius and placing a hand on his shoulder. "It's my honor."

Darius looked up and then rose.

Colt engulfed him in a hard hug. "Thank you, my brother."

Darius thumped him on the back and then released him.

"As touching as that was, *feelings* won't solve this problem," Patrick sniped.

Colt glared at him as we took a seat.

"Give us a moment," Marjorie commanded.

There was complete silence, but The Assembly's expressions looked as if they were somehow conversing.

"What's happening?" I whispered.

Declan dipped his mouth to my ear. "They can mind-speak to one another."

My eyes bugged. "Seriously?"

Declan nodded.

All at once, The Assembly turned to face the crowd.

"We will vote," the wolf shifter informed us. "Whether to give the girl thirty days to manifest or if she will be cast out of Emerald Bay."

My spine jerked straight as the guys growled.

"Quiet," he snapped, then turned to his right. "Saoirse, how say you?"

She gave me a warm smile. "Thirty days."

A little of the pressure eased in my chest.

The wolf shifter nodded. "I say cast out."

The panic was back.

He turned to his right. "Delphine, how say you?"

"Thirty days," she said serenely.

"Raphaël, how say you?"

I knew his answer before he even spoke.

"Cast out."

The wolf looked to Marjorie. "You are the final vote. How say you?"

Marjorie's gaze met mine. There was the same searching I felt before, only this time, there was a heat that took root in my chest. It was just shy of pain, and then suddenly, it was gone.

"Thirty days," she said. "Use it wisely."

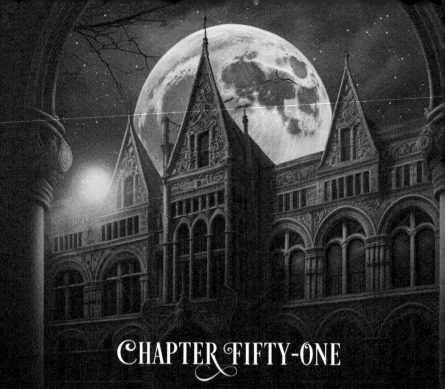

CHAPTER FIFTY-ONE

I PULLED MY LEGS UP TO MY CHEST AND LEANED BACK ON the couch. Declan pushed in on one side while Ronan trapped me in on the other. "I'm not going to break."

"We know," Dash said from his spot on one of the beanbags.

He looked adorable with his sandy brown hair askew and glasses off-kilter. Just the sight of him had my insides warming.

"But that doesn't mean that we won't want to take care of you," Colt said from a chair as he typed on a laptop.

I glanced at Trace, who stood by a window in the lounge, staring out into the forest. "Are you okay?"

His gaze snapped to me. "You told my parents you wished permanent hemorrhoids on them. I'm just fine."

Declan chuckled, tracing a design on my thigh. "That was pretty epic."

I bit my lip. "Am I gonna get in trouble for that?"

Ronan snorted. "No. I think you're safe."

I picked at a minuscule piece of lint on my sweatpants. "What do you think happened to Maryanne?"

Colt looked up from his laptop. "She's on her way out of town."

My brows lifted. "Really?"

He nodded. "I've still got men on her. The vamps cut her off and dropped her at the bus station."

I winced. Not that I felt bad for Maryanne, but I knew this would only make her angrier at me. Hopefully, some distance would afford me protection, but I'd have to watch my back.

"Can't imagine Alister or Patrick being thrilled that she wasn't honest with them," Ronan muttered.

Dash laced his hands behind his head. "I'm surprised she didn't end up drained of blood and thrown over a cliff."

"Too many people watching too closely," Trace muttered.

I shivered, and Declan wrapped an arm around me.

"I think that's enough depressing talk for one afternoon," he warned.

Dash sent me a sheepish smile. "Sorry, Leighton."

"It's okay." I worried my lip between my teeth. "Do you think what Saoirse said was true?" I hadn't voiced the question yet. I'd been too scared. But I couldn't hide from it anymore. If there was a chance I could be what the guys needed, I had to take it.

Colt shut his laptop. "She wouldn't lie. Not in that setting."

A little more of that traitorous hope took root in my gut.

Ronan shifted in his seat so he was facing me. "Colt's right. If she sensed it in you, then it's there."

"How do we access it?" I asked, my heart hammering against my ribs.

Dash leaned forward, resting his knees on his elbows. "I'm going to do some research. See if I can find anything in old texts."

"I'm not sure this is something research will fix," Trace said.

Dash frowned at him. "It can't hurt."

Trace shrugged. "True, but I think Leighton needs to know what magic *feels* like. That will help her access her own."

Something about his words had an idea taking root in my brain. I straightened on the couch. "Would you guys be able to shift in front of me?"

Colt's brows flew up. "Sure, there's a spell protecting the property that keeps humans from seeing us in our animal forms. But why?"

"The night I first realized you were all these amazing magical creatures, I felt something in the air. I can't really describe it."

Trace grinned. "We should've thought of this earlier. If she's not seeing people access their magic, how would she have the first clue how to tap into her own?"

I pushed to my feet. "Can we do it now?"

Declan chuckled as he stood. "Want to play with beasts?"

I rolled my eyes. "You're not beasts."

His eyes bled to silver. "You sure about that?"

A shiver ran through me, but it was one of excitement, not fear. Dash grabbed my hand. "Let's do this."

We headed through the house and to the back lawn.

"Colt, why don't you go first?" Dash suggested. "You're a little less frightening. She did think you were a lost dog, after all."

I pinned Dash with a stare. "You're all awful for letting me do that, by the way."

Colt laughed. "Sorry, LeeLee. But you give one hell of a rubdown."

I just shook my head.

Colt turned away from us and began pulling off clothes. I nearly swallowed my tongue when he shucked his pants, and I had a nice shot of his tight, round ass.

"You're staring, Little Bird," Trace whispered huskily in my ear.

I still didn't look away.

A second later, there was a cracking sound, and Colt dropped to his knees. A faint shimmer took over his body, and then there was no human being in front of me, but instead, a wolf.

Colt's tongue lolled out of the corner of his mouth as he jogged toward me.

"Are we sure he's ready for this?" Ronan muttered.

Colt snapped his teeth in Ronan's direction.

"Just asking," Ronan shot back.

Colt came to a stop in front of me, sitting almost as a dog would.

He was so beautiful. With those same familiar hazel eyes.

"Can I pet you?" I whispered.

In answer, he bumped my hand with his head.

I laughed and began stroking him. Colt lay down, and I followed, crossing my legs and scratching his belly.

"Why'd he get to be the wolf?" Dash muttered under his breath.

"What does it feel like when you shift?" I asked Ronan and Declan.

"There's a moment of pain, but then it's complete bliss," Declan explained.

As I pet Colt's fur, I could feel a hint of the hum I'd felt the night I'd seen him shift for the first time. "There's something. It's almost like pins and needles."

Dash nodded, hope lighting in his eyes. "That's how I feel when I cast. It starts in my fingertips and spreads up my arms."

Excitement bubbled deep. "That's what I'm feeling, too."

Colt let out a rumbly growl as if to say *I told you so.*

I looked up at the twins. "Can I see the dragons now?"

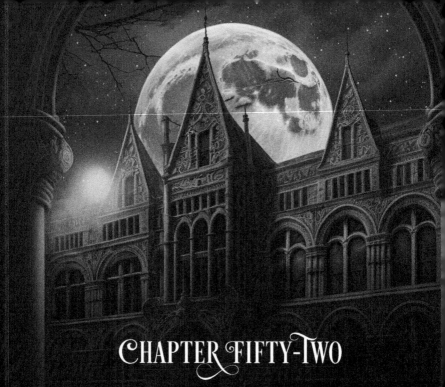

CHAPTER FIFTY-TWO

I STARTED LISTING TO THE SIDE AS I WALKED DOWN THE school hallway, and Dash caught me around the shoulders, righting me. His brows pinched. "In bed early tonight."

I shook myself out of the stupor I'd found myself in. We stayed up late last night. Probably too late. But I kept feeling like the magic might be within reach if I just tried a little harder.

All weekend, I'd spent time with Colt as a wolf, Ronan and Declan as dragons, and even stood with Dash as he cast some spells. Each time, I felt that buzz take root, but eventually, it just died off. As if something were keeping it from fully connecting. It was driving me crazy to feel so close and yet so far.

A long day of classes hadn't helped. And the fact that I'd likely failed my French quiz just now wasn't cheering me up any, either.

"I'm fine," I mumbled.

"Super believable," Dash muttered.

"God, she looks like shit all the time. It's embarrassing that they even have to be seen with her," Chloe said loudly to Mimi and Grace.

I wanted to shut my eyes and make her disappear. But her barb landed. I knew I looked rough today. I'd slung my damp hair into two braids this morning, not bothering to cover my dark circles with makeup.

Mimi snickered. "She looks like Pippi fucking Longstocking with those stupid braids."

Dash's fingers toyed with one of my braids as he dipped his head. "I've always had a thing for pigtails."

Grace's face screwed up. "She looks ridiculous."

"And you look jealous," Ronan said as he strode toward me and Dash. He lowered his mouth to mine, giving me a quick kiss. "Giving 'em hell, Firecracker?"

I tried to smile, but it didn't quite reach my eyes. "Missed you."

He nuzzled my neck. "Missed you, too."

Chloe stomped her foot, the action making her look ridiculous. "She's conning you."

"Keep telling yourself that," Dash shot back.

She stormed toward us, her eyes narrowing on me. "You'll never be powerful enough for them."

Pain churned in my gut, mixing with a healthy dose of fear. Because I was worried Chloe was right.

"Go blow dry your hair in the bath," Ronan shot back at her.

Chloe's cheeks reddened. "You're going to be sorry about the way you've treated me. You're going to have to *beg* for my forgiveness."

Dash waved her off. "Yeah, yeah, run along."

Expletives flew from Chloe's mouth as she stomped down the hall.

"Such a winning personality," Ronan muttered as he led the way to my locker.

I stayed quiet as Dash grabbed my books, and we headed for the exit.

I didn't meet any of the guys' eyes as we reached the SUV. Instead, I just climbed inside. Everyone else followed.

Colt slid behind the wheel and turned on the engine, but he didn't back out. He twisted in his seat. "What's wrong?"

I shrugged. "Just tired, I think."

Trace turned to face me. "No lies, Little Bird."

I bit the side of my lip. "What if I can't do this? What if I'm not what you need?"

Hearing my deepest fears out loud hurt more than I could possibly express.

Colt leaned between the seats and took my hands. "We're just beginning. You feel when magic's present. That's a start."

"But I don't have the first idea of how to access it. Maybe that means I'll never be able to ground you."

Declan squeezed my shoulders. "You have to keep the faith. We're trying to find out more. See if we can find someone who manifested later in life."

"We only have thirty days," I whispered.

They all knew it, but we had to face it.

Trace let out a low, rumbling growl. "The thirty days is bull-shit. If we get close to the deadline, we leave. That's it."

"I can't make you guys run, leave your home, your people. No," I argued.

"It's not a choice, Firecracker. *You're* our life now. The only life we want," Ronan said.

My chest cracked. Everything hurt.

I wanted a life with them so badly, but I wouldn't let them fall because of me either.

Dash took one of my hands and squeezed. "For now, we take things one day at a time. If you don't sleep and eat prop-erly, you'll never be able to find your magic. So first up, naps and a snack."

I knew the fact I was running low on energy didn't help my mood, so I took a deep breath and nodded. "Sounds good."

I'd just hope that the next few days would bring a breakthrough. If they didn't, I'd reassess.

"I wouldn't mind a Baldwin snack," Declan muttered.

Ronan snorted. "You're always hungry."

He shrugged. "Baldwin makes damn good food."

Colt backed out of the parking spot. "Tell him that and you'll have him on your good side for life."

"Does that mean an endless supply of cookies?" Declan asked hopefully.

"Probably," Colt answered.

Declan shot a fist in the air. "Hells yeah."

Something about the move made him look like a little kid, and I couldn't help but laugh.

Declan pinned me with a mock glare. "You laughing at me?"

My lips twitched. "Maybe."

Declan leaned over the seat and nipped my bottom lip. "That's a punishable offense."

My blood heated. "I don't mind a little punishment."

Trace groaned. "Could we dial it back a notch?"

I winced. "Sorry."

Trace shook his head. "Too tempting for your own good, Little Bird."

I blushed, but a secret part of me was too pleased by his words.

Colt made the drive home in no time, but he slowed as he approached the gates. "Who's that?"

A red Volkswagen Bug that looked as if it had seen better days was pulled to the side of the gate, and a woman faced away from us, talking to one of the guards.

Colt pulled to a stop, and the guard walked up to his window.

"She wanted a word with you," the guard explained.

The woman turned, and I saw it was Saoirse. She beamed a mischievous smile as she strode toward the SUV.

"What can I help you with?" Colt asked stonily.

Her grin only widened. "It's what I can help *you* with." She peeked through the open window. "I want to help Leighton come into her power."

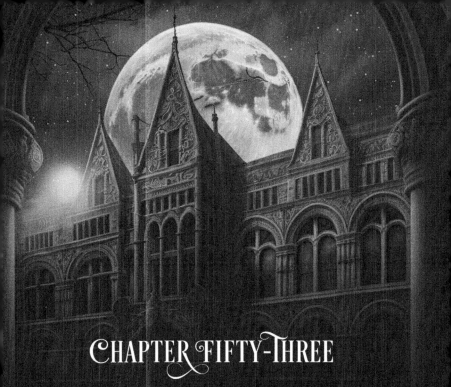

CHAPTER FIFTY-THREE

RONAN LET OUT A LOW, MENACING GROWL. "AND WHAT makes you think we would trust you?"

Saoirse's amber eyes danced. "You shouldn't. You know better than anyone that sometimes it's the people closest to you that you shouldn't trust at all."

It was Declan who let out a growl this time.

Saoirse held up a hand. "I didn't mean you, Declan. I meant your father."

The twins stiffened.

But it was me who was breathing fire. "If you knew what their miserable excuse for a father was doing, why the hell didn't you do anything to stop it?"

Her face softened. "Believe me, if there was something I could've done, I would've."

"You could've tried," I gritted out.

"And if I had, I would've been removed from The Assembly.

We aren't allowed to meddle in the rulers' affairs unless the actions are sanctioned, and I had no proof."

Ronan squeezed my shoulder. "She's right. We didn't have anything that would guarantee my father's guilt."

"And the person behind her in succession would've voted with Patrick's wishes in mind, not justice," Declan said quietly.

I refused to believe that there wasn't *something* she could've done, but at least she wasn't simply standing by, thinking there was nothing wrong with the situation.

Saoirse held up her hands. "I've been searched, and I'd like to help."

Our SUV was quiet for a moment, and then I spoke. "Okay."

"Little Bird," Trace warned.

"We have to try *something*," I said. "This is the best we've got."

"Fine," Colt grumbled. "But you'll be escorted around to the backyard." He jerked his chin at the guard, who nodded.

Saoirse grinned. "A strapping, handsome escort? Twist my arm…"

Declan snorted.

Colt just rolled his eyes and drove through the gates. He parked, and we piled out.

"Stick close," Dash warned, guiding me around the house.

Excitement bubbled low in my belly. Maybe this was just the ticket.

It took a few minutes for Saoirse and the guard to arrive. She was beaming, and he was scowling.

"What's wrong, Louis?" Colt asked, instantly on alert.

"She pinched my ass," he grumbled.

I gaped at Saoirse.

She held up both hands. "His backside was just too tempting. Apologies, Louis. It won't happen again."

Louis muttered something under his breath about horny old ladies, and Saoirse just cackled.

"You said you wanted to *help*," Ronan gritted out.

"Yes, yes." She rubbed her hands together. "Do you feel your magic?"

I shook my head. "But I can feel it when others are using it."

Saoirse made a humming noise. "Interesting."

Dash studied the older woman. "She feels it the same way I do when I'm casting. That pins and needles feeling."

"When do you experience it most?" she pressed.

I worried the corner of my lip. "When someone has shifted or when Dash is casting. Trace hasn't used his magic around me much."

Saoirse tapped a finger to her lips as she turned to Declan and Ronan. "How do your dragons react to her?"

"They'd die for her," Declan answered instantly. "They crave her touch, happiness, and safety above all others."

A wistful, almost longing look took over Saoirse's face. "The beauty of a true-mate bond."

Something tugged deep in my chest. "Do you have a mate?"

She turned to me. "I did many moons ago, one of the few lucky ones."

"Few?" I asked.

Saoirse nodded. "Female dragons are extremely rare nowadays. We fear they're dying out altogether. It makes the true-mate bond extremely rare."

I remembered Declan mentioning female dragons were rare, but I had no idea just how much so. I glanced in his direction. "Isn't Sam one?"

Declan nodded. "She's one of only three in our generation."

I sucked in a breath. "That's so sad."

"It is indeed. But that's a problem for another day. First, we must find your magic." She grabbed my hand. "I apologize for this."

That burning hot pain was back. I cried out as I crumpled to the ground, but Saoirse didn't let go.

The guys charged forward but then ran into some invisible force field as they tried to get to me.

"Almost done, my dear. Hold on."

I whimpered as the guys cursed.

Then Saoirse released me.

I struggled to catch my breath as Dash lifted me onto his lap. He brushed the hair away from my face. "Are you okay?"

"Fine," I croaked.

Trace stalked toward Saoirse, purple fire swirling around his hands. "You come into our home and you *dare* to hurt our mate."

"Now, Trace," Saoirse said. "I needed to understand the block more clearly."

"I don't give a damn what you think you need. You're going to die for hurting her."

Declan and Ronan grabbed hold of Trace, trying to hold him back. But he was so furious they were having trouble.

I scrambled to my feet, hurrying over to Trace, even though pain still radiated through my body. "Trace, don't."

His breathing was ragged as he struggled for control. "She. Hurt. You."

"It was necessary," I said softly.

He didn't look like he agreed.

I placed my hands on his cheeks and guided his forehead down to mine. "I'm okay."

Trace breathed me in, dropping his head to nuzzle my neck. "Little Bird…"

"I'm completely safe."

His body shuddered, and his arms came around me as the twins released their hold.

"I've never seen anything like it," Saoirse whispered.

My eyes flicked to her.

"Calming an incubus in the throes of a rage? It should be impossible. Even for their mate."

"Leighton's special," Ronan said with a grunt.

Saoirse studied me and Trace for a moment. "This is the key. When your mates are in danger, you'll find your power."

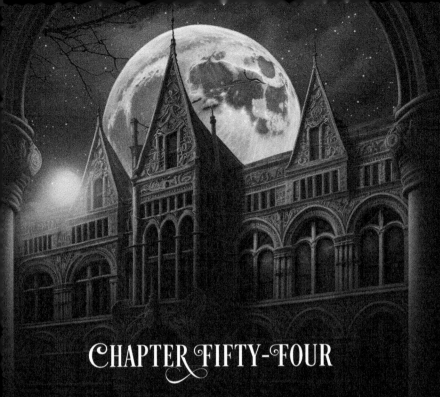

CHAPTER FIFTY-FOUR

MY MUSCLES ACHED AS I PULLED MYSELF OUT OF THE POOL, my clothes clinging to my body.

"Now!" Saoirse yelled.

I thrust my hands outward, but nothing happened. A burning sensation built behind my eyes. The Dragon Lady, as I'd begun calling her in my head over the past week, thought my magic would manifest if my walls were broken down enough. That meant killer workouts that put Dash's to shame. Running, hand-to-hand, extreme cold, extreme heat, and very little sleep.

My teeth began to chatter, and Ronan moved forward, glaring at Saoirse. He opened his mouth, and golden fire spewed out. It encircled in the most delicious warmth. I'd been startled the first time I'd seen it, but now, I knew the flames wouldn't hurt me. I wanted to sink into their warmth and never leave.

A few seconds later, the flames subsided, and I almost fell over.

Colt swooped in to steady me with an arm around my waist. "I think we're done for today."

"We need to keep pushing," Saoirse argued. "We're running out of time."

Her words had my stomach cramping. "I can keep going."

"No," Declan clipped. "We've stood by long enough. This is ridiculous. Whatever this farce is, it isn't working."

My shoulders slumped.

Colt nuzzled my neck. "That isn't on you, LeeLee. We just need to try a different approach."

Saoirse's mouth thinned, but she nodded. "Take tonight to rest. We'll meet again tomorrow."

She didn't wait for an answer. She simply headed around the house toward her red Beetle, Louis trailing her at a distance.

"Come on," Dash said, a hand rubbing up and down my back. "We need to eat."

I didn't say a thing. I felt like such a complete failure in that moment. The burning behind my eyes intensified, but I forced my feet to carry me toward the house.

Trace held the door open, a scowl on his lips. I couldn't deal with his angst on top of my own, so I averted my gaze.

Food was already on the table when we arrived. As delicious as I knew it was, I didn't taste a thing as I ate. Didn't hear a word spoken. I was too lost in my thoughts and barely able to stay awake.

I didn't even notice that someone had stood until my chair was pulled back and I was being lifted into strong, tattooed arms.

"What are you doing?" I slurred as I looked up into violet eyes.

"You're going to bed," Trace growled.

"I need to do homework," I argued.

"Not tonight, Little Bird."

There was a pain in his voice that stopped any argument on my lips. Instead, I let myself burrow into Trace's hold. "I missed you," I mumbled. "Will you sleep with me?"

The lack of rest had loosened my tongue, but I couldn't find it in me to care.

Trace gripped me tightly. "You've got me. Always."

⌒

I blinked against the bright light, feeling as if I were emerging from a coma. It took a few moments for my surroundings to come into focus. I was in my room, in my bed, surrounded by the guys, but they all looked as if they'd been up for quite a while.

"What time is it?" I mumbled.

Dash glanced at his watch as he reclined at the bottom of the bed. "A little after noon."

I jerked upright. "Noon?! We're supposed to be at school. Why didn't you wake me?"

Trace grunted from his spot on my right. "You needed sleep."

My eyes narrowed on him. I had to admit that I felt better than I had in weeks, but that just gave me the energy to be annoyed. "That wasn't your choice to make."

"As your mates, it will always be our job to take care of you," Colt said calmly.

I transferred my glare to him. "I do have free will, you know."

"Of course, you do," Declan agreed. "But don't use it to be an idiot."

I gaped at him. "You did not just say that."

He simply shrugged.

I started to get up, but Trace grabbed the back of my pajama top and pulled me back against the pillows.

"I don't think so," he barked.

"You can't hold me hostage."

Dash's brows lifted. "Watch us."

The corner of Ronan's mouth kicked up. "I've got an idea for how to keep her in place."

His hand slid beneath the blankets, and he cupped me between my legs. I instantly stilled, my body heating at his touch.

Ronan's thumb swept back and forth. "Going to be a good girl and stay put?"

My breaths started coming faster. "I haven't decided yet."

Ronan chuckled, the sound skating across my skin.

Dash grinned as he tugged the blankets down. "Gotta make it worth her while, Ronan."

Colt moved to his knees, his hands going to the bottoms of my pajamas and tugging them free in one swift motion.

The cool air had goose bumps peppering my skin as I swallowed hard. There was something about being so exposed with all five of the guys present, something about how bright the light was, that just turned me on more.

Declan's hand skimmed up my leg. "So silky."

I squirmed in place.

"Still," Ronan commanded as he unbuttoned my pajama top.

I instantly stopped squirming.

A second later, Ronan pulled my shirt free, and I was completely bare.

My breaths came in short pants, and I could feel a phantom energy swirling in the room. My eyes sought out the violet ones next to me.

Trace didn't touch me, but his eyes were pure, blazing purple. "Little Bird, you are pure temptation and sin."

Wetness pooled between my legs.

Dash leaned forward, his fingers dipping between my legs. "Already aching, Mon Coeur?"

"Yes."

I wasn't ashamed to admit it, either.

Ronan traced a finger in circles over my breast, closer and closer to the peak. "Get her ready for my brother. He needs her."

Declan's eyes flashed silver, and my core tightened. There was something about that giving over, not as though I were a possession, but as if I were a part of them both, and they were finally ready to be united.

Dash's finger slipped inside, stretching me in lazy circles.

My hips moved of their own volition.

Colt squeezed my thigh. "Not yet, LeeLee."

Ronan pinched my nipple, and I let out a whimper.

"She needs more," Trace gritted out. "I can feel that feral need wrapping around my dick."

"Hell," Dash cursed. "She's squeezing the life out of my fingers."

"She's ready," Ronan growled.

Then I was being tugged toward the end of the bed. Declan stood there, eyes pure silver as he shucked his tee and sweats. His hand skimmed down from my neck to between my breasts to my belly. "Love you, Leighton."

My eyes burned. "Love you. All of you."

Declan gripped my thighs as Colt circled my clit with his finger. Dash bent his head to take my nipple into his mouth, and Ronan kept twisting the other with his fingers. Trace simply watched, as if the sight were enough to unravel him.

"Are you with me?" Declan growled.

"I'm with you," I breathed.

He didn't need anything else. He simply slid inside.

My back arched as I let out a moan. The stretch was delicious, just shy of pain.

Dash sucked my nipple deeper, and my core contracted.

Declan cursed and began to thrust.

They were everywhere, my guys. I was lost in a sea of sensation, yet somehow, just shy of what I needed.

Declan angled his hips, thrusting deeper. As Colt circled my clit, my legs began to shake.

"Please," I begged, but I didn't even know what I needed.

Ronan growled. "She needs you, too, Trace."

Trace cursed, but then his mouth was on mine.

Liquid fire lit in my veins, sweeping through me in an inferno. Every touch was heightened. Every sensation intensified.

I cried out into Trace's mouth as I clamped down on Declan. He came on a shout, arching into me. The world around me shattered into a million pieces, and I knew when we put it together again, it would look completely different.

CHAPTER FIFTY-FIVE

"SOMETHING'S DIFFERENT," SAOIRSE SAID, tapping her finger to her lips as we all stood in the backyard.

I pressed my lips together to keep from laughing. I was sure I looked thoroughly fucked after my lazy afternoon.

Colt cleared his throat. "We let Leighton sleep in."

Trace snickered, but Saoirse seemed oblivious to it. She simply nodded. "Obviously, a little rest agrees with you."

I made a humming noise, not trusting my own voice.

"I want to try something a little different today," she continued.

"What?" I asked, eager for anything new and different that had a shred of hope of working.

"Clearly, stressing your body out didn't spark a magical response. I'm wondering if you need to connect with your being more."

My brows furrowed. "How am I supposed to do that?"

Saoirse lowered herself to the grass gracefully. "Sit."

I did so, but not nearly as gracefully.

"Once you have fully bonded to your mates as their anchor, you will take on some of their magical abilities. But there should be flickers of it in you now with the amount of time you all spend together."

I worried the corner of my lip. "Will I shift?"

Saoirse shook her head. "No full transformation. But you might gain their increased senses of sight, hearing, and smell."

I grinned. "So, I'll be a human lie detector like they are."

She chuckled. "With some practice, it's possible."

"I'm in."

Saoirse just laughed harder. "Glad to hear it. Now, close your eyes."

I did as she instructed.

"Listen to the world around you. What do you hear?"

I let the sounds roll over me. "The waves crashing into the rocks. The wind. A bird."

"Good," Saoirse praised. "Now, pull that focus into yourself. What do you hear from your own body?"

I had to think about it for a few moments. "My breath. My heartbeat."

"What do you feel?"

I kept breathing. "My hands on my legs. The sun on my face."

"Deeper," Saoirse urged.

"The beat of my heart reverberating through me."

"More."

I worried my lip. "My blood moving through my body."

"Even deeper," Saoirse whispered.

The world around me melted away as I disappeared inside myself. It was as if there were a whole new layer to my being that I'd never experienced before. I could see it but not quite reach it. It was like a sea of sparks at the very center of me.

I reached out, trying to touch it, but something kept me from getting through.

"Holy shit," Ronan muttered.

My eyes flew open. Sparks flew around my hands. They were a mix of colors. Golds, silvers, greens, and purples. My guys' colors.

Then they simply disappeared. Disappointment coursed through me. "How do I get it back?"

Colt's hands landed on my shoulders. "Don't push it, LeeLee. That was amazing."

"That was magic," Declan said with a grin.

Giddy excitement coursed through me. "I have magic."

Ronan grinned. "We always knew it."

Dash studied me for a moment. "I think this might be because we were all together today. Connected in a way we never have been before. It lit something inside of you."

A mischievous grin spread across Saoirse's face. "Now, that's my kind of homework."

I blushed.

Dash knelt in front of me, his hand lifting to my cheek. "The secret has always lay with us. It wasn't with us being in danger. It was in us simply being one."

My throat burned.

As he released me, my gaze found Trace. I didn't miss the fear in his expression. It made my chest ache.

I climbed to my feet and crossed to him. I pressed a hand to his chest. "This is good. Don't run on me."

He swallowed hard. "My magic could hurt you."

"It won't," I vowed.

"You don't know for sure."

"You have to have a little trust," I whispered. "Please."

Trace dropped his forehead to mine. "I trust you with my life. It's me I don't trust."

⁓

I let my toes sink deeper into the sand as I walked, Ronan on one side, Declan on the other. The moon was bright, casting more than enough light for us to walk by.

"How do you feel?" Declan asked.

My lips tipped up. "Aren't you tired of that question yet?"

He gave me a sheepish smile. "Today was a lot. You can't blame us for asking."

I got it, I really did. I felt it in my own ways, which was why I'd begged the twins to get me out of the house. Their version of that was a walk where the house was still in sight.

"I feel…hopeful. And terrified that I won't be able to move past those baby sparks."

Ronan dropped a kiss to my temple. "This is just the beginning. You need to give yourself time to work up to more."

I kicked a clump of sand. "We only have twenty days left."

I had to voice the thing that none of us had said.

"Twenty days is a long time," Declan assured me.

But maybe not long enough.

Ronan slid his hand into mine. "We know what works now. Resting, taking care of yourself, and being together."

"Orgasms," Declan added helpfully.

I couldn't help but laugh. "I certainly like that last one."

"Me, too," Declan said, waggling his eyebrows. Then his body jerked, eyes going wide. He began convulsing as he dropped to the sand.

"Declan!"

Ronan shouted, but then he was falling, too, and I didn't miss the dart sticking out of his shoulder.

I screamed as loud as humanly possible, praying that Colt would hear me from the house.

A sharp sting lit my neck, and I batted at the sensation, but it was too late. The world went blurry around me, and then there was nothing at all.

CHAPTER FIFTY-SIX

MY HEAD THROBBED IN A STEADY BEAT, AS IF THERE WERE a tiny marching band practicing on my skull. I struggled to open my eyes, trying to find some relief from the pain. I blinked against the low light.

The space around me came into view slowly and all at once. Dilapidated wood walls. A broken window. A single-room cabin. One that had clearly seen better days.

I lay on a bed, but it smelled musty and wrong. It was the scent that had the panic setting in.

I jerked upright, and the world swam around me. I lifted my hand to my head, but it tugged the other hand with it. Bound. My wrists were bound with a zip tie.

My stomach roiled. This wasn't happening. Not again.

Memories assailed me, and tears sprung to my eyes. Declan. Ronan. Fear gripped me. I had to believe they were okay. Some part of me knew I'd feel it if they were gone from this Earth.

I tried to steady my breathing, counting to four with each inhale and exhale. I wouldn't be able to escape if I was hyperventilating.

The cabin door swung open, and a figure stepped inside. "Fucking finally."

I knew that raspy voice. It was hardened by years of cigarettes, booze, and drugs. That sickness in my belly intensified.

Maryanne stepped further into the cabin. "Don't try anything stupid." She lifted a gun. "I'll get more money for you unharmed, but he'll still take you with a hole in your leg."

My mouth went dry. "Who will take me?"

Her lips twitched. "Wouldn't you like to know?"

My fingernails dug into the backs of my bound hands. "My mates will come for me, and they won't make your death a kind one."

Maryanne's face hardened. "I'll be long gone by the time they figure out where you were taken. Kicking back on a beach in Costa Rica."

She scowled at me. "You've put on some pounds, girl. Weren't exactly easy to move. Hasn't anyone told you that no man likes a fat bitch?"

Rage burst to life inside me. I was sure I had filled out and grown curves now that I wasn't being starved, thanks to her.

Maryanne shrugged. "Guess it doesn't matter what those guys think of you now because you won't be seeing them for a while."

I didn't play into her game. Maryanne loved to hold information over my head. Loved to make me dance to get the things I needed for survival.

So, instead of playing into her hands, I stayed quiet and waited. Watched. I studied the cabin out of the corner of my eye.

My feet weren't bound. I'd have to make a run for it and pray she didn't shoot me. If I could knock her down, I'd have a better shot at escape. But a distraction would help.

Annoyance flickered across Maryanne's features. "Don't you even want to know who I'm selling you to?"

I shrugged. "It doesn't really matter, does it?"

Her cheeks reddened. "I'm getting half a million for your sorry ass."

"Good for you," I said as if I didn't have a care in the world.

Maryanne stalked through the room and slapped me hard across the face. "You're going to live in torture for the rest of your days."

The coppery taste of blood filled my mouth as my head snapped back. I let the pain wash over me, not fighting it but letting it fuel me. I'd need that rage.

"That vamp seems pretty obsessed with making sure you never have a moment's peace," she snarled.

My body went cold. I should've known it was Damien. Of course, he'd be happy to pay a pretty penny to get his hands on me again.

Maryanne grinned triumphantly. "His father doesn't even care. Just wants his boy to be happy. Sweet, really."

I launched myself off the bed and into Maryanne. She shrieked as she tumbled backward and landed on her ass, but I didn't wait. I just ran.

Nausea and fatigue coursed through me, and I knew whatever Maryanne had doused me with was still in my system. But I had adrenaline on my side. I pushed my muscles harder as I charged out of the cabin.

It took a second to register my surroundings. We were on a tiny beach that was surrounded by thick forests. *Crap.* I had no idea where I was.

Maryanne screamed from behind me, already getting to her feet.

I couldn't wait. I had to go. At first, I headed for the woods, but the heaviness in my muscles told me that was a mistake. She'd catch up to me in no time.

The moonlit ocean caught my eye, and I changed tack. Maryanne had always been deathly afraid of water because she didn't know how to swim. If I could just make it to the water, if I could swim around the little jetty, I'd be free.

"I'm going to kill you!" she shrieked.

My bare feet hit the ocean, and I ran into the lapping waves.

But I underestimated just how much the woman who was supposed to be my mother hated me. She hit me from behind in a tackle. We landed in two feet of water, and she pushed me down.

Shouts sounded from the forest on shore, but they were so far away.

I clawed at her arms, kicked and bucked, but it was no use. My muscles didn't have the fight they needed.

Maryanne's face contorted above me, both in rage and the waviness of the water. Her fingers tightened around my throat as she pushed me deeper.

My lungs burned. Fire like I'd never known before. Some part of me called out to my guys. Wanting them to know I loved them. And then that fire swallowed me whole.

ALSO BY TESSA HALE

Supernaturals of Castle Academy
Legacy of Shadows
Anchor of Secrets
Destiny of Ashes

Royals of Kingwood Academy
The Lost Elemental
The Last Aether
The Queen of Quintessence

The Shifting Fate Series
Spark of Fate
Mark of Stars
Bond of Destiny

CONNECT WITH TESSA

You can find Tessa at various places on the internet. These are her favorites…

Website
www.tessahale.com

Newsletter
www.tessahale.com/newsletter

Facebook Page
bit.ly/TessaHaleFB

Facebook Reader Group
bit.ly/TessaHaleBookHangout

Instagram
www.instagram.com/tessahalewrites

Goodreads
https://bit.ly/TessaHaleGR

BookBub
www.bookbub.com/authors/tessa-hale

Amazon
https://bit.ly/TessaHaleAmazon

ABOUT TESSA HALE

Author of love stories with magic, usually with more than one love interest. Constant daydreamer.

Printed in Great Britain
by Amazon